## Daughter of the House

CATHERINE GASKIN was born in Ireland, grew up in Australia and, after spending eight years in England, married an American and settled down for ten years in New York. She and her husband then moved on to St Thomas in the Virgin Islands where they lived for two years, and they now make their home among the Wicklow Hills in Ireland.

Catherine Gaskin has now written eighteen bestselling novels; *Family Affairs* is the most recent.

CATHERINE GASKIN

# Daughter of the House

*Collins*

FONTANA BOOKS

First published in 1952 by William Collins Sons & Co. Ltd
First issued in Fontana Books 1971
Fifteenth Impression September 1980

© Catherine Gaskin 1952

Made and printed in Great Britain by
William Collins Sons & Co Ltd Glasgow

# PART ONE

---

## I

Maura couldn't tell, when she lifted herself on to a stool at the bar in The Stag on that night of late summer in 1949, that she was going to fall in love with the man who sat two stools away from her. She had always thought there would be a warning of some sort, but there wasn't, so she merely smiled at Jeremy behind the bar, and asked for a gin.

He looked along sideways at her. 'We've been expecting you since six,' he said.

'Couldn't get away from the office.'

'Traffic bad?'

'It's as congested as hell on the Southend road. Everyone's making for the coast to catch the last week-end of the season.'

He shook his head. 'The summer isn't over yet.'

She shrugged and sipped the gin, deciding that whatever Jeremy said about the summer not being over, at the end of her ten days here she would put *Rainbird* up on the slips and close the cottage for the winter. She sat quite still, facing the rows of bottles and glasses, and letting the fatigue of the drive down from London fall away from her. Without turning her head she pictured the scene within the room; the deep, comfortable chairs occupied by the nightly regulars—to whom she would presently nod with a pleasing sense of familiarity—the polished brass upon the walls and the few pieces of old china gleaming chastely from the mantel, and below, the big hearth which in summer Jeremy's wife, Willa, filled with flowers—perhaps now already blazing with early chrysanthemums.

This call at The Stag before the last short drive up the lane to the cottage, had long ago become custom. It established the fact of her arrival in the village; it was in that way much more than just a courtesy to Willa and Jeremy, who were her friends. In the morning she would go down to the boat-shed, and old Able would greet her there with inquiries about the cause of her lateness at The Stag this evening. This attitude of theirs, sometimes irritating, was at least solid. It gave to her the blessed sense of belonging.

Jeremy came back to her. 'Weather all right in London?' he said.

'Bit thundery, I thought, Jeremy. You know how it's been all this summer—we live expecting the weather to break. I was glad to get out of it.'

'Your father's well?'

'Yes, he's well. He loathes the heat, of course, but he never lets it force him to alter his habits.'

'And Chris and Tom?'

She nodded and smiled. 'Father passed a rather important brief on to Chris this week, and then suggested that he stay behind in the evenings and work on it. Chris didn't like it much—but I must say he settles to work more easily these days.'

'And what news of Tom?'

'Nothing new—still at the Ministry. He's going to leave it in the spring and go back to Ireland.'

'He doesn't come here very much, Maura?' He questioned her with the statement.

'You know what it's like, Jeremy . . . they all think I'm impossibly independent and smug about the cottage, so they leave me to get on with it. Though, I think Tom's secretly rather approving of anything that's independent. He's the last person in the world to try to push around.'

Jeremy let the remark pass without comment, though certainly he had long wondered about the exact relationship between these cousins, and whether they would ever marry. They could not be said to be in love—at least not in the way Jeremy remembered he had been in love with Willa—

but there was a comfortable friendship, which, lasting through the four years since the war, seemed likely to drift into marriage.

Looking at her, and becoming aware that the man separated from her by the two empty stools was also looking at her, he remembered that he had neglected to make them known to each other.

'Maura, could I introduce Johnnie Sedley, who's staying here. Maura de Courcey.'

She turned towards him.

'How do you do?' he said. The introduction was acknowledged with the formality of an Englishman, with the difference that he spoke with an American accent. He was blond and wearing a loose white T-shirt in the fashion that seems to belong solely to Americans.

'Willa told me you were coming,' he said. 'She's been in here several times this evening looking for you.'

'Have you been here long?' she said. It was conventional, and she felt a little foolish, but there was nothing else to say.

'About ten days,' he replied. 'I suppose I'll stay until the weather changes.'

'I thought most Americans didn't let weather interfere.'

'I'm not "most Americans" '

'I'm sorry.'

Abruptly he slipped across the empty stools to the one beside her. 'Oh, hell, I'm sorry. I didn't mean to bark like that. I just get so used to the line the rest of the world takes about Americans being the eternal tourist, that I begin seeing it where it doesn't exist. This happens to be my particular part of the country, and I like to imagine everyone else can spot the difference a mile off.'

'Oh . . were you here during the war?'

'No. I did a post-graduate course at Cambridge before the war—and my great-grandfather's family lived near King's Lynn.'

'Then I'm doubly sorry,' she said, and laughed a little.

He thought she looked nice when she laughed, though he had decided in those first minutes when she had lifted

7

herself on to the stool and asked for a drink, that she wasn't in the least beautiful or even handsome.

Jeremy said, before he moved away from them, 'You should tell her about your third cousin, once removed, in King's Lynn. Maura would like that story.'

'Oh . . . my cousin,' he repeated. He looked down at his glass, twisting it, and moving it backwards and forwards across the bar, examining the wet smear it left behind.

'Yes, my cousin's a nice little woman who lives in King's Lynn, as Jeremy told you. When I was at Cambridge I went to find out what had become of the Sedleys—there'd been no contact after my great-grandfather went to America. I found the place where they used to live, a rather nice farm with one of those very small, half-timbered manor houses. It had been sold about twenty years before, and the people sent me to a Miss Janet Sedley who ran a library in King's Lynn. She didn't know what to make of me, at first—I was American and she hadn't spoken to many Americans before. And besides I was at Cambridge, and that was suspect, too. But we got on quite well, and the Sunday after that I took her over to Cambridge for the day. I think she enjoyed it—at least I didn't drive a little red sports car as she expected. She told me primly that her father had died "without male issue," and she couldn't cope with the farm. She was rather gentle and Victorian. She's still alive, and very old now—I went to see her last week. It was rather funny—touching, I suppose—to see how proud she was of all the American servicemen she'd given tea to during the war. She told me far more than I ever knew before about Kansas and Little Rock and Atlanta. As I said . . she's a nice little woman.'

Then he raised his head and looked at her.

'I suppose you think I'm naïve and slightly ridiculous —like all Americans are about their connections in this country?'

'Why do you have to spoil it?' she said. 'I think Miss Janet Sedley is a nice little woman, too. And I don't think it's ridiculous to be pleased about discovering where you belong. You've lived here—you ought to know the English better.'

'Yes . . . yes, I should understand the English much better than I do. But somehow I manage to put my foot into it, and follow immediately afterwards with the other foot. Like now.'

'You haven't done anything very dreadful,' she said, a little flatly.

And the American, watching her, knew why her mouth drooped from its firm, too-straight line. He knew his last remark should have been gentler, and wondered how it was that anyone so pleasantly restrained and normal as she appeared, could be so easily startled and made afraid. He regretted the uncompromising bluntness of what he had said, regretted his lack of manners, regretted most of all that he had caused her to withdraw from him. He tried to think of something to say to her.

'Yours is one of the yachts down at Able's boat-shed?' he asked. '*Rainbow* . . . do you call it?'

'Yes, that's *Rainbow*,' she said, pleased with the trifling matter of his having remembered the yacht's name. 'It belonged to my father's cousin, who lives in Ireland. Every summer before the war I used to sail with him.'

'And now?'

'He gave *Rainbow* to me,' she said simply. 'During the war he had no one to come sailing with him—both his sons were away. And then, afterwards, he didn't seem to care so much for it. The last time he sailed her was on the trip over here. We brought her over together.'

'He's still alive?'

'Oh, yes. He's not old—really. I often wonder if perhaps he doesn't regret parting with her.'

'Not to you,' he said briefly, with little intention to flatter or please. 'Any fisherman in the village will tell you she's in good hands.' He stopped, and then said, 'If you need a crew any time you can count on me. I'm always around.'

'Thanks, I'll remember.'

He said quickly, 'I didn't mean to butt in.'

9

'You're not butting in. I'm always glad of crew. Not everyone has the time to go with me.'

'Just as long as you didn't think . . .'

'No, I didn't.'

It was at this moment a girl in the private bar began to sing. Maura turned towards the open door, as Johnnie did, to get a view of her. She seemed very young, and she was sitting at the piano, playing softly. She sang softly, too, but her voice was rich and low, and it reached them through the mingling sound of that crowded room. The song— *Smoke Gets in Your Eyes*—was thick with sweetness . . . as sweet and hushed as if she sang to a child. Maura felt she didn't care that most of the people in the room had dropped into silence; she was singing because she enjoyed it, and she didn't give a damn about anyone there.

And when she finished her song and began fingering around on the piano for the start of another, Maura saw suddenly how lovely she was. She wore a white cotton dress, and sandals on her bare feet, and Maura felt that the skin of her arms would be wonderfully smooth to touch.

'She has a beautiful voice,' she said. Then louder to Johnnie, 'Do you know her? Is she staying here?'

'She's my wife.'

She flushed, because it seemed blundering to have taken it for granted that he was here alone. But he had always said 'I,' and never 'we.'

'I'm sorry,' she said, with some confusion. 'I didn't connect . . .'

'No, of course not. Why should you?'

Gradually the talk in the bar had recommenced, but the girl's voice was still quite clear above it. She was singing *Always*.

'She's very beautiful—your wife.'

'Yes.'

At the same time he slid off the stool and faced her. 'I'll be seeing you around,' he said. 'Don't forget I'm ready to be crew whenever you say so.'

'I won't forget. Good-night.'

The suddenness of his going was unexpected. She knew an unaccustomed sense of loneliness as she saw him bend over his wife. The girl rose, smiling slightly, and Johnnie caught her hand in his own. They walked towards the staircase that way. With the narrowness of the stairs she was forced to move ahead of him, but his hand still rested on hers as it gripped the banister.

Maura waited impatiently for Willa, and at the end of ten minutes she saw her come through the private bar. Her face was radiant with her smile; she had a crisp, brown, little face.

'We thought you'd never make it this evening. Mrs Burnett expected you before six.'

Maura smiled back—the very sight of Willa, the catch of eagerness in the other's voice, could make her feel less tired. 'I know. I've been badly held up.'

'Glad you got here,' Willa said gently. Then added, 'How long are you down for this time?'

'Until next week-end—at least I'll stay if the weather holds as long as that.'

A trace of emotion, of regret, crossed Willa's face. 'How quickly the summer passes. It seems such a little while since you got *Rainbow* out for the first time in the spring.'

Then she put the thought away from her. 'What are you drinking?'

'I won't have another, Willa, thanks. I think I ought to get on to the cottage.'

Willa looked at her carefully. She saw that her dead white skin was stretched with fatigue, and her eyes and hair seemed even darker than before because there was no animation in her face. The fine lines, usually creases of laughter, were tight under her eyes.

'You're tired,' she said.

Maura nodded. 'It's more than just the journey. Father and Chris have both been working hard, and that means I work hard too. But Father got fed up with my languishing about; he said if sailing my cranky little boat would make me less irritable, then I'd better get to hell and do it for a week.'

'You're not irritable—that would be a change.'

'Fractious, then. There's no difference, really But we'll all three of us, you and Jeremy and I, get out in *Rainbird*, and then nothing matters.'

Willa's mouth twisted. 'The last sail in *Rainbird* always means the end of the summer for me now. I hate it when you go.'

And Maura, gazing at her small, neat face, wondered for which of all the dear things she did and said, one loved Willa most Her gaze rested upon the other with affection and contentment.

'I've been talking to your Johnnie Sedley,' she told Willa.

'Yes . . . I wondered if he was still here when you came. What do you think of him?'

'He's nice—but he's awfully touchy.'

'About some things, yes. But Jeremy and I like him a lot.'

'Yes, so did I. He wants to come sailing.'

'If you've got room you should take them both. They'd love it—things must get rather dull for them round here. His wife is sweet. Did you meet her?'

'I saw her.'

'Lovely creature, isn't she?'

'Yes—quite lovely.'

She slid off the stool. 'I must go—I'm nearly dropping. I'll be sailing to-morrow afternoon if you want to come.'

'Yes—call in on your way down. Jeremy might be able to come, too.'

'Fine.' She called across her shoulder to him. 'Good-night.'

'Good-night, Maura.'

There were a few casual salutes to her as she moved through the crowd. Willa came to the door with her, and stood gazing out into the darkness. Then she blinked in the sudden glare of the headlights which swept the squat, timbered building. She raised her hand to wave, watching the car out of sight along the village street. Inside, the barmaid was calling for last orders.

## II

The homecoming to the cottage was finally achieved, Maura always thought, when the first preliminaries were done with. When she had taken her bag upstairs and read the note from Mrs Burnett, when she had brought coffee and biscuits from the kitchen and set them down on the table beside the sofa, she was at home. She considered the books and the piano and the record cabinet—all these were very dear to her; they were the accumulation of the past four years, representing a maturity hard-wrested from the years of war.

She reached for her handbag and found a cigarette. Her father, Desmond, had been rather pitifully discountenanced by this purchase of the cottage. He had not wanted it, as he never wanted anything which might drive even the slightest wedge of separation between him and his children. Too much love had always been his trouble, and a jealous counting of every small mark of their affection until they were twisted and bound, and seemed at times almost strangled by it.

Maura could not think of a time when she had not worshipped her father. He was an uncomplicated, though amazingly shrewd man, believing in himself with a single-mindedness which carried him through difficulties often far greater than he knew. Maura buried her shoulders deeper among the cushions. Desmond was very secure in his knowledge of the love of his children, but they had, both of them, suffered too long under the burden of his brilliance and energy. He seemed always to spur them to efforts beyond their capabilities, and because they loved him, had strained themselves for his sake beyond their powers. He had always been confident that his gifts would be reproduced in his children, and he, so ostensibly sophisticated, at the same time astonishingly naïve, had been bewildered by their failure.

She remembered clearly his shock when she had bought

this cottage and a second-hand car on her discharge from the army. It had taken all her accumulated service pay, and the little money she had had before the war. He had been hurt, and the months that followed were difficult. When Tom and Chris had come down to help her paint and redecorate it, he was silent—not even offering his advice, as she had expected, when she went to the sales for the furniture. It had taken much tact, and even more time, to convince Desmond that his London house was her home still. But even when this conviction grew on him, he could never resist the temptation to lavish luxuries, small or immoderately large, upon her, increasing the ease and excitement of her London life in order to draw sharper and finer contrast between the two. She had, long ago, detected this subtle cheating in him, and had indulged his vanity by allowing it to appear secret still. All his life, she thought, no one had ever hurt her father unnecessarily.

But his final giving-in had been graceful enough, and even, in time, he had given her presents for the cottage, as the carpet and the piano had been. Maura even guessed that he respected her more for having fought against him and won. Her time at the cottage he never interfered with, and almost never did he ask her about it. In this feigned indifference, she thought, he showed his hurt like a child.

But the arrangement worked well enough—at least, well enough to allow her to be happy at the cottage And there was the unhoped-for gift of *Rainbird*, and exquisite days, like days taken from time itself, sailing on the estuary. This would have held her to the place, even without the companionship of Willa and Jeremy. But always at the back of her mind, like a warm current of contentment, ran the thought that she had Chris and Desmond to return to, that the solidity of their lives would anchor her again. And there was also her cousin, Tom.

She wished she could have fallen in love with Tom four years ago, and married him, as he had wanted her to do. But it was like waiting for a wind to stir on a hot, breathless day. There was no movement towards him, no sudden restless need for him—in the way she had never yet felt a great need of any man. In the spring, she thought, Tom would give up his job at the Ministry and go back to Ireland. And in the spring she would be thirty.

She stubbed her cigarette into the saucer, and began to make the first unwilling movements towards going upstairs.

### III

Johnnie turned his head a fraction so the sun didn't shine directly in his eyes. His body leaned with conscious relaxation against the seat, and the fingertips of one hand gently stroked the steering wheel. Comfortable, and with no apparent need for hurry, he yet strained for the first sounds of Irene's coming, for the lateness of the hour, and the restlessness of the morning had seized upon him; he knew a need for movement, a desire to catch up with what had already slipped by.

He pictured how Irene would look when she appeared, running towards the car with swift, smooth movements. Her face would be as alive as the morning itself, no more subtle than it, no overtones of shade obscuring it. She was happy so long as her activity was in some way linked with his, and she didn't mind showing it. She was delicate, and still strongly emphatic in the way she loved, determined in her own particular fashion to make their marriage a matter of simplicity and ease. He turned as the door opened and she stepped out into the sunlight. Instantly she raised her face in a kind of gesture of appreciation towards it, as if she were made glad and happy by the single fact of its being there.

Willa was behind her, but, in her direct manner, she didn't stop for any purposeless overtures. She came to Johnnie's side, and her face wore its fascinating smile.

'Johnnie, I'm going up the hill a bit. Would you drop me?'

'Sure,' he said, and opened the door. 'We're not heading for anywhere in particular. Where do you want to go?'

'I want to see Maura de Courcey. The cottage is about half a mile along the lane.'

He nodded. 'Ready, Irene?'

She came, slipping in beside Willa on the front seat. The Sunday morning village was aloof and unconcerned as Johnnie turned the car and swung away from it. Twenty minutes earlier it had been alive with the steady movement of people towards the church. Now he was anxious to escape from the close environs of the single street, from the closeness of people, from the Sunday-bound village into countryside where the day of the week didn't show.

'Turn up on the left,' Willa said, and he obeyed, sounding the horn impatiently.

The summer hedges were tall and thick above the lane. Johnnie could see nothing beyond or behind them. The feeling of bound closeness which had oppressed him in the village would not go. He felt a prickle of irritation.

'Why should anyone want to live here?' he demanded of Willa abruptly. 'It's shut in. You can't see a thing.'

'Maura's cottage is at the top.'

He nodded silently.

Irene said, 'Does she live there alone?'

'Yes.'

'How lonely.' She glanced across at Johnnie. Willa saw her visibly reassuring herself of his reality, his presence. 'Does she come often?'

'Almost every week-end of the spring and summer.' Then Willa recalled what Maura had said about closing the cottage, and she added thoughtfully, 'We miss her badly when she goes—Jeremy and I. We've grown used to counting the weeks by her comings and goings.'

Then she said, so low they could scarcely hear, 'Maura is part of the summer for us.'

Glancing down, Johnnie saw a faint twist of unhappiness in her face. He guessed suddenly that she regarded the other's going as a flight from accustomed routine, and

16

that, momentarily, her independence was a thing to be envied.

Irene's gaze had strayed to Willa's face; she read thoughts there that roused her interest. But when she questioned the other again, her tone possessed a quality which divested curiosity of its inhuman touch. 'What does she do —in London, I mean?'

'She has a degree in law. She works with her father and brother.'

Irene accepted the information. Her features were tightened and concentrated as she thought about the woman to whom she had not yet spoken, as she tried to fix the points of that personality. Irene's mind flickered over the few details she possessed, counting them swiftly. She said at last, 'And she sails, doesn't she? She owns the boat— what's it called, Johnnie—*Rainbird*?'

'Yes,' said Willa. 'She sails and listens to music and cooks a little—none of them too intensely.'

The hedges finished abruptly at the top of the hill. Johnnie stopped the car before the cottage, and turned to look about him. Suffolk on the other side of the river was neat with hedged fields and church spires, but the scene belonged wholly to the life of the estuary. The changing, twisting, baffling stretch of the Stour was the significant point of the landscape. Tidal creeks, slipping secretly through the fields, until now never guessed at, were mercilessly sought out and exposed by the sun—shallow waters glinting like dull grey satin under a net of tall rushes and weeds. There was a view of green marshes and woodlands, and of a flight of solan geese rising with a bold sweep from glistening mudflats.

Johnnie looked back towards the cottage. Maura was walking down the path towards them. He thought her altered from the person he had remembered two nights ago at The Stag. She was freer, for one thing, movements easy and without strain. She smiled at them without that trace of weariness.

'I thought you'd forgotten, Willa.'

'How long is it since I've missed a Sunday-morning

gossip with you? Not once this whole summer.'

Irene had got out of the car to allow Willa to slip over past her. Willa motioned towards her now. 'Maura, you haven't met Johnnie's wife, have you? This is Irene Sedley —Maura de Courcey.'

They smiled an acknowledgement to each other, and Maura caught a suggestion of unexpected shyness in the other's face It destroyed her first image of Johnnie's wife —the self-possessed young woman who had sung in the crowded bar of The Stag as if it had been deserted, whose head had turned only in answer to Johnnie's touch. She regarded them both with interest, and then, without fully knowing why she allowed them to break into her hour alone with Willa, she asked them to come in.

They offered a first polite refusal, and then with no more hesitation, followed Willa inside the cottage. They found their places easily in the room; Willa went to her usual chair, Irene leaned against the mantel. Johnnie stood with his back towards them, staring through the window down towards the river.

'I like the view,' he said. He gestured to include the room. 'It's nice here.'

His words touched her; they managed to overcome the fact that they had talked to each other only a few minutes, and he was simply and naturally appreciative. For a second she allowed her eyes to stay with him. She thought, until he spoke, his face was faintly arrogant. There was a suggestion of arrogance, too, in the way he wore his clothes —feet thrust into worn, loose sandals, his white T-shirt drooping carelessly about his hips. His straight, fair hair hung with frank untidiness upon his forehead.

But he had caught her gaze upon him, and grinned to show that he was aware of it, and to make her aware of it also. She smiled back, turning to where the drinks stood upon a side table.

When she had handed around the glasses, Maura took a seat facing Willa and Johnnie. Irene had begun to wander about the room, glass in hand, reading book titles, pausing with a vaguely defined gesture of delight before the vase of purplish-blue salvias, and at last stayed motionless beside the piano, her body resting against its curve. Gazing at her in her attitude of graceful ease, Maura knew an instant of recognition, a near-certainty that she had seen Irene before. Impossible to name time or place. Or was it, she wondered, simply that all real beauty was familiar? One recognised it because its image was always there, at the back of consciousness, only waiting to find its counterpart until it was brought forward.

The talk between Willa and Johnnie forced her attention back to them.

'. . . a bomb that was meant for the Harwich docks fell in the field behind it,' Willa said, 'and stopped the clock. It's never been working since. It was a good thing they'd taken the stained glass away.'

Johnnie said, 'I remember the stained glass from the first time I saw it.'

'You've been in the village before this?' Maura asked him.

'Yes, sure. I came over one week-end from Cambridge. I came over with two men from college and we had some sailing with people they knew. I even stayed at The Stag. It didn't look quite so smart in those days.' He grinned at Willa. 'I told Irene I'd take her to a completely unspoiled East Anglian village. She didn't expect the plumbing to work—it didn't last time.'

'But it hasn't changed all that much?'

'Not a bit—except for the church clock and the plumbing at The Stag. But it's not the same as before—the change is in me, not the village. I don't quite know what I expected to find by coming back here.'

Maura said slowly, 'I wonder what it is we all look for when we go back to the past. I wonder if we hope we'll find a part of our past selves that was better than we are now —a sort of happier ghost.'

'Whatever it is we hope for,' Johnnie said, 'we don't find it. Perhaps that's a good thing.'

But as he spoke he looked at where Irene stood. Without knowing why she should do so, Maura's eyes followed his.

Still resting in the curve of the piano, Irene had turned, and they couldn't see her face. But they were made aware of the tenseness of her body, and a faint hostility. There was even, Maura thought, a suggestion of pain. And it was then that Johnnie's gaze caught Maura's for just a second, and held it. Neither expression changed by a fraction, but when the glance was at last broken, they had advanced a step towards familiarity.

Willa was conscious of the whole happening. She tilted her glass slowly, wondering what to say. During that few seconds' break in the conversation, something had happened individually to each of the three, and she alone had been outside it. Her apartness from them did not trouble her; only Maura's entanglement roused in her a faint sense of disquiet. She herself possessed no desire to learn more of the relationship between Johnnie Sedley and his wife. They were happy together, and that was as much interest as they held for her.

But with Maura it was different. Why, Willa wondered, did Maura always make herself vulnerable and open to every passing breath of others' emotions? Willa knew a feeling of unrest and fear at this prodigal showering of Maura's sympathies, deciding that she could not see her go deeper into the situation.

She spoke and her words were a deliberate provocation to more talk, and thus a release of Maura's emotion. 'If war should come again . . .' her face held a courageous acceptance of what she feared and dreaded. '. . . it is these years, these days—Sunday mornings like these—that will be our ghosts. *These* will be the times into which we'll try to retrace our steps.'

Johnnie said, 'But our memories cheat us. There's so little accuracy or truth about what we remember. Four years ago we had a war, and now we sit here, and in our hearts we can't believe we may be on the brink of another. And yet our memory of peace wasn't any more true when we went back to it. The world had changed so much that when we tried to pick up as we left off and found it wouldn't work, we ceased to believe what our memories told us—we ceased to believe, in fact, that anything like that had ever existed.'

Maura shivered in just a second's comprehension of his meaning—that nothing was so permanent in one's mind that its memory was indestructible, or untouched by decay. She wanted to protest, even vainly, against it.

But it was Irene who spoke, who made them feel her desperate conviction. 'It seems so important to me that we should strive to hold a memory of everything that has ever happened to us—and to believe in it. It's only the memory of the past which gives the present its value.'

It was a grave little speech, strained and conventional, and it drew all their attention to her, to her vague unhappiness. This faint grief became her wonderfully, gave her face a rigid, uncompromising beauty. She seemed unbelievably young then, and they knew that the memories of before the war were childhood ones for her. But she had the courage to urge Johnnie to preserve his own recollections, even though they did not contain any thought of her.

Irene's agitated beauty was so compelling it seemed impossible Johnnie did not turn his head and see it. His inattention was not unkind, merely that he was absorbed in a thought no one else could share. He walked a solitary way, as they all did at times, and Willa reflected that Irene would have to learn the loneliness of waiting for his return. Johnnie's years of war would forever cut them apart. His wife could know only what the war had made him, never what he had once been. Willa wondered if love had made her jealous of that part of him she did not possess, of the idle thoughts no woman ever shares, the wayward, vicarious pleasures he did not expect or want her to understand.

Irene broke their mood of unease. She slipped on to the piano stool, and her fingers traced through a strange little tune—scarcely a tune at all, so soft, so low and hesitating. They began to talk in disconnected scraps which the string of notes threaded together somehow. There was no melody in what she played, nothing the mind could fasten on and hold. A few chords, a little run played over and over, and then off into a tune which she didn't finish. And all of this so softly they had to strain to hear it.

Johnnie, glancing over his shoulder, exchanged a brief smile with her, and the moments of her unhappiness were gone.

## IV

All the light drained smoothly towards the horizon. Fragments of cloud crumbled round the pool of colour which the sun had left behind, and Johnnie wondered if it meant that rain was on the way. The dusk had given to the countryside its own touch of intimacy—so that he, with his alien's love of England, was, for just these moments, almost a native, with a native's sense of possession and pride.

He was alone, because the desire for quiet which beset him sometimes at this hour had driven him from the crowded rooms of The Stag. Irene, who knew this mood, had let him go unprotesting. He never asked what she felt of these hours when his bafflement was uppermost, when his searching for peace seemed never more urgent. He felt shamed, sometimes, when he considered his endless demands upon Irene's gentleness and courage. She was too young, he thought, to suffer so much because of this germ of discontent which sickened him.

The evening and the deserted lanes, had given him some of its quiet, blunting the edges of his restlessness. His feeling for solitude was gone, replaced by an urge for talk and company, but not the sort which greeted him back at The Stag. So he turned up the lane which led to Maura's cottage, not hesitating, but still with no great certainty that his need could be met.

When the high dark hedges broke, he found the windows of the cottage lit, and the sound of music halted him. He listened for a time, then moved forward more slowly. The door remained open as it had been that morning, and he stood within its deep frame and gazed into the sitting-room. He could smile now at his own arrogance in coming here wondering if Maura could recognise his mood and fall in with it. He felt humbled and corrected as he watched her, so surrounded with the evidence of the life she led here, so serene within its circle.

She was absorbed in the music, unaware of him. Her face in profile was strained and concentrated, but there was a smoothness about her body which told him she was at ease, and happy. Her hands moved with a certain controlled skill through the familiar Brahms rhapsody. They were eloquent of all the efficiency he had ascribed to her in his thoughts. She was wearing slacks and a dark sweater, not ungracefully, and he guessed she had been sailing. The glare of the standard lamp was pitiless to her white face, but it emphasised her startled eyebrows and the black fringe of hair. She was faintly dramatic, he decided, and then smiled to himself at the thought, imagining it was the last quality she would have claimed for herself.

The music came to an end, and inelegantly she wiped the sweat off her palms by rubbing them against her thighs. He knew he must say something, knew that this intrusion upon her privacy would go beyond excuse if he didn't speak now, though his instinct was to remain silent, to go on watching her.

'You play extremely well,' he said.

She turned, and seeing him, rose, at the same time smiling her delightful, swift smile. She was excellent at pretending that his visit was wholly expected.

'You're much kinder than I deserve.' she said simply. And then, 'I hope you haven't listened too long. It hasn't been good.'

'Only the last—and I liked it.' He wanted to see her face, but she stood with her back to the lamp and it had become a whitish blur.

As he advanced into the room, she turned and took glasses and a bottle from a cupboard. She came and handed him one, and he bent and smelled the old, good brandy. They took the chairs which faced into the empty hearth.

'This is my father's choice.' She indicated the brandy. 'He has tastes I can't afford.'

Johnnie took his first, slow sip, and then he grinned across at her. 'He must be a good guy to know.'

His smile found an instant reflection in her face. High cheek-bones and the corners of her mouth flashed upwards. 'Father is the whole world's idea of a good guy. He's unhappy if everyone doesn't think that about him.'

'And does everyone?'

'Almost everyone.' She looked into her glass. 'I do.'

The thought seemed to agitate her. He watched her as she rose, placing her glass on the hearthstone. She paused, as Irene had done that morning, before the vase of salvias. She had withdrawn from him, beyond his reach. The brief moment of their intimacy was shattered, its bright promise unfulfilled.

'I sailed all afternoon,' she said. Her tone was casual, a stranger's once more. It was simply talk and nothing more.

'Who was crew?'

She gave him one quick look that carried a recollection of her promise to take him on *Rainbird*. 'I went to Dedham to pick up young Peter Brown. I take him whenever I can. He's sixteen, and wild about boats.'

Not waiting for his reply she dropped down at the piano and once more took up the rhapsody. It was again a barrier between them, but less unkind than the other. The wedge of her withdrawal was driven deeper between them, until he wasn't able to bear the exclusion any longer. He came and stood behind her.

As instantly as if he had touched her, her hands left the keyboard and slid dully into her lap. She twisted until she could look at him fully.

'Have you ever heard of my father?' she said.

'Yes, I know about him.'

She rose, and went back to her seat before the fire. 'In a minor way he *is* famous, I suppose.' She took up her

24

brandy glass again and sat staring into it.

When he was a very young K.C., Desmond de Courcey had figured brilliantly in a *cause célèbre*, and he had dug his heels in hard to the small fame it had brought. He had pursued his luck unceasingly, unendingly until a sufficient number of spectacular trials had made him safe. Johnnie could remember his name spoken at Cambridge, and occasionally it had found its way into the American press. His personality was exotic enough to make him worth writing about, apart from his cases—and in the early days Desmond had played up to this with a flamboyance that made him conspicuous. This had been gradually dropped, when his reputation was secure, for a smoother, more even approach to his work. 'Tailoring himself for the Bench' was the phrase used of him, and those who didn't like him said he would preside there with as much ostentation as had marked his career thus far. Ostentatious or amazingly shrewd, he was still a man of absorbing interest, and his daughter, when she spoke those words, was fully aware of her father's fame, was proud of it, and concerned for everything that touched it. But she would know, Johnnie thought, the frailty and longing which lay behind his fabulous exterior.

'My brother and I,' she said, 'have suffered all our lives with the very excess of his loving, and of our loving him. No ordinary children could match his talents—and we are very ordinary children. We would have given our souls to bring him a show of success—even the lightest reminder that we were, after all, his children. But, you see, we're just impossibly mediocre—not bad, not good. And Father still minds about it terribly.'

'And you—do you mind?'

'I mind for his sake. He's so full of a great love of living, but success is always part of it. He surrounds us with the kind of living his success has brought, and closes his eyes and rather pathetically trusts that somehow Chris —and myself—will succeed in just the way he has done.'

He was acutely aware that some love of drama in her was forcing its way to the surface. She lay back in the chair, long legs outlined by the slacks, white face sharp against the high neck of the jersey. Under her eyes he could see the tracery of fine lines which the glare of the lamp revealed She was consciously tensed. It was almost deliberate, he thought, this attitude of near-despair. And then he recalled her Irish background, and wondered if this appeal to his sympathies wasn't something too deeply inbred for her to control or subdue, even if she had wished to. If she and her brother, Chris, were to be mediocre, then they would be mediocre in a grand fashion. The story would be touched and tinted just so slightly, until it had the aura of dramatic failure about it. He guessed that in these last moments she was nearer her father than at any other time, drawing strongly on that native ability, surely inherited from him, to charm the senses of her hearer, to twist their hearts with sympathy, and have a vicarious triumph in doing it.

'Father's life has been so much harder than ours,' she continued, unaware or perhaps careless of how much of herself she had given away. 'His father was an Irish farmer with a few acres of what must have been principally bog. I suppose it all adds to the romance of Father's career to consider that he began in such a way—he's never tired of telling people that he went through Trinity on scholarships and a shoe-string. In any case, whatever he had to do without when he was a boy has bred in him an undying distaste for everything that doesn't cost a lot of money. The simple life has no sort of appeal for Father. He likes big houses and big cars—and the extreme of comfort. When he was at college he even managed to get himself piano lessons—God knows how. From a family that couldn't distinguish one note of music from another, he's made himself into a rather good musician.'

She leaned forward to give her words emphasis. 'When one lives with him one is possessed by him, utterly. He is even at the root of my attempts to play the piano.' She shrugged. 'But I'm not good—never will be. I suppose because I haven't his gift to begin with, and lack the confidence he has to sit down before a room full of

26

people and attempt something that only a virtuoso plays.'

There was no response from Johnnie, and coming out of her absorption in her own words, she looked up at him. She knew that his thoughts were no longer with her, but following a train she herself had invoked. Reflectively her eyes rested upon him. He stood with his faintly arrogant slouch against the mantel, his loose clothes appearing to emphasise rather than blur the lines of his body. His thoughts were very much his own. He pulled them about him closely, retreating into a world of loneliness, unbroken, unrelieved by any single contact. Maura herself was now excluded, much in the manner he had been earlier. She was stung to alertness and the need to draw him back to her

She watched him in silence as he moved towards the piano, and watched, also, the lines of his head as he bent over it. Diffidently he touched a note; it cut sharply into the quiet. He raised his head as though listening for an echo back from somewhere, his lost expression still with him. His hand dropped away. He turned and came back to her.

'Maura.' It was the first time he had used her name. He made it soft and mysterious.

'What is it, Johnnie?'

'How could it be,' he asked, 'that when I stood in the doorway there and listened to you playing, I told myself that all this had happened before—that I'd been through this experience at some other time?'

'Yes . . . why are some things we've never seen before as familiar as what happened yesterday?'

'I don't know, either,' he said simply. 'Perhaps it hit me like that because when I was a kid at high school I used to think it would be a pretty fine thing to play Bach and Brahms.'

'Why didn't you?'

He shrugged. 'Musicians are an unknown quantity in my family. It never occurred to anyone that I might like to try, and I didn't have the courage to try myself It was the same at college—I was meant to prepare myself for

27

a business career, not turn into a *dilettante*. Even at Cambridge, which was my father's big concession to the acquisition of fine arts, I did a course in economics.'

'Is it too late—even now?'

'Much too late. Having once wanted to play the piano doesn't matter so much now. Learning to play Bach belongs back in the days before I went off with all the other guys to find out what war was really about. I discovered that if you didn't get killed you lost out somewhere else—you lost your fancy ideas about Bach, and a lot of other half-baked plans you'd got. And sometimes you lost any inclination to go back and do the job scheduled for you.'

He turned directly to her. 'And so look at me. I'm thirty-six, and I'm loafing in a pub in Essex because I haven't got the guts or nerve to tell my father I don't want his bloody firm—and I can't make myself go back and settle down to it. Since I came out of the Navy I've tried it, and I just can't stick any more.'

'What are you looking for, Johnnie?'

'Looking for? That's just it . . . I don't know what I expect from all this.'

He shrugged. 'I guess that's why I'm here.'

He said no more. The brandy glasses were refilled, and cigarettes lit. Maura knew he hadn't intended that she should question him further, nor did he ask for sympathy or seek understanding of any kind. There was no suggestion of fear or dread in him. She felt that when he was ready his decision would be taken without help from anyone. She was strangely content with the confidence he had given, desiring no more than that.

Presently Johnnie went and searched among her records, selecting the Beethoven clarionet trio. Its theme of sheer impudence pleased them; they laughed aloud, delighting each other with this swiftness of intimacy. Johnnie whistled it flatly, and then broke off at the sound of thunder at the end of the valley.

'Oh, blast!' Maura said. '*Rainbird*'s uncovered. I had

to drive Peter back to Dedham in a hurry, and we left her as she was.'

Johnnie stood up. 'Get your coat. We'll go and do it now.'

In the hall she put a worn mackintosh about her shoulders, and took down the torch from its hook. They went into the garden, and the scents of the flowers rose to their nostrils, with a heavy, cloying odour; the gate creaked under Johnnie's hand. On the road their footsteps were loud and small stones rattled in the ditch as they passed. More thunder came, and the first movement of wind. The air cooled suddenly; the breeze hardened. High white ridges showed briefly in the clouds, then merged with the following dark piles. They caught the smell of the river and the mud-flats.

The anchorage lay within the opening of a narrow, nameless creek. Four small yachts were company to each other. Able's boat-shed, with its cluster of rowing dinghies gathered about it, was closed and in darkness. Maura flashed her torch around, and she and Johnnie drew *Rainbird*'s dinghy towards the river. At the water's edge they drew off their shoes, and pushed out into the shallows. On board, Maura lit a lamp and put it down on the deck; its rays ploughed long tracks in the water, greenish and thick. Johnny followed her murmured directions as they worked with the tarpaulins.

The rain began to fall as they finished. The hard drops slashed into their faces; their bare feet were chilled. They climbed into the dinghy, and Johnnie took the oars; in the shallows they turned out together, drawing it clear of the tide mark. Johnnie watched as she fumbled with wet fingers at the strap of her sandal. And then he bent and fastened it for her.

On the hill the wind was stronger; the darkness was like pitch until they turned the last bend of the lane and they could see the light in the windows of the sitting-room. Johnnie swung the gate open, and stood back to let her go through.

She paused beside him. 'Good-night, Johnnie.'

'Good-night, Maura.'

The wind and rain carried away the sound of his foot-steps as he walked down the lane.


## V


Their falling in love was unspectacular. They were never alone, so that learning to know each other was accomplished during crowded evenings at the bar of The Stag, and long days of sailing the quiet stretches of the river. Their loving lay in such simple things that they did not fully recognise it until it was too late to avoid the pain of its sudden discovery.


Johnnie turned away from the empty silence of Maura's cottage and took the road which led over the hill into the valley beyond. He had little hope that he would find her there, only the fact that *Rainbird* was still at her moorings, and Maura's car stood outside the cottage. He made no excuses to himself for his deliberate seeking of her company; he simply wanted to find her and talk to her.

At the top of the hill he paused. Here the sound of the sea was cut off, and the thick smell of wood-smoke replaced that sharper, more alien tang in the afternoon air. The peaceful unconcern of the scene affected him strongly, like a stab of unease and discontent. He gazed around him, seeking her.

He saw her directly he raised his eyes to the fringe of the copse on that nearest hill. The scarlet rug blazed boldly on the hillside, and each one of his senses seemed to recognise the form and stillness of the figure which lay upon it. He started to skirt a field of plough, startling a herd of grazing cattle into brief movement, racing across the last space of pasture which separated them.

'Maura!'

She heard him coming, and sat up to watch him. He

reached her and flung himself down breathless beside her, face pressed into the rug. She could hear his intakes of breath; the sun on his pale hair held her fascinated gaze. He betrayed nothing when he turned upon his back and grinned up at her, eyes closed.

'Guess I'm out of condition.'

She wanted to slap the flatness of his chest, push her fingers through his hair. She looked at him, at his tanned face, looked at the whiteness of the skin which an ancient tear in his jersey revealed, and she felt as if her whole life had waited upon this first moment of loving him.

Then he opened his eyes and saw her concentrated stare upon him. She turned her head away.

They did nothing, clinging fast to silence to calm them, and to take away the urgency of the moment. It was a pause of dangerous weakness, when the restraint they imposed upon themselves waited to be shattered by the eyes fixed upon her averted face. He tried to imagine how it would be to kiss her.

They had looked away from each other, and upwards, and so together watched a heron's gentle flight down towards the river. In the hush they believed they could almost hear the rustle and brush of soft feathers. It headed, then, with sudden purpose towards a bend of the river hidden from them, and passed from sight.

Johnnie said, 'The summer has been long.'

It meant nothing, his remark, but Maura nodded willing agreement, grateful for the sound of his voice, sane and ordinary, utterly unrelated to that single look which had passed between them. True, what he had said—the summer had been a jewel. She recalled the long hot days, pavements in London burning beneath her feet, but days gladly endured in order to see the white glare of the sun on *Rainbird*'s sails, to ride without effort at night on the smooth, starlit channel. She heard again the noisy good-humour of the crowds that jammed the parks and the cries of the children fretted by the heat. The myriad colours of their dresses were as unreal as paper flowers. But a summer to remember, just the same—a time to fling one-

31

self down on sun-warmed grass, to breathe in the heavy scents of the scarlet poppies in the cornfields. Too many good things to remember each with sober clarity; too much sun and heat, too many colours. And now, at the very end of it, this day's gift to her.

And Johnnie himself, looking at her, began to wonder dully what it would be like to grow accustomed to missing her. He thought of the utter madness of it all, of having known and loved her within a week, to share her life in just this small way for ten days, and never see her again.

'Will you stay on here—you and Irene?' Maura's body was still, her voice as quiet as the passage of the heron.

'For a while, I suppose.'

She turned to look at him. As if he sensed her questioning, he closed his eyelids, and rolled on his side.

'Johnnie,' she said.

His eyelids flickered. 'Yes?'

'Why don't you go back?'

'Go back?' His voice was quiet, but with an edge of apprehension in it.

'Yes—go back.'

His body stiffened, and he opened his eyes. 'Maura, do you think it's right to go on doing something because you're just not strong enough to hold out against its imposition on you?'

She met his gaze. 'How can I say?'

He sat up abruptly. 'Then I'll tell you. Perhaps you'll have some idea whether I'm doing the right thing or not.'

He fell back against the rug.

'It's easiest to begin with my great-grandfather, the one who came from King's Lynn. His father was a small squire, and he was not normally the sort of person who needed to go to America—except that he married a woman who made it impossible to live in England. She was a servant—either in his own house or on a farm close by —and not the wife for the son of a gentleman. The story that her mother was a gipsy may even have been true— but they said she was beautiful. His family never heard of him again—one of the reasons, being, I suppose, that he was a poor man all his life.

'I imagine the way he was brought up made my grandfather shrewd and careful—it's fantastic to think how unlike his mother he must have been. He borrowed money and started a small textile factory in Pittsburgh. He never lived as a rich man—but my father had the sort of education a rich man's son has. The place was big when he came into it, and then was the time to bring in the schools of chemists. My father built what must have been the biggest textile laboratory in the States then. He went to the financiers for his money, and risked a hell of a lot on it. Well, you know about synthetics and nylon. He had huge war contracts, and at the end of it he was sitting pretty.

'But you know what happens to concerns that grow big —they get that way by buying up smaller firms, they have subsidiary companies, they have labour problems and strikes. It takes a particular kind of man to sit at the centre of all that, and know which way to jump, know the wrong time to take out a loan and know how big a staff canteen ought to be. My father is that sort of man. He took the business from a small, going concern, and made it into something so big that he only gets round to shaking hands with all the managers once a year. But he loves it—it's his whole life. I don't think he would have got married if he hadn't wanted children to carry it on.

'That's the whole trouble—it would have needed four sons to carry on, and there was only me, and one girl. I came back from Cambridge and worked with him until 1941.'

He lapsed into silence, and when she thought he would say no more, he continued slowly, 'I might have been all right if it hadn't been for the war.

'War is a strange thing, Maura, when it's played out on a lot of little islands. You seem to spend a hell of a lot of time just sitting down waiting, but when things happen, they happen with uncomfortable speed. But the waiting is tough—you drink or gamble or do nothing at all. I had too much time—and I began to ask questions that hadn't occurred to me before. And one of them was whether I'd got any real obligation to go on with a job they'd planned for me when there were a hell of a lot of things I wanted much more to do.

'Things started with a bang when I got home from the Pacific. I was "good old Johnnie" and a fine little hero because I'd flown a plane for the Navy without much distinction. When the flag-waving was over I was meant to go back to my desk—and then I discovered it was much worse than it had ever seemed when I thought about it in the Pacific. I wanted to marry a girl I'd been writing to all the time I was away. I think she loved me, and she tried damned hard to understand why I was different, but she saw only my father's position, and a complex absence of plans for myself. She was the sort who needed roots—she had to know her place in society, had to know what was going to happen to-morrow. She wasn't willing to gamble on marriage—and I suppose she was right.

'I stuck at it somehow—my father and I were always taking planes to New York or Chicago, and either lending money or borrowing it. The actual weaving of textiles hardly seemed to come into the picture at all. The whole trouble, as I looked at it, was that I'd grown up the son of a rich man, and I'd never known the firm when it was small enough to have any kind of personal atmosphere about it. My grandfather took to textile weaving from the sheer necessity to make money, and then the whole thing gathered momentum, and turned into a force that had to expand or fold up.

'I used to like the trips away from the plant. I always made them as long as I could. I liked New York best because that first year after I was out of the Navy I used to see a lot of a guy I'd run up against once at a college debate. I bumped into him again in Leyte. I think I envied him more than anyone I knew. He'd written two novels, and when he wasn't in New York he was in Europe as a foreign correspondent. He fitted that kind of life as well as anyone could—in fact he just didn't want any other kind of life. He belonged to New York like no other place in the world. His father was a Czech immigrant, and his mother first generation American of Irish parents. He was born and brought up on the Lower East Side. Mark's high-paced, and he doesn't want to be tied to any one place or woman or job. He doesn't possess anything he can't pack up and take with him. I haven't seen him for more than eighteen months—he's been living in Vienna and Florence—but I think about him a lot. Though in a sense I blame him for my restlessness getting worse. He always did what he wanted with his life . . . sometimes I didn't want to see him . . . it made me sick with envy just to hear him talk.'

'What would you have done—if you'd been free?'

'Don't get me wrong—I didn't want his kind of life. I think I would have farmed, if I'd been able to choose. A small farm I could have worked on myself. I would have taken anything that was small. In my case I guess the wheel has come full cycle again. I want to start with something as small as my grandfather did.'

'Does your father know all this?' she asked.

'Almost everything—they think I'm a rehabilitation problem, and if I went to Europe for a year I'd be all right. They expect me back when I've looked at enough cathedrals and galleries.'

'Are you going back, Johnnie?'

He looked at her. 'Would you?'

'It isn't any good having someone else answer that for you. Are you going back?'

'I guess so—when I can stick it again. My father's tired and pretty sick. I'll have to go back and have one more shot at it. But if it's still no go, then I'm finished with it for good.'

'And what of Irene?'

'Irene? It doesn't matter to her what my decision is. If I wanted to live in a caravan she'd think that was all right, because she's one of those rare creatures who are loyal and unselfish enough to want to fit into the pattern whatever way it changes.'

'She's very lovely . . . Irene,' Maura said. 'I think she's the loveliest thing I've ever seen.'

'Yes,' he agreed, 'she's very beautiful. And she's gentle and kind.'

He looked down at Maura, but it was like gazing at her through a glass.

'We've been married two years. We'd known each other only nine weeks.'

Without her bidding he went on :

'She was one of the dime-a-dozen photographer's models who hadn't got the right kind of push or temperament —whatever it is—to get herself into the big time stuff. Poor kid, she had no family, and she'd come from the South to New York—dead scared and dead lonely. When I met her she was sharing an apartment with three other girls.'

His eyes turned away as he recalled the crowded spaces of that stuffy little apartment west of Central Park. There had been noise and good-natured laughter, and damp underwear hung in the bathroom, and Irene had lived out her days in the midst of it, not liking it and trying to like it. But she'd possessed the kind of courage which made her stick, even when she knew she hadn't the qualities which would have brought her into the full-page ads. and she knew she would never be photographed in the necklace from *Cartiers*. Beautiful she was, but then beautiful girls were too common a commodity in New York, and she had the kind of face that went with furs. He remembered how she had talked of all this one hot evening when they had sat together on the fire-escape—it was the only place in the apartment where they could be alone. The noise of the night-city had risen about them, and close at hand, the intimate, daily sounds of the apartment-dwellers, the voices, the radios, the clatter of dishes in a sink. The Manhattan sky burned brilliantly above them, a dull pink reflection of the lights of the tightly-packed city. From the direction of the Hudson they caught the faint siren of the New Jersey ferry. He had asked Irene to marry him, and she'd turned her young face thoughtfully upon him.

'Is that what you really want, Johnnie?'

It was the only time she had ever questioned his love, accepting it from that time on as she gave her own. After their marriage he found her grave and sweet and gentle, much more than he had known, startling and shaming him sometimes by the very strength of her tolerance. He thought of her now with gratitude, and with his new awareness of Maura at his side, he knew that this meeting on the hillside must be their only one. He rolled on his side, closing his eyes before the pain and knowledge of it.

And Maura, looking down that little valley, thought of the American girl, and she knew, without him speaking of it, that Irene's loyalty would embrace whatever change in his way of life he decided to make. Maura had not Johnnie's memories to bring back the noisy stimulation of the great, glaring city—but only an intuitive knowledge of how their love must have grown out of the very environment which enclosed them. Her eyes turned to welcome the sight of a skein of wild duck pushing a dark wedge in the northern sky. She followed them as long as they could be seen, and then her attention returned to Johnnie beside her. His face had dropped into repose, no longer restless and urgent as it had been while he was speaking. She knew his seeking bewilderment, but she could give no help. She felt the inadequacy of love, of her own love, which did not even have the power to search his heart and know its compelling desires. She wanted to lay her hand upon him, even lightly, to draw him back from his solitariness. But it remained still and unmoving in her lap.

The afternoon shadows had slipped down the opposite slopes and now advanced upwards from the hollow of the little valley. A faint blue was gathering in around the trees and the farm-houses. There was a happy peace here . . . an intimacy in which they had shared, but there was also a serenity far removed from their wild longing for each other, removed from the frantic restlessness of Johnnie's story. As they stared ahead and the slender shadows grew, they were more alone with each other, and less a part of the valley. Their aloneness increased, and awareness of each other. It was imperative that they either speak or break the power of their silence by movement.

Maura rose first, looking not at him, but at the darkening outline of elm trees against the farthest hill-top. Then Johnnie rose also, more slowly, and gathered up the rug. They began the descent of the hill.

## VI

Willa had drawn her chair close to the fire they had lit against the chill of the wind which rose from the Stour. Occasionally she prodded with her foot the piles of white ash which had collected on the stone hearth. They were burning Maura's store of driftwood; the flames which shot upwards were violent, incredible colours—as mad and improbable as a winter sunset. Maura sat on a low stool close to her feet; the heat had slightly scorched her cheeks until they were flushed to unaccustomed brightness. Watching her, Willa was moved to wonder at what it was that so claimed her thoughts, what had caused the shade of preoccupation, almost apathy, which had fallen across her face.

She voiced at last the thought which had been uppermost in her mind since she had entered the cottage. 'I'll miss you terribly,' she said. 'The winter is so long, here—nothing to break it up.'

Maura glanced at her, struggling to remove the fog of dullness from her eyes. 'I know,' she said lifelessly. 'I can't stop myself wondering what will have happened to me—to all of us—before I come back again in the spring.'

Willa's face twisted strangely. 'I wish you weren't going. I wish it wasn't the last time.' She sat forward, closer to Maura.

The other stirred. 'Willa?'

'Yes?'

'You're happy here? You're quite happy?'

'Why do you ask?'

'Why?' Maura shrugged vaguely. 'I suppose I wonder if you're not sometimes restless and lonely. I think I distrust your contentment, and wonder if it's as true as it seems.'

'Yes, I'm happy.' Willa spoke without false emphasis, as if there was no need to point up her words. 'I am happy here. How could it be otherwise when I remember what it was like during the war? I can't think of it again without knowing the awfulness and misery of those years. I never believed marriage could last through a time like that, and settle down afterwards to the ordinary, blessedly monotonous existence we have now. I thank God for every day that goes by in which nothing happens. I thank God for the very boredom of it all.'

Without looking directly at her, Maura caught the faint and uncertain movement of the other's hands as if she groped in the air before her for the words she sought. 'I used to wonder how our marriage would turn out. I'd never known Jeremy when he wasn't in submarines, and drinking all the time he was ashore. Poor Jeremy, he never seemed to realise that no one would despise him for being afraid—it only mattered that he kept going back to his submarine and he stayed sober and did his job as well as it could be done. It was a marriage made when we were all afraid and unsure—and to cling to each other for comfort and hope was natural. How right it would seem later, when there was no more danger or uncertainty, was something we had to risk.'

Her face relaxed into a look of tenderness. 'Jeremy's happy—I know that. It's right for him here, Maura, and I think he realises it. An occasional flutter at Newmarket and a day in London are the extent of his excesses. And for myself'—she shook her head—'I polish glasses and clean tables in the bar, and I wouldn't care if I never had another exciting moment in all my whole life.'

Maura listened, touching the fire gently with a poker. A magnificence of colour sprang out briefly and died again. For just a moment she was fiercely envious of the content in Willa's voice, of the serenity of her eyes. But it was right, she thought, that Willa should have such things from life, because she wasn't smug or ungenerous about them, because she could understand without questioning, and give sympathy almost without words.

Maura said quietly, poker still in hand, and her eyes fixed upon the bright blaze, 'Willa, I must tell you something.'

'What is it?'

She laid down the poker and turned. 'I've decided I'm going to marry Tom.'

Willa fixed her gaze thoughtfully upon Maura, watched the colour come and then drain sharply away from the other's cheeks. She saw the determination there, and the touch of arrogance which might have been Desmond's own. She knew it was pride which held Maura's eyes upon hers, would not release her until she had spoken.

She said quietly, 'I'm glad, Maura. You and Tom—I think you're right for each other.'

Maura turned back to the fire, speaking quickly, 'Yes, we'll suit each other well enough. Cousins, at least, have the advantage of a common background—we'll know what to expect from each other.'

'It will please your father.'

Maura caught her words eagerly. 'Yes . . . yes, it will please Father. He's always hoped it might happen . . . always said he knew what was good for me. He's tried so often to make me realise one can't expect too much from marriage.'

'Expect too much?' Willa spoke sharply. 'What do you expect?'

Maura shrugged. 'I don't quite know. Perhaps I've thought there ought to be something different about marriage. Something exciting and challenging which kept one looking forward to to-morrow. I begin to see now one is lucky to achieve a passive kind of happiness.'

'There's nothing passive about happiness. It won't stay static, either. It's got to be worked at all the time.' Willa's tone abruptly took an edge of authority. 'Do you really have much idea what you're talking about? Marriage isn't a matter of knowing what to expect from each other, or of easy phrases about passive happiness, either.'

'But remember, Willa, all marriages are not like yours and Jeremy's. You've got to try to come down to other people's level. I suppose there does exist for everyone the one person with whom it might have been possible to have this . . . ideal of mine. The chances are a million to one you'll ever meet him—or if you do it's probably too late.'

Willa said quickly, 'Maura, what are you talking about?'

She answered flatly. 'I'm in love with Johnnie.'

She repeated her words, but they were now a wild outcry against the suddenness and tyranny of her love.

'Oh, Willa—do you realise what's happened to me? I'm in love with Johnnie.'

Willa's hands fell limply into her lap. 'What will you do?'

'Do?' Maura bent her head with a gesture of pain. 'What else can I do but what I've decided?'

Willa's voice was low with distress. 'But are you sure? How can you know you love him? You've only known him a week.'

'Does that matter?' Maura demanded. 'Does that matter in the least? Time isn't a measure of loving. How long did it take you to decide you loved Jeremy?'

Willa swept aside the question. 'And what of Johnnie?'

Maura's head rested in her hands. 'He loves me—I'm sure of that. This afternoon—we both knew it. It was there as plainly as anything that was ever put into words. But he won't say anything. Neither of us will.'

'Do you think,' Willa broke out, 'that marrying Tom is going to help you forget this?'

'I don't want to escape the memory of loving him. That's part of it.'

'That's not fair to Tom. You're not a good liar, Maura. You can't pretend to love him.'

'There will be no pretence. Tom knows that I don't love him. He doesn't expect my love because he has none—except the affection we have for each other—he has no love to give himself.

'He has told me about it, 'she continued. 'He was in love with a girl in Italy during the war. I imagine it was the greatest and most wonderful thing that ever happened to Tom. She was killed—and Tom being what he is, he knows he'll never love like that again.'

Suddenly Willa cried out, 'A marriage can't be made like that—in cold blood You must think about it—at least you must tell Tom about Johnnie, and give him the chance of making the decision himself.'

Maura said dully, 'There is no need for Tom to know. I mean never to see Johnnie again.'

Willa's agitation dropped to a faint despair She knew the look of near-obstinacy which possessed Maura's face. Foolish and impulsive at times, she was never more so than at this moment, or never, perhaps, so appealing. Had Johnnie himself, she wondered, grown to love these very imperfections, to know her rashness and generosity. But she was courageous, and she had faith in herself and Tom to make this marriage. There were resources in each of them to meet the demands of the other. She thought that had these two, Maura and Tom, been able to love each other, then marriage between them would have been something of worth. But they would go on giving the best of their passion and tenderness to their separate and vanished ideals. It all seemed such a terrible waste.

Willa knew there was no more to say about it. Maura, in a mood like this, was beyond persuasion. She said quietly, 'To-morrow is your last day—you'll go sailing alone?'

Maura nodded 'It's much better that way. I've promised myself I'll never see him again. I'll be leaving here as soon as it's daylight on Monday.'

The words already contained the note of her departure. They almost seemed the herald of the winter. Maura threw some more wood on the fire, and they watched—each absorbed by the thoughts which ran between them—as the flames clutched the dry edge of the sticks The wind flowed softly around the house, its sharper gusts a faint echo of Willa's sigh. They knew they needed the comfort

42

of each other, feeling vaguely that beyond this one hour, beyond even the circle of the firelight, there was waiting for them more events than they could, for the moment, comprehend. Unwilling, perhaps unable to move, they remained there as long as the pile of driftwood lasted.

# VII

There was plenty of time all that next day aboard *Rainbird* to think about her decision to marry Tom. It was a day of wind and sun—catspaws of wind which darkened and ruffled the water of the river long distances ahead, a day which brought a light of bliss to Peter's Brown's eyes as they slipped off on a lee tide.

There had been many mornings like this in Maura's life—like this one, but possessed of the infinite variety of winds and tide and sky known to a sailor. But as the wooded banks slipped by, her mind was back with all those other mornings of sailing with Tom and his father, Gerald, among the islands and bays of the Irish coast. Much of Maura's childhood memories belonged with Tom and with the leisured busyness of holidays at Rathbeg. Desmond's cousin, Gerald, had given all that crowded world of horses and dogs, farm and garden, to Maura and Chris to love and possess in no less a degree than his own children. Chris was the chosen companion of Harry, Tom's younger brother, and to them belonged the silent and concentrated hours of fishing in Harry's dark and beloved little mountain lakes, where rising trout made the only ripples on those still waters. Between all four of them existed a deep, but casual and undemonstrative friendship.

The essential difference in their two fathers, Desmond and Gerald, lay back uncounted generations ago, when Cromwell had sacked the country. Gerald's ancestor had turned Protestant—the story told against them was that it was to keep a favourite thoroughbred mare, rather than for the sake of their farm-lands, that he made his decision. But the sense of possession was strong, their land-hunger a continual, gnawing ache, and through the following generations, as the wash of political strife had swept about them, they had contrived by whatever means came to their hands, to hold what they had fought for. If the means were sometimes doubtful and not much to their liking, they were prepared to pay that price for the security of Rathbeg and its acres. For a restless, younger son's part in the rising of 1798, a portion of their land had been confiscated. Through the next century it had been gradually restored at infinite cost and trouble—and for the reason of their loyalty to Parliament at Westminster. But Home Rule was an established fact, and Rathbeg prosperous and untroubled when Maura and Chris had first known it. The only awkwardness they had known was that of their cousins' opposite religion.

Desmond was a descendant of the Catholic rebel, Michael —the patriot who had been executed, and for whose recklessness Rathbeg's lands had diminished so abruptly. He had left one son, Desmond's grandfather. Desmond himself had been the youngest of eight children, and could remember too vividly the overcrowding of the tiny farmhouse where he had grown up—far away from Rathbeg— and the wretched and paltry yield of its infertile acres. He had hated the barren hill-slopes he had helped to farm, and the quarrelling, noisy life of the farm-house. His escape to a law-course at Trinity had been made on money borrowed by his mother, and the scholarship which his brilliance—coming suddenly in an otherwise dull family —had won even against the prejudice aroused by his religion. Once out of Trinity he came to London, not caring about his obscure and humble beginning in a law firm, but only conscious of his freedom from the servile poverty he feared and dreaded.

When his children, Maura and Chris, had been old enough he had sent them on visits, not to his own brothers, but to his cousin Gerald, at Rathbeg, in order that they should learn of the kind of Irish life he had never known. He had no scruples about where he owed his loyalty—he knew too well the things he needed and meant to have for his children. Maura guessed that, almost since she was a child, Desmond hoped for a marriage between herself and Tom.

But, perversely it seemed to Desmond, as they grew older, they grew a little apart—not less friendly, but as the range of their interests widened, they were less absorbed in each other. They knew the plan made for them, and Maura at the age of eighteen, and Tom two years older, had agreed that it was impossible. Tom was at Trinity then, Maura preparing for her law course at Cambridge, and they both knew, or said they did, that they would never be in love with each other. Tom had come to London and joined the Army at the outbreak of war, and Desmond had thrown them together with cool deliberation all during the period while Tom waited for his posting to North Africa. His disappointment was plain when Tom went away and there was no talk of an engagement.

Chris followed Tom's Division out to the desert, and followed it also to Italy, while, Desmond, at home, had managed to have Maura, now in the legal section of the Army, transferred to London. Chris being beyond his reach, he clung to Maura with fierce possessiveness.

At last, on leave in Florence, Chris wrote that he had caught up with Tom. He wrote of the change he found in his cousin, while from Tom's letters she read almost the same words of her brother. Each had tried to assess the quality of the change in the other, the extent, the direction, and had failed—their scratched out sentences perhaps stronger than the words they might have used. They spent two leaves together, and Chris was with Tom when the news came that Harry had been killed in the Normandy landings. Only his hurried, unpolished letters could tell them of Tom's grief, until there came Tom's own letter to her, with its few lines recalling to her Harry's love of Rathbeg, and Gerald's immense loss. After that he never spoke of Harry again.

And it was Chris who wrote to them that Tom had been seriously wounded in the fighting on the Gothic Line. It was a head wound which didn't heal quickly, and he was sent back to England when he could be moved.

Maura called a brief order to Peter as they made for the mouth of Harwich harbour. Outside the breeze hardened, but with no signs of bad weather about, she gave in to Peter's demands that they keep heading north. Her mind was with Tom and on the months following Chris's letter to her, begging her to see Tom as much as possible, and telling, though briefly, of the Italian girl whom Tom had loved. She had been killed, he wrote, in a raid on the hospital where she nursed.

Maura gazed about the expanse of hard, glittering sky which surrounded her, remembering how it had been when Tom came back. She was unprepared for the austere changes which the years of absence had made in his handsome face, and wondered why she had never before seen the fineness and strength of his hands. She recalled, also, her unaccountable shyness before the stranger he had become; visits to his hospital in Reading were hours of discovery. There was too much change in Tom to be weighed up immediately or completely. She grew closer to him, and yet seemed to learn no more of him; his reticence still screened the years of the war. He talked much of Harry—Maura was shamed to realise she had guessed so little of the intimacy which had existed between the brothers—and he talked of Rathbeg. And here his love was passionate and voluble—his plans for Rathbeg and his longing to return there. She knew that consideration for Rathbeg would decide every other question in Tom's life from now on.

Maura was granted leave at the same time as his discharge in the autumn, and he took her to Ireland with him. They went immediately after the Japanese surrender, when the world was in the midst of its waiting pause, and their own affairs, after so long a period of being subject to bigger issues, suddenly assumed overwhelming importance. The five lost years demanded compensation. Tom sought it in Rathbeg.

There had been at first a tentative, wary acceptance of the things he saw, then followed his wild joy at the per-

46

manence and beauty he found there. Maura saw with wonder his rediscovery of every remembered scene—the treasured images he had carried with him through these five years renewed and restored to him.

And then, for the first time, he talked to her of the girl, Gena, whom he had loved. He talked to her one evening as they walked on the flat shores of the lake, with the mountains behind them leaning backwards into the autumn haze. There seemed little to tell her—they had been in love, wildly in love. They had been lovers, he said, and she had refused to marry him, feeling the thread of war binding them together more strongly than would be so in peace-time, afraid—as she could never make him be—of the regrets which might come to them when they faced the end of the war and his return to England. She had been simple, and very proud, he said.

His face, as he talked, had been aflame with memory, animated and stirred as Maura had never before in her life seen it. She knew, for all his brief sentences, for the few words in which he had chosen to tell her the story of his love, that all the vitality of his nature had been poured into it. He had expended himself upon it—having loved once in that fashion she knew it would never return for him again. She felt that he was patient because all need for impatience had passed.

They had their three weeks together there—and never, it seemed to Maura—had the Irish countryside been more lovely, the sky more tenderly stooped towards the mountains, the lakes throwing back their reflection more softly. Never before had the wild, lonely bird-calls been so haunting, so much far-away magic. They rode often in the grey Irish rain of the autumn, and out in the bay in *Rainbird* they watched the mist come swirling down from the highest peaks, over Rathbeg and its wide stretch of land, roll out across the water towards them. They hove to, with that grey vapour clinging close about them, moisture gathering on everything they touched, dripping with melancholy patter from the shrouds and forestays. The silence was complete, and they stood there, side by side, feeling

47

the immensity of it pressing about them. They had never been more alone than on that wet dock, or closer to each other. Tom's hand dropped lightly on hers but still they did not speak. Their communication was instant and as perfect as it can be between two people. Their common blood, as well as the common love of the land which lay unseen in the mist, drew them together strongly. They remained thus, unmoving and wrapped in silence, until a faint breeze tore the mist apart, cutting a way clear to their anchorage, giving them one brief glimpse of Rathbeg and the friendly trees surrounding it. They weighed anchor, and slipped forward quietly.

The days dropped away swiftly to the end of Maura's leave, but those moments never lost their significance. Although Tom must stay behind at Rathbeg until he was stronger, she could sense the formation of plans, a purpose which had not been in him before. Her visit ended with Gerald's promise that she should have *Rainbird* for her own—they would sail her to England in the spring, he said.

She felt the deck of *Rainbird* firmly beneath her feet now, and remembered that it had all happened four years ago; in that time Tom had come to England—against Gerald's pleas that he stay with him—to study agriculture, and at the end of his course, had taken a job in the Ministry. Gerald had to be content with his explanation that he was going to learn all that anyone could teach him about farming. He planned to go back to Ireland in the summer—and he wanted Maura to marry him then.

She knew that Tom loved her, not in any passionate sense, but because he loved no other woman. They could trust each other, knew each other's mind with pleasing thoroughness. There was sureness and serenity in the life they would have together. But as yet she had hung back from a definite promise to marry him. She hung back because on that one occasion when he had revealed his love for the unknown Italian girl, she had seen for the first time, what love might be. In none of the passing encounters of her Army days, nor in Tom himself, did she ever find the qualities which could have awakened such an emotion in her.

And now, in loving Johnnie she knew what it was she had desired. In this single span of time—swift enough to count the days upon her two hands—she had tasted the full measure of love, and had learned that she would never know its like again. She would go on loving Johnnie without purpose, without hope.

And suddenly looking up and catching sight of Peter Brown's young and untroubled face, sharp now with a kind of ecstasy and wet with spray from the short, sharp waves which the steadily hardening wind had begun to kick up, she suffered a twist of almost unbearable pain. She called an order to heave-to, and reef.

## VIII

The light had gone from the sky when *Rainbird* entered the estuary again. Darkness fell rapidly, wrapped the shallows and mud-flats in shadows, and only where the banks sloped up sharply were the outlines of the trees blacker than the sky. Maura looked at them, her mind and body aching from the battle she had fought all day with the pain of losing Johnnie, and the anguish of her decision. Out there, during all those radiant hours of sun and wind, his face had seemed to ride before her, swinging back and forth with the dip of the mast and forestay. It had haunted and tormented her, until her mind was too dazed to comprehend it any longer.

She could not remember having eaten or drunk all that day, but Peter's calmness told her that somehow she had managed to give no strong indication of the incredible tumult in her heart. But the storm had exhausted her; her body had become a vague and alien shape surrounding the vacancy of her mind. Her one desire was to sleep and be allowed to forget her pain.

They had a fair breeze, and *Rainbird* slipped quietly up the river. Peter padded around the deck with soft move-

49

ments, preparing to anchor when they reached Able's boat-shed. Maura caught sight of his face, and knew his expression—a sober and regretful reflection that he would not sail again until the spring. He glanced upwards, and she felt he was offering a strained, awkward gesture of gratitude for the fairness of the day, for the exultation he had known during their swift passage across the water. She tossed a half-smile of affection and understanding towards him and he responded. At that moment they rounded a bend in the river, and Able's anchorage came into sight.

Johnnie stood with a lamp beside the closed door of the boat-shed. The sight of him struck her with terrible familiarity, brought flooding back into her brain all the emotions she had believed were lost in her weariness. She was tired, but now immensely alive again—alert with an impossible, blinding alertness.

'Ahoy!'

'Ahoy, there!' Peter's high young voice drifted over the water.

He slipped into a dinghy and rowed out to them. Peter greeted him cheerfully with a swift account of the day's sailing. Johnnie returned his greeting mechanically, turning as he did so towards Maura and raising his lamp high so that its rays lit his face as well as her own. His eyes questioned her. The air of defeat and hopelessness which hung about him was mercilessly plain to her. She knew that he also had spent a day of unfruitful turmoil, but he expected no answer to his problem from her. He simply looked at her, and they knew each other's misery.

They exchanged a few words, commonplace—neither knew nor cared what they were saying—and then all three set to work in silence. When *Rainbird* was ready they loaded the dinghies with gear, and Peter rowed the smaller one ashore; Johnnie and Maura took *Rainbird*'s own. They secured the boats above the high-water line, and Peter started up the hill towards the main road quickly. He was catching the last bus from the village to Dedham; it was only a few minutes off the time. Maura and Johnnie, their arms loaded with gear, followed him. Calling over his shoulder to them, Peter talked with deliberate cheerfulness of his return to school.

'It's been a terrific summer,' he said. In the darkness Maura could sense that he was smiling towards her. 'Seems ages before we'll have *Rainbird* out again, doesn't it?' He paused, then added swiftly, 'You'll be still wanting crew next summer, Maura?'

'You know I depend on you, Peter.'

'Thanks.' Then he added, 'Look, I'll have to dash. The bus will be along any second now. See you in the spring, Maura.' He dumped the gear he carried into Johnnie's arms. 'Good-bye. Good-bye, Johnnie.'

A few yards away from them he stopped and came back. He addressed Johnnie.

'I forgot. I won't be seeing you again. Hope the trip back to America is good. Wish I were going with you. Good-bye.'

Then he sped on ahead and out of sight.

Now they were alone and each was afraid of the other's silence, and still afraid to speak. Their tiny span of time was drawing to an end; they were each pitifully conscious of the minutes running out, slipping away from them. And yet there was nothing special to do, or to say. There was nothing more significant or important than their love, and they couldn't speak of it so they walked on with the night close about them, and the anguish of their hearts and minds much louder than words.

They reached the cottage, and Johnnie helped her to stow the gear in the hall.

'You're leaving early in the morning?'

'As early as possible. I'll have to get a day's work in at the Chambers.'

She was glad of the dignity they both found to resist senseless questionings.

She stood by the open door. 'Good-bye, Johnnie.'

He held out his hand. 'Good-bye, Maura.'

The light contact of their hands was a swift undoing. Johnnie stared at her with an expression of uncertainty, then caught her in his arms. When he kissed her, it was

51

the kiss that all these minutes of silence had led up to. It was a kiss of passion, and still one of farewell. He did not release her immediately, but pressed his face close to hers, as if he wanted to memorise its feel, wanted to store it up against the time when he would be without it.

Then abruptly he stepped away from her, turned and walked down the path. It was too dark to see him go, but she heard the sound of the gate as it closed behind him.

# PART TWO

---

## I

Desmond noticed that the leaves of the trees along Hanover Terrace had begun to tighten, and their tips were brown, and he wondered if Maura had noticed it as well. Incredible, he thought, how much he minded not having her at his side to say these things as they occurred to him.

He walked up the steps and let himself in with his latch key. The door swung behind him with a loud noise, and the man, Simpson, was in the hall immediately.

'Good-evening, Simpson. Is Miss Maura in?'

'Good-evening, Sir Desmond. Miss Maura arrived about an hour ago.'

'Good . . . good! Where is she . . . in the drawing-room?'

Simpson took the discarded hat and gloves. 'I believe she's upstairs, Sir Desmond. She mentioned being tired, and talked of having a rest.'

A flush rose on Desmond's face. He half-hesitated, and then said, 'Can you tell me if her car came back?'

'Oh, yes, sir. She put it away in the garage after she had left her bags.'

'And Mister Chris—has he been in?'

'He's been in, sir, and left again.'

'Thank you.'

Communication between the master and servant was sparse. Desmond's servants were always highly-paid, efficient and anonymous. He had chosen to have them that way, and so he turned and mounted the stairs, and he was lonely. The day stretched backwards from him, and it seemed lonely, also, because during it he had treasured this promise to himself of an hour alone before dinner with Maura and Chris. And they unknowingly had failed him here, and had given him solitude in place of the company he craved. He knew his resentment was unreasonable, and disliked it the more for that. Pouring himself a whisky, he felt tired and dissatisfied.

Children were the very devil, he thought. He settled firmly in the chair before the window which gave him a view of the sunlit park and the crowds on the edges of the lake. There were sailing boats out—the season had lasted much longer this year, and he calculated that the man who hired them out had made money. He was full of soreness and irritation, and the boats seemed to him like silly toys, sprawling and languid, for there was little wind. He moved, frowning and fingering his glass, not liking much what he saw from his window. This was the park when it belonged to the crowd, not the view he had paid for when he bought the house. Desmond wanted no feeling of belonging to the crowd.

The thought brought him back to Maura and Chris again, for now they seemed identified with that indifferent crowd, drifting past his very windows and caring nothing for him. Chris gone out again—and Maura lying upstairs when she must surely realise how much he wanted to talk with her, how long the ten days of her absence had been to him. He resented even the mishap which had brought her home at this hour, instead of having the day at the Chambers as she had planned. At nine-thirty, when he had reached his rooms, she had been on the phone to tell him her car had broken down near Colchester, and she was waiting to have it repaired. (Impossible old car, he thought, but he wasn't going to buy her a new one to have her racketing down to that blasted country cottage every time she had a free half-hour.) Unwillingly he had agreed it was better that she wait there than come on by train. But having counted upon her presence, he had missed her too keenly all that day. His sense of grievance grew stronger.

He was peevish because he knew his devotion to his daughter was servile; away from him, beyond his touch and reach, she was a persistent ache from which he had no peace. At times he might have wished her ascendancy less strong, and himself more free, but he was too long accustomed to his bonds. He was fearful and cunning in his relations with her, seeming to give her licence, as in the matter of the cottage, but drawing her back again to him, surely and persistently.

And Chris also was at fault—leaving the Chambers before him, coming home to shave and change, and going already to pick up Marion. He guessed that they would leave it as late as possible before dinner to return to the house. They would go wherever it was they went to drink; probably to some dark little pub—only they wouldn't notice it was dark—and they would sit there talking about things that concerned themselves, and certainly not him. It left him so much alone here—alone and sitting here like a fool awaiting Maura's pleasure.

He twisted in his chair, turning his back upon the glitter of the lake and the colour of the throng. There was much simplicity in Desmond's nature, and the room now before him gave him supreme satisfaction. He knew it was beautiful, and he knew it represented all the things he had made from his life. He did not despise himself because this room was the showplace of his achievements and possessions.

All his life gifts had been flung into Desmond's lap to make what he could of them. He had enormous luck, but far greater than that, he knew, was his genius for evaluing what fell within his hand's reach. People and opportunities were twisted to become vehicles for his talent to ride upon. He was a huckster of his own gifts, and with them he had purchased the magnificence which lay around him. It was his own created world, the one in which he chose to dwell.

There were two mirrors to reflect the scene, to reflect Desmond himself as he sat there. They diminished it all —the room was compact and minute like a doll's house, and he a tiny stuffed figure in his chair. It seemed as if he gazed upon himself from a very far distance and from a past time. He had long ago recognised the fact that when an ambitious man ceases to look to the future, it has little more for him to wrest from it, and now this was true of himself. It was a recent habit of his to slip back to the early London days, and back further than that—to the Trinity days in Dublin, to the darkened and exaggerated memories of his boyhood.

Trinity had been his great awakening and his testing ground. Ability, he undoubtedly had, enough to leave any competition behind, but he had to learn quickly that it was his sole possession. After the rebel Michael's break from the family at Rathbeg, his children had dropped into complete obscurity; lack of education and the money for it, as well as unfavourable marriages had brought them lower. At the time of Desmond's entry into Trinity, his father was a small farmer, existing on mortgages and working harder than a labourer in his own fields. The background might have ruined him for his uncouthness hung heavily upon him; the necessary restrictions of his life had never even given him the glimpse of what he might be, or what might wait for him. When he came to Trinity he knew only books, and the hands which handled them were hardened with plough, shears and reins. But there was enough of breeding still in him to make him aware of this; it was urgent then for him to find the opportunities to pull himself to the level he sought. The most potent and promising of these was his friendship— never strong or binding, but there nevertheless—with his cousin, Gerald.

Gerald had been born at Rathbeg, and would some day own it. The cousins had never met in their childhood, had no particular knowledge of each other's existence, but their meeting at Trinity Desmond counted as one of the most important happenings of his young life. He had no vision of the future—none save a strange, innate conviction that Gerald's influence, however slight now, would remain with him always. He had never admired or wished to imitate anyone so much as Gerald, who was all that Rathbeg was, all the power and prosperity which Desmond's family had cut adrift from so long ago. The difference between them now was great, but he was beginning to recognise the first development of the talents which lay within him, and he had begun to conceive a time when they might be almost equal. He never lost that idea.

It was Gerald who took him on that cold and memorable winter's afternoon to the house of Francis Healey, a professor of languages at the College. Healey was a cultured, quiet man, full of humour and gentleness, but his French wife made him remarkable in that academic circle of Dublin. She was forty then, dark and small, with irregularly-shaped features which caused some to say that she was ugly. But whatever charm, whatever fascination she possessed, it drew people about her effortlessly; the vigour of her wit had become a byword. They had little money, she and Francis Healey, and the poverty and worry of their five small children she shrugged off with cool, outrageous courage. She was gay and brilliant—the first woman of her kind that Desmond had ever known.

And then he fell in love with her. He didn't know why he should love her, or what return he could hope for, but loving her was almost against his will, something too natural to stop or prevent. He carried the frustration of it with him all that winter, coming to her house two and three afternoons in the week, and always hoping her shabby, faded drawing-room would be without its usual collection of students. She was kind to him—he would feel himself softened and comforted in after years to remember her kindness. He was awkward and inarticulate before her, with the manners of a country farm-house still upon him. But she eased his shyness from him until he could talk to her, and some of the force of his emotion found relief in that fashion.

He did not tell her she was to him as exciting, as strange and foreign as anything he had ever imagined. Could she know, he wondered, how removed she was from the women of his experience, his mother and sisters, the girls in the cottages upon the bare hills and slopes; did she know that for him she was the world beyond Ireland, beckoning and compelling—that her charm and pretty manners were the product of a way of life he had before this viewed with almost a peasant's scorn and near-apathy? But he thought she did know all of this; she was wise as well as kind, aware of his unspoken love, and trying to soften the pain of it for him. He had never believed how tender a woman could be until she had shown him.

Understanding his craving for what he had missed far better perhaps than he knew it himself, she began to help him with piano lessons. Herself a rare and accomplished musician, she wanted to give to him of her talent, because it was the only thing she had to give. She took that ability of his to strum folk-songs and ballads, and began to reshape it, guiding, explaining, while it was gradually revealed to him that all music could be a love song. He accepted it with ease and gratitude, knowing exactly what it was she intended, working to please her, and supremely conscious of the relief this expression gave him.

If she did not love him, or acknowledge love, she was ambitious for him, using her power to drive him far harder, with less pity, than he had the will to do himself. Through his years at Trinity they continued in that manner—he knew her only as a woman surrounded by her young family, oppressed by money worries, and yet she was teacher as well, arbiter of all the graciousness and polish to which he would ever aspire. She possessed him wholly, and made his obedience to her unquestioning. He didn't know why a woman so much older, a woman not beautiful, should so possess him. But her influence was there, and continued long after her death during the winter of 1917, when Desmond was serving in France.

He was never freed from her, the memory of her gaiety and wit led him to seek it in other women; his gaze towards them was merely the search for the intelligence and animation of her dark little face. He never found it when a woman returned his gaze, because he had once been too swift a prisoner to Elise Healey's enchantment.

It was unfortunate for Mildred Stirling that she fell in love with Desmond then. He was ready for no woman's love, least of all a love like Mildred's. She had inherited a fortune too young from her father's railway shares, and she had not yet learned of anything it couldn't buy. She was a V.A.D. in the hospital camp in France where Desmond was sent with a slight wound. By the time the wound was healed, and Desmond went on leave to England, she was desperate in her love for him. The grace and charm he had learned from Francis Healey's wife was becoming habitual—and he had never been unkind to a woman—so that she was never fully aware of his indifference. Five days after he left she had managed to get leave, and she found him in London alone. Because there was no reason to refuse, he let her take him to her brother's house in the Cotswolds. She had courage of a kind, and a gambler's spirit; before he left again for France she had his promise to marry her.

She was not a vicious or greedy woman—she merely made the mistake of loving and believing love itself could awaken response. It was not her fault, or Desmond's either, that their marriage should have failed so miserably or so early. Desmond had loved once, and passion and tenderness both were spent in that love. Mildred might struggle as she pleased against the truth of it. They returned to London, and she grew to fear the ambition which drove him to work with consuming energy, grew to fear the dullness and silence of their house while he was away, but still to fear far more the hours in the evenings when he sat at the piano, never turning once to look at her quiet, hungering face. Maura, born in the second year of their marriage, brought little change to their lives. At Chris's birth Mildred died, never having known Desmond's eyes upon her with real awareness, never experiencing, even briefly, the return of her love. She was almost glad to die to be freed from its pain.

Weeks after she was dead Desmond awoke suddenly to her loneliness, and was appalled and shamed. He tried to recall her fair, handsome face and scarcely a memory remained to him. He began to wonder of what she had talked and how he had answered her, but no word of their conversations was remembered. It had all vanished; all their talks and plans—if they had ever planned—all the evidence of their life together. He looked among her possessions, seeking the woman she was, and found little to guide him. He could look at her portrait and it told him nothing. Desmond knew, had always known, that he could never have loved Mildred, but as the enigma of her continued to baffle and confuse him, he began to see that she might have been an interesting woman to discover.

He successfully resisted the attempts of Mildred's only brother to have Maura and Chris brought up with his own children. In that first year after her death, that year of acceptance and adjustment, he laid the foundation of the obsession which they were to become. He began to see how these children might be all he had wished for himself. Their ordered, luxurious nurseries were to wipe out the memory of the crowded farm-house, their clothes were the finery which in his own childhood he had never glimpsed. Mildred's solid middle-class breeding would show in them, he thought, and there might even be from him still a trace of that pride of the land-owning class which he had known in his cousin, Gerald. His plans for them kept pace with his own career. They would be clever and poised, he thought, remembering and hating his own early uncouthness.

He brought them down much too early from their nurseries to mix among the people with whom he now filled his house. The unmovable coolness which Mildred had given them withstood the influence to which they were exposed. They remained pleasant children, concerned in their own affairs, and slightly indifferent to the distinguished company their father entertained. They displayed none of his own brilliance, being intelligent but not outstanding, pleased with small and mediocre successes. But they were increasingly dear to him, and when, after a meeting with Gerald in London, they went one summer to Rathbeg, his dream for them seemed satisfied. His own childhood was then, at last, buried.

His thoughts deliberately sheered away from the subject of Maura and Tom. He rose with a faint gesture of irritation to pour himself another drink, but the action helped him not at all. What obstinacy, he reflected, could possibly keep them apart, who seemed made for each other, whose thoughts fitted together with an invariable ease? Could they be such fools as not to see what lay before their own noses? He frowned down at the glass in his hand, and it was a very moderate helping of whisky he took—less than he would have liked. Then he strode across the room and opened the door. There was no sound from the landing above where Maura's room was. He advanced half-way up the flight of stairs.

'Maura—Maura, are you awake?'

Her voice came to him, indistinct behind the closed door. 'Coming, Father. Be with you in a minute.'

Gratified, he returned to his seat in the drawing-room, first selecting and pouring the pale sherry he always kept for Maura. He added the other half of the whisky to his own glass.

She came quite soon. He heard her step on the stairs, and then the sight of her in the red gown which had been his gift. He looked at her with satisfaction, believing that such colours were made for dark women, and that if Maura didn't have beauty there were other ways of making her memorable.

She bent to kiss him; there was nothing perfunctory in the gesture.

'Have I been ages? I meant to be here when you came in. But lying down was fatal—it was almost impossible to get up.'

As she spoke she moved to the table where the glass awaited her. It was a movement of long custom, and something in it warmed Desmond's senses. In it he saw the love between them which had established such routine, her unspoken love which accepted and conformed to his desires. It was precious to him, this evidence, although he knew he exposed himself to chance hurts by the very importance he gave it.

'My darling, I'm used to waiting upon my children.'

She smiled at him, because she knew he expected it. And she said, 'It's good to be home,' because this also was expected. 'The cottage is shut now—I don't go back until the spring.'

His returning good-humour swept through him warmly. 'It's always good to be home,' he said. 'These week-end places are all right, but one needs a home. You've got to have a place where you know you belong.'

And then he saw, looking at her face, that his words had been wrong. They had wounded her in some unexpected fashion, and his pleasure was grown cold. She wore an expression of grieving and bewilderment, as if she were utterly lost to him. It terrified him, this alien waywardness. He wanted to stretch out his hand to her, his best-loved child, and call her to him. As if fearing him she turned towards the window, so that the expression, Maura's very self, was hidden from him.

'Has work been heavy at the Chambers while I was away?' was all she said.

Helpless and afraid, he was forced to answer as she compelled him.

## II

The El Greco burned brilliantly against the white wall. Tom gazed at it, finding there a passion and still a perfect detachment, a quiet grief which smote him each time he saw it. The saint's figure was human and tired.

Desmond had hung it bravely in the bare white dining-room, permitting no other colour to detract from it. Theatrical it might have been in effect, but the picture withstood that criticism. It remained there, giving a point to that austerity of white—magnificently alive, and Desmond's stroke of boldness was justified.

Tom could only turn from it to Desmond himself, who sat with a woman on either side of him, bending towards them from his height. He was splendidly handsome, Tom thought, heavily built, with huge hands, one spread now upon the table, the other enfolding his glass. His head was flung back occasionally as he talked, and the white hair upon it seemed unreal, too thick, too crisp. He was easily the most remarkable person of the ten who sat around the table. Even the high-cheeked face of the Judge on Maura's right grew less distinguished beside Desmond. Well aware of his power, he accepted it naturally—and the small, pleased murmurs of the women beside him had long been a part of his life.

Tom knew all this, but knew, also, much more about Desmond than many other people. Gerald's memories of his cousin at Trinity were clear and sharp and he had related them to his son. The great bulk of a young man desperately ill at ease, with the uncouthness of the farmhouse and the fields hardly yet touched by poise, was uppermost in Tom's mind. This much his father had told him, and the evidence of how far from that point Desmond had come, was more astonishing to Tom because of his greater knowledge of the man.

He was essentially simple, Tom thought, with the guiding motives of his life clear and easily discovered by anyone who sought them. He cared only for his work and his children. His sympathies remained curiously free from even the slightest encroachment of another force—in some fashion he had achieved a complete divorcement from anything which was not one or the other. People—ordinary people—touched him hardly at all; he was impersonally solicitous of his servants and employees, kind to them, but barely able to distinguish between them, admittedly disinterested in them as personalities. Tom had wondered if anyone as genial as Desmond could be called inhuman, and yet the word had sometimes occurred to him. A disaster—even a war, Tom recalled—was real to him only in so far as it concerned or endangered his children. He went abroad to look at pictures, to hear music, and returned, bringing almost nothing of feeling or memories—his heart was never touched or moved by contact with mere strangers. All his curiosity about people, all his

63

passion and imagination were consumed in Maura and Chris. Even the realising of what further ambition was still left to him became a hold on them; he would accept, in time, a place on the Bench, and they would feel he had done so to please them.

There came the short interruption of the women's departure, the scraping of chairs and the sounds of their voices on the stairs. Then the men drew together, close about Desmond, and Tom sat back in his chair, striving to escape the fumes of the Judge's cigar. The fifth man present, a tired, burned-up little scrap with brilliant eyes, a painter whom Desmond had met in Italy, tossed a conversational opening to Tom, who followed it listlessly. He felt vaguely sorry for the man, who later would undoubtedly try to sell some pictures to Desmond, and who was now so obviously uneasy in the chilling, slightly overpowering company of the Judge. Tom blew his cigarette smoke high, leaned further back and studied the Florentine, his nervous gestures, and his dislike of the port. He wished he felt more inclined to talk, but his mind was following the quiet and softly spoken battle which Chris, beside him, was losing.

Chris's fair and handsome face—Tom sometimes thought it absurdly babyish—was flushed and earnest. How was it, Tom wondered, that with the experience of a war behind him Chris could still wear that expression of a child's naïveté? In moments like this he was curiously like the portrait of the fair woman, his mother, which hung upstairs.

'Wait a while, Chris,' the Judge was saying. He was, in his English fashion, indifferent to the presence of the little Florentine across the table—the one person who had possibly not been aware, since his arrival in the house, that Chris was engaged to the Judge's daughter.

Desmond did not hasten to put down his glass, but still he gave his son no time to speak before him.

'I think it's wiser, Chris. In two years your position will be immeasurably better. Marion is a sensible child— she knows what these early years mean to any barrister.' Desmond gave the faintest nod of deference towards the

64

Judge. 'None should know better than Marion.'

And Tom, seeing Chris's dumb and impotent rebellion, was sorry for him, and for the fate of that love, so recently known between himself and Marion. They would wait, Chris and Marion, because they were weaker, so much weaker, than the two who now decided for them. But in the time of waiting their love would be tested and strained as it should not be. They were slight creatures, both of them, too easily swayed by the forces now lined against them. They were in love, a conventional, romantic love, unimpassioned and slightly timid—and they should marry, Tom thought, and have their cool happiness before the danger of some other love, more demanding and exciting, should take either of them. But they were here, caught in this intrigue of Desmond's jealous possession of his son, and they wavered and lost before it. Shrugging his shoulders, Chris gave up the struggle, and Tom, seeing the gesture, was disturbed and irritated. Maura would not thus have given in. He wished now that some sudden, wild visitation of her strength could have claimed Chris, and made him cast away the prudence of their advice. But nothing happened—he merely went on staring sullenly at the table.

Tom turned again to the Florentine, and spoke to him in his own language, his desire now being to make some happiness, some pleasure in place of Chris's disappointment. He watched the man's face relax, and he dropped back in his chair; the tobacco-stained fingers were no longer restless. They talked together about Florence, and the words, falling upon the ears of the others at the table, seemed rich and exotic, and coloured with more warmth than words usually have.

Tom's gaze fell upon Maura, standing beneath the Rembrandt which her mother had bought in the first year of her marriage. She talked earnestly to the Florentine's young wife. They had grouped themselves there, both dark—but unlike in the contrast of their pale olive and white skins—against the splendour of the portrait of the fair Saskia, with her soft, rich smile, half-amused, half-shy and her delight in the brilliance of her costume. In that brief moment of entering the room Tom saw them thus, the two women unconsciously posed, and the third, the painted one, smiling above their heads. Then the composition of the piece was broken by the eager movement of the Florentine towards his wife and the comfortable familiarity of her talk. Maura stayed with them only a few seconds.

She turned then towards Tom, and he came to her, laying his hand gently and unhesitatingly upon her arm, and leading her towards the windows. She chose the chair, half-turned to view the room, which Desmond had sat in earlier that evening. There her stillness was almost the stillness of the portrait, something betaken to herself to shut away the low sound of talk in the room, the dispirited unhappy face of Chris—to shut away the story that Desmond was relating to the young woman, who with Marion's mother, had shared their conversation at dinner. Tom knew that for some reason Maura was in revolt against all of it, against this life of her father's, the adornments she wore which were his gifts, against the close oppressiveness of his love.

Why, he wondered, had Desmond not seen this in her face, why, on this day of her return, had he not known the change in her? Surely love like his could not gaze unseeingly at her, not sense this new demand in her nature. She was looking for something, or someone—even, he thought, with her still body and eyes, she was searching. Or perhaps the search was already ended, and only its memories disturbed her. Whatever it was, whatever had happened to change her in the ten days of her absence, this newly awakened life appealed strongly to all that was left of adventure in him. Maura was stronger—less easy, but stronger. Her slight aloofness which held her back from a desire to know other people to the limit of their natures, seemed at last shattered. He was excited because she appeared to have shed that inhumanity, that faint coldness inherited from Desmond—in these few days had stopped merely observing and learned to partake. But if Desmond had indeed seen all of this he would still cling to the old beliefs, the old faiths, trusting that they could never be entirely supplanted. Tom knew it was true, that of all those here, only he would find the new person of Maura more interesting, more absorbing.

The Florentine had asked Desmond to play, and the room fell silent as he took his seat at the piano. It was typical of him that he didn't flinch from the virtuoso thunder of the Brahms-Paganini variations—someone less confident would have hesitated, but he didn't. Tom watched his body bent slightly back from the keyboard, listened to the early development of the theme, as sharp and clear as a carillon of bells, but all the time he was outside the music, and his thoughts with Maura, and the change he found in her. His desire to be part of the stillness of her was more distinct and real than ever before. He looked down at her unmoving face.

But the music found him, and he grew restless with the wild tarantella movement of the fourteenth variation. It was a whirlwind of sound, catching him up pitilessly, pushing him forward and forward, pounding him with huge chords.

The unquiet mood of it stayed with him until Desmond began on the fourth variation of Book Two—the loveliest, Tom thought, of them all. The tender little grace notes fell softly, swaying into the waltz-like rhythm of the melody; it had a breathless beauty, warm and sad, unbearably sweet.

Tom leaned towards her and spoke, his voice lower than the sound of the music.

'Maura.'

'Yes?' she answered in a whisper.

'When can we be married?'

'I think, Tom . . . whenever you like.'

She had turned her face to him, and their eyes met in friendliness, and the little variation went on, more gentle and caressing than he had ever known it before.

# III

Maura saw the first little curled brown leaves, wondering where and how Johnnie saw them. They circled above the lake in Regent's Park, and she wondered if he watched them drift down the tidal creeks of the Stour, past the sloping wooded banks, past Able's boat-shed, and disappear into the grey wide spaces of the estuary. Was Johnnie still there, still listening to Irene playing at night in the bar of The Stag, or had his restlessness caught up with him, and driven him on? Would he have wanted to stay, she wondered, now the East Anglian countryside was swept with winds from the North Sea? The lights would be lit early at The Stag, and a fire in the grate where the chrysanthemums had flamed the first time she had seen him. Did Johnnie care for the tightening circle of acquaintance-ship which winter brought to the inn—evenings no longer interrupted by casual visitors in cars which stopped for half an hour and were never seen again?—or was he stifled by the closeness of that rural community, and were the villagers regarding him no more as a summer stranger and beginning to ask questions? And was Irene, that child of the city, bored and lonely; and did Johnnie know it without her saying so?—for Irene, of course, would never have spoken of it. With the coming of the autumn had they perhaps gone south—gone to France, to Italy, to Spain; were they jostled in the smelly, colourful market-places of North African ports? How little she knew of Johnnie when she did not know instinctively where he would have chosen to go.

She reminded herself, looking at the leaves, that knowledge was not necessary to love, but rather love itself created desire for knowledge. She reminded herself also that wherever Johnnie was, whatever he was doing, her knowledge of it would not halt the perceptible advance of winter, or of spring itself, or of her marriage to Tom when the summer came. It would have been simple enough to have asked news of him from Willa, but merely knowing of him would not have stilled the disturbance of her heart, or prevented the silent calling of his name. When the frosts in November blackened and tightened the tree branches, it would not help her to know that he gazed on hard blue seas, or on valleys where flowers still bloomed.

She had promised herself during that last day aboard *Rainbird*—that last bright day of wind and sun, and the sight of Johnnie's lamp when they returned to the boat-shed—that she would never see him again. But a promise could not hold back thoughts of him. She wondered if with greater knowledge they would have found each other less lovable, or if—as she hoped it might have been—their flaws slowly revealed might have drawn them closer. Perhaps her brief memories had the unreality of perfection. There was too little that was ordinary about their ten days together, the one afternoon upon a hillside, the only kiss they had given each other. There had been no time for disenchantment, or for the familiar to become commonplace.

She thought that some day she would tell Tom about Johnnie, perhaps when years of peace at Rathbeg had released her from the desperate want of him. Of Tom's understanding she was sure—his own love had been given and spent in one complete gesture, so that only tolerance and generosity and affection remained. She wished that Johnnie might have known Tom, have known what serenity lay ahead for her with him. It was comfort for her to reflect, during the short winter days when desire for Johnnie was sharp and unrelenting, that Tom's children would eventually and finally take his place in her thoughts.

Broken ice glinted dully in the water, and they stood on the bridge and watched it. They watched it in silence— in a half-lazy, half-weary silence which their walk and the sharpness of the cold air had brought them. The light was going rapidly; the park emptying of the people who had paced beneath the dripping trees an hour earlier, of the few children whose cries had broken the winter quiet. Desmond's gloved hand upon the rail lay motionless, as still as the duck upon the banks of that forlorn island in the lake.

Maura stared downwards, stared at the ice which slipped beneath the bridge in the slight movement of the water. She sensed, rather than saw, the dusk that gathered into the trees, and when she lifted her head she knew she would see the lights in Hanover Terrace. A man appeared on the path at the side of the lake; he bent his head into his overcoat, and his footsteps were hurried and unheeding of what was about him, as if dusk had caught him unawares, and he was suddenly cold and irritable. At last they heard not even his footsteps, and the silence was complete. It seemed strange to Maura that Desmond should utter the sigh which she had held back for his sake.

Instantly she turned to him. 'What is it?'

He did not answer her look. 'My dear, Christmas and anniversaries are bad for sentimentalists. I'm not wise enough to look forward to more anniversaries, but always back—and that's bad, too.'

'Why?'

'Why not?' He sighed again, exaggerated but effective. 'My dear, can't you conceive of all the mistakes I've made —even all the ones I've made and have yet to find out about? It's hard on sentimentalists.'

'Have there been mistakes—many?'

'Who knows that there haven't been? Mistakes with

you and Chris . . . you might have been quite different.'

'How different? You and I can stand here and say nothing and be happy with each other. Can there be a mistake about producing that?'

'Yes, I know . . . I know. Many of the things I've done *have* been right. Next Christmas you'll be with Tom at Rathbeg.'

'I know . . .' She moved her own hand upon the rail until it was close to his, not touching because the moment was already too charged with whatever emotion Desmond struggled to hold back—the sense of failure which might yet come, the mistakes made, or the dread of losing her to Tom.

He looked at her hand near to his and said nothing. They stood there in unaffected intimacy, and farther down the lake the dark shapes of two ducks came out of the growing dusk. Maura watched the wedge-shaped ripples fan out, thinking that Desmond was a sentimentalist of a formidable stamp. Whatever qualities he possessed, with them he commanded love from herself and Chris, not only respect. But he was no fool as sentimentalists are. He might label her going to Rathbeg a sentimentalist's dream, if he wanted to give a name to it, but it was no poor match for her. Long ago Desmond had known what friends she and Tom could be, and if not lovers—she could see him give his cynic's shrug of the shoulders which immediately belied the sentiment he claimed—lovers were rare enough in the world, and friends perhaps even rarer.

For no obvious reason the ducks turned and made back to where they had come from, the curving ripples had a suggestion of finality and sadness. She wished they had come nearer, bringing their friendly brown shapes to banish the aloofness of this half-hour of dusk. Their squat little bodies in the water retreated farther and rounded the point of the island. Their going was part of the scene, like the gradual blotting out of that fine dark filigree of bare branches as the light left the sky. There was no movement of people, the benches and paths were deserted, and the only sound was the steady clop-clop of the tiny waves against the stones beneath them. Then distantly they heard the roar of a high-powered car going towards Baker Street, but it was not part of their world, or part of this blank, cold stillness which hung on them. It was the indefinable few moments when the winter afternoon gave place to evening. Maura leaned against the rail, lost in a momentary trance which the cold had brought to her. This was a time in which her life seemed regulated and planned beyond her control, and there was nothing to do but slip along with it, as quietly and easily as the ducks had vanished beyond the bend of the lake. The order of things was inescapable; growing up close to Tom, but needing to love Johnnie before her decision to marry could be made. And of all this, Desmond standing here beside her, went unaware, believing that his patient years of planning had come to their own inevitable conclusion. She pressed herself closely against the damp wooden rail, and closed her eyes.

Desmond felt the movement in her body, and the shiver which followed it. He grasped the hand which lay near his, and she opened her eyes quickly and turned to follow him.

And then they caught the sound of footsteps on the path beside the bridge, and the sound of voices. They hesitated, not knowing, either of them, why they did so, except for the feeling that this was an intrusion on their privacy. But it was momentary only, barely a pause in Desmond's movement; Maura completed her turn from the darkening lake, and so was facing Johnnie and Irene when they stepped on to the bridge.

Irene spoke first. 'Maura!' They could see that quick, instinctive clutching at Johnnie's arm. It was a gesture of excitement and surprise. 'It's Maura!'

Maura's brain was dull and icy. She fumbled for words. 'You're in London . . .' Then stupidly, clumsily, 'I didn't expect. . . .'

It was Desmond who calmed the panic which touched her. 'My dear, I haven't met your friends.'

'I'm sorry.' She was calmer, almost apathetic, again watching events pass out of her hands, herself only the instrument to perform the introductions mechanically, knowing that someone else, Desmond, Irene, Johnnie, would shape this meeting, decide its outcome. Fear washed about her, leaving her no other emotion but the desire to escape from all that was to come, all the future struggle, the pain, all the things that would spring from this meeting. All the past months had been purposeless in their endeavour to leave Johnnie behind, because she stood now upon this bridge where a few moments ago she had experienced, if not peace, then absence from disturbance, and find herself now speaking to him, drawing in every detail of his appearance, searching his face for change, and being conscious through all this that their love had never lessened, but had lain waiting, treacherously it seemed, for their second meeting. In fact, all the months might have been merely a preparation for this. The cold peace of the afternoon was roughly snatched away.

Maura turned her gaze away from Johnnie and looked at Irene. She stood with face upturned, wrapped in a fur coat which made her beauty exquisite, and talked to Desmond. She answered his questions easily, questions about their stay at The Stag—and Johnnie and Maura stood silently beside them, quite apart from everything which Desmond and Irene found to say to each other.

Desmond was enormous beside her, and he was smiling down at the loveliness of her face in the dusk. Maura waited patiently and saw it happen; saw Desmond's capitulation to that beauty, to the unaffected sweetness of her voice and eyes, and for once she wished that Irene might have been dull and ugly, stupid, ungraceful. Then Desmond might have let her go unregretfully, and she, Maura, need not see them again. But all this was impossible because Irene was beautiful, and because the fact they were Americans and alone in London on Christmas Day would appeal to Desmond's sense of hospitality. It was like watching something which had happened many times before to see Desmond take Irene's arm and wheel her gently as they started in the direction of Hanover Terrace.

They were left to walk behind Desmond and Irene along paths wet with the moisture which dripped from the trees.

'How long have you been in London?'

'Three weeks.'

'You didn't stay on at The Stag?'

'The weather broke about a week after you left. There wasn't much sailing.'

As they walked Maura looked backwards, hoping to catch a glimpse of the ducks, but they were indistinguishable against the thin dark mass of the island.

'Where did you go?' she said.

'Where?' He paused and seemed unwilling to reply. 'We loafed about. At least I did—you know how good I am at loafing.'

'No,' she said quickly, 'I don't know. I don't know how good you are at anything. I don't know you at all.'

He halted and gripped her arm, making her stop also and face him.

'That's right—so you don't. You really don't know a damned thing about me, do you?'

He dropped her arm and resumed his walk. 'We're so conceited—all of us, about ourselves. Somehow I imagined you'd know, or guess, just what I would do when I left The Stag. But, of course, you didn't. How could you?'

She stood still, and he, walking on, was forced to stop and come back to her.

'Johnnie, you're not to talk like this. How could I know what you would do—however much I wanted to know?'

'I'm sorry.'

They walked on. Maura could see Desmond bent slightly over Irene, in that manner he had towards women to whom he enjoyed talking.

Then Johnnie said, 'Hell, Maura, I'm sorry. We went to Florence first. That was good—for a time. I knew it a little before the war. Looked a bit different, and the people are hurt and suspicious. But it was good, just the same, to go back to all the things I'd seen before, and find they weren't so different after all. I guess it's the permanency of old things that we all cling to. Then we got caught up with the American colony. A tight little bunch who have grown so Florentine that some of them speak English with an accent. But for some reason they still dig out the Americans who stay there longer than two days. God knows why, because it keeps them suspended between two worlds, and not wholly belonging to either. They all seemed slightly pathetic to me. It was unfortunate we got mixed up with them, because it left us no alternative between being rude about their invitations or getting out.'

'You left?'

'Yes, of course. What else? We went to Venice.'

'It was nice there,' he continued, 'until the morning I saw Mark Brodney drinking coffee outside Florians. Do you remember I told you about Mark?'

'Yes.'

'He's been away from New York for a long time. He told me he was free-lancing, and he'd finished another novel. He had just the same effect on me as always. I was dissatisfied and fed up—more than ever I didn't want my kind of life, and I didn't know what else to do. In a kind of way he made me feel a fool, because I was so much less sure of where I was going than he. If he had even told me I was a fool, or told me I was right, I would have known what to do. But he just sat there and listened. In the end Irene went back to Paris to wait for me.'

'Wait?'

'I took my time. Walked when I felt like it, and thumbed lifts when I wanted to move on quickly. I stopped at a couple of farms and did odd jobs. Some places didn't want me at all—they were rather suspicious of Americans who didn't arrive in big cars. I expect it seemed funny to them that anyone who had good dollars in his pocket should want to work for a few francs. But I made out. Got to Paris after two months.'

'But why, Johnnie?'

'Because I needed to. I needed to shake off my idleness for a while, and yet still be free from the sort of work I didn't want to do. Raking out pig-pens and mending fences seemed much more desirable just then than drinking highballs and sleeping at the wrong end of the day. A final fling, Maura.'

She knew what it would have been like for him—thumbing lifts out of Florence and heading back north towards France, leaving the car and walking when he had liked the country. He would have done a lot of walking in those two months, calling at farms to buy food, and eating it where he chose. It seemed right for him—even with bad weather and growing colder as he went farther north, that sort of life would have suited him. He belonged with scenes like that; she remembered him aboard *Rainbird* and how much at ease he had been there, light hands when he had taken the tiller, and quick, unclumsy movements on deck. That was all Johnnie's world, even dark winter mornings working close to the warm breath of animals belonged to him as much as the days she recalled they had had together in the sun.

'I'm not trying to glorify them, Maura—the people I met on the road. They were just ordinary people, greedy, vicious, fearful, just as people everywhere are. But it was easier to recognise it, and that helped you get past it. I learned a lot from them. But it was only two months after all, and I was conscious of the end of it all the time. I couldn't loaf around any longer; I had to take a train back to Paris. Even with Irene willing to follow any crazy whim of mine I knew that whatever I did, finally I must go back to the job I was trained for. It's just one of the truths you run away from, but which sticks all the time. We came over to London because I figured it was a nearer approach to home. I've taken a job with the *Financial Times*.'

'Why that?'

'I took it because it was offered to me. It isn't much of a job, but it's getting me ready for going back to my own. I guess we'll hang on here for another six months.'

They walked faster now, to draw closer to Desmond and Irene, and in the terraces opposite the lights had strung out. In the top window of a house Maura could see the outline of a woman as she paused in the act of drawing the curtains, to stare into the darkness towards the invisible lake. A car passed them quietly, and they crossed the road to Hanover Terrace. The sound of their footsteps was dulled by the wet leaves which clung to the pavement. They were almost at the end of the terrace when Johnnie spoke again.

'I didn't mean to see you again.'

'I know that.'

'I didn't come to London because you were here. I can't help what's just happened—perhaps nothing on earth would have stopped it. But I'm going to stay. I can't run out on you, too.'

'No, not from me.'

They said no more. Desmond had opened the door, and bunched together, they moved into the hall.

The house was not part of Maura's mood that afternoon; it had no place with her memories of standing on the bridge with Desmond and the dim beauty of the water. It did not belong with the terrible bewilderment of seeing Johnnie again. It was the house of Desmond, half-filled with people, warm and brightly lit; and the tinkle of spoons and women's laughter in the drawing-room. Tom was in place there, and Chris and Marion, and all the familiar figures—even Irene, seated next to Desmond, was not a stranger here. It was only the face of Johnnie which was new, because her imagination had seen him almost everywhere except in this room. Johnnie was her love of all that was removed from the world of Desmond; he was the toughness and independence which Desmond had not been able to subdue. He was free—at least for the present time —of everyone who was like Desmond. But it was the final submission of all revolt to see him here—his tanned and hardened skin the evidence of his two months' freedom —yielding now to the claims which were reasserting themselves. She looked from Desmond to Johnnie, thinking that love was itself the sale of freedom.

They came together at last, Tom and Johnnie, when the tea things had been carried out, and smoke was already beginning to thicken the atmosphere of the room. Tom sat beside Maura, and Johnnie dropped down into an easy-chair facing them. His action was one she had seen a hundred times, but she missed the familiarity of the salt-water stained slacks, and the worn sandals. This figure in the dark suit was a clear indication of the person she had never known, and Johnnie against another background, fitting into another world, was different—as she herself must seem different to him. He bent forward to light the cigarette she held in her hand, and then towards Tom. Maura watched their heads close together as the tiny flame sprang up.

'I hear you're going to live in Ireland after you're married,' Johnnie said.

'I've been away from Ireland long enough,' Tom said. 'I'm tired of being there only on visits.'

Johnnie's eyelids flickered for just a second. He slipped his lighter into his pocket slowly. 'You farm, don't you?'

'Yes.'

'How large?'

'There's about two thousand acres I'll work myself, the rest is let out.'

Johnnie said nothing for a little while, and Maura's eyes strayed to his hands. There was a deep gash across the knuckles of one which was not yet healed; where the palm was revealed she could see the yellowed skin of callouses. When he saw her eyes upon them he turned them palm upwards, and looked at them also.

Then he turned them down again and said to her, 'What will you do with your time there?'

'I imagine she'll have little enough of that on her hands,' Tom said. 'It's amazing how occupied one can be in Ireland with a great number of things that don't seem like occupation at all. That's the fascination of it.'

He added, 'We're bringing *Rainbird* across, of course. You have seen *Rainbird*, haven't you?'

Maura said quietly, 'Johnnie was my crew mostly the last time I stayed at the cottage.'

'Yes—I'd forgotten.' Tom had not forgotten. He had been told in those first minutes after introduction that Johnnie had sailed with her, and he had remembered it, she knew.

'Maura will hunt, of course,' he continued. 'She says she never will, but it makes no difference. In the end she'll give in. We all succumb to the madness of it.'

Johnnie nodded slowly. 'I guess you do.'

'It is a madness,' Tom said, 'because you go crazy with the excitement of it. It doesn't leave you with the memory of thrills or rides to exaggerate when you're too old to ride to hounds any more, but the feeling of power because you've learned the country from the dangers of it, and because you've seen how it looks when you're cubbing before daybreak. People like Maura do it in the end because they can't bear to be shut out.'

Tom's voice had grown urgent as he talked, and when he stopped there was a quietness between them, so that Johnnie's tone, when at last he spoke, seemed dry and reserved. 'I guess they do,' he said.

Then he looked at Maura. 'Will you miss London? It's a big change.'

Tom answered for her. 'Maura is half-Irish, and she's no stranger to Rathbeg.'

Johnnie got to his feet slowly. 'You're right, of course. The Irish have made my own country by the very power of their adaptability. I just wondered, though, how it worked the other way round.'

He inclined his head in Irene's direction. 'I think we'll move off now, Maura. Sir Desmond has more than enough extra guests on a day like this.'

She made no attempt to detain him, but stood beside her father when they were leaving and heard him urge them to come back again, watched them walk down the stairs.

Irene's hand on the banister was pale and small. Then she went back to the drawing-room, and to her seat beside Tom. He lit another cigarette for her without saying anything, and she was grateful for the quietness of him, the very peace.

## V

Sudden rain, with black clouds which blotted out the light, had wiped away this first touch of spring. The early days of April were too early, Maura thought, to take the pale sunshine seriously, or to think much about the strong smell of the earth when one went into the park. It always ended in this anti-climax of rain, running down the windows, dripping from the trees in the terrace. Even now she could hear, without turning to watch it, Desmond's move to lay more coal on the fire, and she knew exactly how he would stand before it, poker in hand, talking to his guests.

She continued to stare at the window, at the rain sliding past them, thinking that when she finally rejoined the group around the fireplace, it would be returning to a pattern and a sight which had become too familiar during these Sunday afternoons of the winter. Johnnie was there, and Irene, with Desmond close in attendance upon her. Tom was there, and Chris and Marion. And Willa Parker sat on the fender stool, toasting her brown face before the fire, and managing to keep Desmond's eloquence a little in check by the good-natured sanity of her remarks. Desmond was always a little uneasy with Willa for this reason, and turned now and again to Irene, sure of her attention.

It was strange to remember, Maura thought, how inevitably Irene and Johnnie had been drawn into this circle, absorbed its atmosphere, had remained held and bound by Desmond's influence and his will. From the first Irene had been a favourite with him, and she much more than merely humouring him, grew fond of him, and patient with the exuberance of his temperament. Maura wondered what particular need in his nature she answered, what response in him she evoked. Certainly she, and Johnnie through her, had been given an appointed place in that household, and Maura was able to see how she may have seemed the second daughter to Desmond—and while loving Maura still he might have recognised in the other woman all the things that it was impossible for his own child to be. He was wise enough to know that one woman could never be all that he desired, and was content to divide what seemed to him perfection among two.

He played greedily upon the fact that they were Americans away from home, and that Johnnie's job kept them in London. There was no escape from his invitations, which became routine as the months passed. They were vulnerable, too, because their flat in Great Portland Street had become for Desmond a stopping-off place after Mass on Sunday mornings, and he would bring them with him, across the park, when he returned to Hanover Terrace for lunch. It seemed in these long, quiet Sunday afternoons, that Irene and Johnnie were as familiar to the house as Maura and Chris, as familiar as Tom, and much welcomed and loaded with his hospitality. He was so naïvely trusting, so sure, Maura thought, that all about him was right, that things were to his ordering and liking. How could he, she wondered, go on insisting, Sunday after Sunday, that the two Americans should be present, and why was it he had never known how long the day was for her, and how swiftly the week went and it was upon them again—until all time seemed Sunday?

Desmond could never know how much she learned of Johnnie during the Sundays of that winter; how much more of him she knew than the person who had sailed with her and drank beer in The Stag. She saw him now as the sort of person New York might have known, not a young man killing time in an Essex pub and filled with a futile nostalgia for the Cambridge days back again. He wore impeccable clothes; when he chose to argue with Desmond or Tom or Chris, he was not readily silenced.

And all the time there was the touch of toughness in him, that characteristic American directness which made the attempts at subtlety the English employed seem faintly effeminate and unnecessary.

These Sundays gave her time to question him, and she remembered carefully their conversations.

'Do you write home often, Johnnie?'

He nodded. 'Whenever there's plenty of good news to give them—like now, I'm sticking to my job and in a few months I'm coming back. I could write them that every day and they wouldn't get tired of hearing it.'

'You're not very fair to them.'

He dropped his careless tone and almost snapped the answer at her. 'Of course, I'm not fair! What else would you expect? One can't help resenting the circumstances, the people who drag you back to something you don't want. Just the same, I know I'm not fair to them. But they should have had more children. A lot of children gives you room to get rid of the disappointing ones without missing them too much.'

'Oh, shut up, Johnnie. Self-pity doesn't suit you.'

He said, 'Of course, it doesn't. They're really pretty swell—my mother and father. Of course they live like all American industrialists, but that doesn't stop my liking them. My mother looks like a doll; she likes to work tapestry and, she sits and talks in her pretty, tiny voice, and stitches away and appears as innocent and naïve as a baby—which in fact she is. My father's always been the big shot in that concern—as much boss in his household as in his business. Only he's as tough as a bit of old hide when he's handling a deal, and treats my mother as if she were a new-born lamb. It must be pretty hard on her now —he's been ill, and I imagine it's a new experience not to have her mind made up for her.'

And she had said quietly, waiting for his reaction, 'Johnnie, why do you stay on here? You know you're going back.'

He had turned to her, and in his face she had seen and recognised that single look that had passed between them once before on the hill that afternoon at the end of the summer. It was not changed at all.

'Give me time, Maura.'

One left him alone when he was like that, because the layer of patience and submission he had painted over his revolt seemed as close to slipping from him as she imagined his tolerance for the confines of his job often were. He suffered this lack of freedom, but not gladly, and the sight of him at parties, polite and interested, passing drinks and finding ash-trays, restrained, hiding restlessness and dissatisfaction, never failed to call back to Maura the memory of him aboard *Rainbird,* his ease and quiet there. It was never the same quiet he displayed now.

She turned away from the window, away from the rain, and looked at the scene before her. They were all there— *en famille*—young people about Desmond, he a part of them and sharing their spoken thoughts, watching for their several expressions, from the slight shades which slipped across Marion's gentle face, to Willa's boldly clear reactions. She watched him now as he went to the piano, Irene following—as he always bid her—to turn the pages. It was completely the family picture, the one Desmond saw before him when he gathered people about him—the one he was determined to create whether or not the principals were miscast.

One could only turn from his unclouded face, and look at Chris and Marion, side by side on a sofa, and wonder if he were not too harsh in his insistence that they wait for marriage. And yet he knew young people well—even in his passion for Chris he had a cynic's knowledge of his son— and he might have weighed the matter of his marriage with justice and wisdom. If the ultimate decision was beneficial to himself, then it was all the better. But they must wish themselves more often alone—on Chris's free days they would want to follow their own inclinations, to talk or be silent, whichever pleased them—but not forced to be either because it was Desmond's bidding. Affection for him held them here because their absence would have hurt him to an absurd degree. They seemed so captive, these two, in the plans which were made for them.

She recalled a conversation with Johnnie on a day soon after Christmas.

'Why doesn't Chris get married?' They had been standing together by the drawing-room window, watching a small procession of three children trail awkwardly behind a uniformed nurse.

'It isn't very practical,' Maura said.

'Why not?'

'My father thinks Chris should be a little better established before he marries. He wants them to wait two years.'

'That's nonsense. Chris and Marion are in love—anyone with half an eye can see that. They're like a pair of kids who've been knocked sideways because they can't have a treat they've been promised.'

She said quietly, 'Chris and I have no money of our own.'

Because he was not able to help it, Johnnie had turned his eyes away from the children, whose cries reached him faintly through the closed windows, and he had looked at the portrait of Maura's mother. It was a bad choice to have placed it opposite the Rembrandt portrait of Saskia—that glowing, colourful woman, voluptuous in the exotic splendour of her costume. One did not turn from her to the fair, handsome face of the other woman and feel that they had known any equality of devotion. And yet it was true, he knew, that her husband had been Mildred's only life, and her children existed only as a part of him, so that they were not mentioned in her will, and Maura did not wear a single ornament which was hers by Mildred's own wish. Desmond had the entire control of her fortune. She would have loved him, Johnnie thought, as Maura did —bound and tied by love that was too close and fierce. He was impatient with it, and stifled.

'I don't see why you and Chris allow this tyranny to go on,' he said.

'My father has never been a tyrant.'

'Perhaps not in appearances, but in actual fact he is.

One can rule just as effectively through affection as through fear.'

'Then it's not tyranny.'

'It is—of a kind.'

'Then it's a kind my brother needs,' said Maura firmly. 'Chris hasn't any part of Father's ability.' She caught his arm suddenly. 'Look at my brother, Johnnie. He's handsome and weak, and in spite of his age and war experiences he's a baby. But he's got charm to help him, and for the next few years he has Father to push him into a safe place that he can't tumble down off. Chris is appealing, isn't he, Johnnie? You want to do things for him, don't you? We all feel like that. But all the same, my father is right—he shouldn't get married yet.'

He said no more because it was useless to talk to Maura in that fashion about her father. And all through the winter he had watched for a single slip in her loyalty, but nothing had ever betrayed her into it. He suspected that in her own thoughts there was often a feeling and movement towards revolt which was never allowed expression. He himself thought Desmond selfish and clever— uncomfortably clever, and from his vantage point carried on his fascinated study of the paradox of this man who had brought his career to its present stage, and the contrasted personality he knew as the father of Maura and Chris. Desmond's procedure in the courts was level and balanced, the precision of the legal mind more and more developed with age and experience. He was fair, and of late years had dropped the flamboyance of style which had made the early trials notable. As the father he was unjust, demanding, jealous, using charm and not logic as persuasion, stooping to the tricks of drama and rhetoric to gain his points, ruling with a harshness the law never employed. But one could not deny him the quality of enthusiasm, and his love for his children was real, however patriarchal and overbearing. His ambition for them was patently obvious to the onlooker, as well as his own intention never to yield the place he held in their lives when they married. Chris was tied to him firmly, and through Tom and Rathbeg, Maura's chance of escape was slight.

The stumbling-block would be Tom himself, Johnnie thought. He was not pliable. It might well be that he would prove stronger than Desmond, and Maura would find freedom by having it forced upon her.

Johnnie turned to study Tom now with quick interest. Irene had taken Desmond's place at the piano; she was singing the Irish ballads he had begged from her. All of them had fallen silent because Irene's voice was undeniably beautiful, and because at the moment there was more than beauty in it. Tommy Moore's verses—frankly sentimental— she was unaccountably able to translate in a fashion no Englishwoman could ever achieve. How was it, Johnnie wondered, she could produce that alien note of sadness which was the essence of the song? Tom's head was bent over her at the piano, and he was unashamed of the emotion on his face.

'She is far from the land where her young lover sleeps . . .'

'Damn the Irish,' Johnnie thought. It was too easy for them, with their soft words and tears that came with no effort. And with their hardness, too, hearts untouched and selfish. Selfish as Tom was selfish. And yet it was not selfishness like Desmond's own, but one he covered himself with to hold back the curious and inquisitive from ever glimpsing his true feelings. It was his defence, this faint disinterest, and he had perfected it. He had, at times, an expression of weariness, as if he no longer welcomed the further experiences he would have, as if he wished living itself were over.

Johnnie had known almost right away that Tom and Maura were not in love. Affection for one another they surely had, an enviable kind of comradeship, but of the necessity of one for the other he was never convinced. Their lives would work out together in simple sequences of order, because they knew each other's worlds intimately and feelingly. They would commit no sins against each other's prejudice.

He had questioned her about Rathbeg and about Tom. 'It will be good for me there, Johnnie,' she said. The words had been low and sincere, as if she meant to reassure him. There was no fear in Maura about her life after she was finally committed to the step of marrying Tom. 'In the beginning I suppose I'll find it hard to stop being busy—except when I've been at the cottage I've never had time for inessentials before. But I don't think I'll ever tire of Rathbeg. I've loved it ever since I first saw it. And, of course, I shall have *Rainbird*, and a house and garden to look after, as well as Tom's father. And then,' she added, 'Tom and I will have children.'

'Children should be important to both of you,' he said.

'Children are part of things at Rathbeg. They've got to be made take the place of Tom's brother, they've got to be the reason for the love and work Tom will expend on Rathbeg.'

'Your children will be Catholic, Maura.'

She nodded. 'Yes, of course. That's what's so strange, and in its way tragic, about the whole affair. My children will be brought up as Catholics, and it all seems to be forgotten that Desmond's great-grandfather left there for that very reason. No one minds now. It's ceased to matter a great deal.

'Of course,' she continued, 'Catholic or Protestant will always matter in Ireland, and there'll be plenty of Tom's friends who'll deplore my arrival at Rathbeg. But they'll get used to it because Ireland is peaceful enough to be able to forget things like that.

'But sometimes,' she added, 'I feel a kind of guilt about the change my children will bring to the house. There's been a Protestant tradition there for a long time, and I wonder if perhaps the reality of Catholic grandchildren will be less welcome to Tom's father than an abstract consent to them is now. In that way, I suppose, Tom hasn't chosen well. The girl his brother would have married, Sheelagh Dermott, was much more the kind of daughter-in-law Gerald needs—though he's loyal to me, and I don't imagine he lets himself think that way.

But she was everything they could want—she was born in Ireland, and must know the temperament of Irish servants—and from what Gerald says of her, she's the sort of woman who can run a house and bring up children with her hands tied behind her back. I haven't seen her since I was about sixteen—she's younger, of course. I imagine she's very lovely. Harry's death must have been harder for his father on her account.'

Johnnie could look at her now and recall that conversation, look beyond her to Willa, and picture them again as he remembered them together in Maura's cottage . . . before Tom's name was ever known to him, before Rathbeg and the fate of Maura's children had any reality or significance. He saw her questioning face beneath the dark hair, the elegance of her tall figure in the soberly-cut clothes she always wore in London. Even familiarity had never given her beauty in his eyes, but there was every known and loved feature to cherish, and she was dearer than beauty could make her.

He felt an overwhelming desire to talk with her alone —to be rid of the eternal clutter of people which overhung them. Not once in all this intolerable winter had they been alone. It seemed, looking back on it, to have been merely a series of images he had seen in mirrors misted with dust. Maura had never emerged clearly from the surrounding clamour—memories of their conversations were not sharp, but always mixed inevitably and irretrievably with the talk of others. And it was impossible to know whether she had done all this deliberately—just as it was impossible to know anything she had felt that winter. The frustration of it had piled upon him, and seemed now to swell and gather in a tumult of anger and disgust. He wondered why he had allowed it to go on—why, in fact, it had ever passed beyond those moments of decision upon the bridge on Christmas Day. And was it the impossible hope of achieving something which held him on here, week after week, in this house where he was never at peace for a moment? What was there to achieve? Maura would never be more to him than in the week he had known her at the cottage. She had reached her greatest height in that time, and the person she presented to him now—vague, deliberately underplayed, was no more real than the merest shadow she had cast.

He hated the nocturne Desmond had begun to play— the Chopin D flat nocturne which had always before been a thing of incredible, impossible beauty—because now he was sick with the sight and nearness of Maura.

## VI

Maura liked the Temple best when, as now, the sounds of the working day were gone. It was locked in the quiet of its Saturday afternoon, and the warm May sunshine woke the colours of the fire-flowers in the bomb sites. They waved high above the fallen stone, giving a touch of grace to the weathered piles. And the little cats of the Temple had made it their intimate jungle, where they stalked or lay in careless splendour on the broad flat slabs, chased each other among the tall weeds, and uttered their shrill cries, certain in their knowledge that this wilderness was their own. Maura loved the little cats—aloof and unfriendly as they were—watched for the strength and beauty of their tense bodies as they perched with their thin, straight tails on the broken walls, or sprawled in solitary ease among the nettles.

She rose now and gathered together her papers, sorted and clipped them, selecting the final, fair copy to leave on her father's desk. There the afternoon sun rested richly; the room seemed dusty and bound with its quiet, the heavy binding of the law volumes were faded with years of standing in solemn patience upon the shelves. The room without her father's presence seemed unfamiliar; the furnishing was dark, for none of his love of colour had ever been allowed to obtrude here. It might have been any room of a hundred throughout the Temple; the worn back of the leather chair might have received its shabbiness from any other man besides Desmond. There was nothing particular about this room to indicate its owner, not a picture or an ornament, and on the desk only the papers she had left and the solid white surface of his unsoiled blotter.

She went and stood by the window where the sun had warmed the carpet beneath her feet. Pump Court, below, was tranquil, and one could look now past the empty spaces of the bomb sites across the smiling green lawns to the Embankment, and the distant grey glitter of the river.

She pressed her body against the sill, and she seemed part of the quiet of the courts and the gently swaying purple and pink fire-weeds. She thought it must be different from any other silence in the world, and she remembered how Tom had told her about the silence when the great guns had suddenly ceased their thunder across the flower-filled North African valleys, and smoke rose with deceptive serenity against the hard sky. There would soon be the silence of Rathbeg for her to learn—the periods of the day with their particular quiet and noise. The silence of the evening and the lake suddenly shattered by a flight of wild duck, and the plovers shrieking above their endangered nest on a bare field.

She knew she would miss all this, her own office here beside her father's and the piles of papers in it; would miss his praise of a piece of work well handled. In the years since the war this place had been her life, and when she was gone, a young man of Desmond's careful selection would have her room, and her name at the bottom of the staircase would be wiped out and replaced by his. As the years passed, her visits to the Temple would become less frequent, and finally there would be no further reason, except memory's prompting, for her coming. Even in the obscurity of her position here she had been happy, and it would be something to remember—perhaps to be sometimes amazed over, that she had worked here among what it pleased Desmond to call the 'greats' of English law. She wondered if her children would think it strange.

Footsteps sounded sharply in the court below, and she

leaned farther forward. A man halted in the entrance from Middle Temple Lane, and when he raised his face to look about him, she saw that it was Johnnie. She stood perfectly still, and her instant reaction was one of dumb wonder and apprehension. She watched as he began an inspection of the court, reading the names on the staircases. At last he was below her, and she could no longer see him. She remained motionless until the first sound of his footsteps on the old timber stairs, and then she crossed the room, through the outer offices, and opened the door on to the landing.

He had heard the sound of her movement, and paused at the bend of the stairs; his face was raised to hers. He hesitated only a second longer, and then raced up the remaining stairs.

'I thought you might have left.'

She shook her head. 'I've only just finished.'

He stood beside her. 'You didn't mind my coming? I phoned the house and they said you were here working. Maura . . .?'

'Yes?'

'You don't mind my coming?'

'No—no, of course not. I'm surprised you've never visited us here before.'

He grinned. 'I don't imagine it's much Sir Desmond's idea of business to pay little social calls in the middle of the day.'

'I suppose you're right.' She motioned him past her in the doorway. 'My father's whole life is based upon the fact that he knows how to work when it's time to work.'

She led the way through the outer office, closed the door of Desmond's room as she passed, and entered her own. 'I was thinking about making some tea. They'll be finished at home. Will you have some?'

'Thank you, I'd like that. '

He said almost nothing while she brought the cups and an electric kettle from the outer office. She was glad of his silence, because there was nothing ordinary about this visit, and commonplaces would have jarred intolerably. It was merely a waiting pause while the tea was being prepared, and when he was ready he would tell her why he had come. But now he moved about the room, fingering ornaments upon the mantel, staring for some moments at the one water colour she had hung. And all the time he was whistling softly, a high, nervous whistle with no tune to it. She did not ask him, as he stood before the water colour, if he recognised the little boat shed they had passed often near the entrance to Harwich harbour. Johnnie had never seen it like that—pale in winter sunshine, with a background of white-caps. It was a relief when he left it, and came to stand before the window—one which shared the same view as Desmond's.

They drank their tea standing together there, saying little, except when Maura pointed to a long, black cat which had laid tentative paws along the crumbling wall.

'That's my favourite,' she said. 'He sometimes lets me feed him. But he's mighty independent, as cats are.'

'What do you call him?' Johnnie leaned forward to get a better view.

'When I think to give him any name he's called Shorty. It's stupid, isn't it. But I've never seen such a tall cat.'

They watched as the cat squatted upon the wall and began to wash himself. Maura saw with pleasure the confident, nonchalant movement. 'Why is it,' she asked, 'that they have such powers of fascination? Whether one likes them or not, they compel notice. They're such demanding little creatures, and they give nothing in return. That one,' she said, pointing, 'doesn't care two hoots for me, but he'll take all I have to give, and wait for more. But I suppose that's a game not only cats play at.'

He put down his cup upon the window-sill suddenly and turned to face her.

'Maura, tell me why it is you go along expecting any kind of treatment from people, and why are you content to put up with it? Who has made you feel that you can only expect second best? Is it Desmond? Tell me?'

A faint colour had risen in her face; she stared fixedly at the cat.

With his hand he caught her face and swung it towards him. 'You're too ready to play second fiddle all the time. You make no claims for yourself.'

'What claims are there to make, Johnnie?' she asked. She spoke steadily, as if his abrupt touch had given her command of herself and, in a sense, of him also. 'Tell me what you think I'm missing. What is it I haven't got for myself?'

He didn't answer her, and she wondered if the firmness of her tone made him aware that he had no right to examine her life in this fashion. She saw a trace of defeat in him, and angry unhappiness. He took the cup from her hand, and placed it beside his own on the window-sill. 'Maura, go and sit down. I want to talk to you.'

'I'm not going to sit down, Johnnie. This is my own ground, and if you've chosen to come and talk to me here, you do it on my conditions. What is it you want to say?'

They stood facing each other, with the sunlight strong on them both. He saw all the tiny, fine lines around her eyes, and thought that she looked older than during the summer. The look of expectation had left her, and in place there was nothing but the blankness she had chosen to show him. He knew that she was not happy. And she, looking back into his face, saw its wild restlessness, and knew his rebellion had reached a point from which he would not readily swerve. It was almost certain now that he would never return to the enforced restrictions of his life. Immediately she knew that she would never again see him in her father's drawing-room, submitting, with his precarious patience, to the demands he had laid upon himself.

'I've come to tell you that I've asked Irene for a divorce.'

And she said quickly, before he could add anything further, 'And what has that got to do with me?'

He took her by the shoulders as if he meant to shake her. 'For God's sake don't act like a fool or a block of wood. You know that I love you, and that's why I've asked Irene for a divorce.'

They looked at each other, and the feeling between them was that shaken agony of the moments when they had kissed in the doorway of her cottage. But now it was strengthened and worsened by all the months they had known each other, by the long Sunday afternoons painfully endured, and the knowledge thus gathered and stored. There was no withdrawal from each other this time—at least there was no possibility of withdrawal until much more had been said.

'How do you think it's been,' he continued, 'getting through all this bloody winter?' He had almost shouted the words, but abruptly his voice dropped. 'Oh, Maura, it's been hell. I shouldn't have stayed in London. I should have gone away.'

He made to take his hands from her shoulders, until abruptly she caught at them. 'I know,' she said. 'It's been pretty well hell for me, too.'

'Oh, God, Maura, I'm sorry!' He kissed her, not passionately, but with the full measure of their distress. They clung to each other with lonely desperation, knowing that outside of each other's arms there was reality to face.

'Darling,' he said. 'Darling, I've made such a mess of things. I should have gone away.'

'The blame belongs to both of us, Johnnie. To me as well as you. I've known what it's been like, and I should have come to you long ago and asked you to go away.'

'It would have made no difference,' he said. 'You see, that's what I've been waiting for. If you had come to me and asked me to go, it would have been because you loved me. We would have been just as we are now—only it would have happened three or four months earlier. I meant to have that admission from you whatever happened. You do love me, don't you, Maura?'

'Yes. Yes, I do.'

He looked at her closely. 'It's been to hear you say that that I came to London. I don't think I was fully aware of it, but those months when I was alone after we left Florence and Venice, I thought of that constantly. I told myself if only I could hear you say that, I wouldn't want any more. I didn't have any definite intention of seeing you —at least I was truthful, as much as I was capable of truth then—when I told you I hadn't meant to see you. But I would have done it, I know. I knew where you lived, I knew the clubs Sir Desmond belonged to—it would have happened somehow, at sometime. That day in the park can't have been such strange coincidence. I suppose I walked deliberately in the direction of Hanover Terrace. If it hadn't been that day it would have been some other day. I don't deceive myself any longer that I would have stayed away from you. And I told myself it was just to hear you say you loved me.

'But it's not enough,' he said. 'I want much more now. I'm not content to have you only say you love me. That's why Irene had to be told—why I asked her for the divorce.'

'Irene loves you, Johnnie.'

'Yes . . . and she must have known for a long time now that I didn't love her when she married me. But she has such courage and dignity, Maura, and we should have stayed quite happily together if I hadn't met you. But she knows all that. And she knows the extent of my selfishness, too—how I married her because I thought I loved her, and didn't wait to find out how real it was. I haven't been fair to her—not in any way. And none of this makes it easier to ask her about divorce.'

'What did she say?'

'Hardly a word. Neither yes nor no. But Irene wouldn't go on with a marriage under conditions like these. We've made a pretty successful partnership so far, but this has busted it wide open. That's where it's all so unfair— because it was my fault in the beginning, and none of it has ever been hers. And the fact that she will be generous over this makes it worse.'

Maura's hands slid away from his shoulders. 'Johnnie, how much have you thought about all this? Have you thought that even if you do have a divorce, I can't marry you as long as Irene is alive?'

With a gesture she silenced him. 'I know you haven't asked me to marry you. I'm telling you I can't.'

He took her back into his arms.

'Because of your religion? My dear, I've thought of that. God, how much time haven't I spent thinking about it! But it doesn't alter the situation at all. I love you in a way that makes it impossible to continue with Irene.'

She put her face down against his shoulder, and stood there silently. Her thoughts were not much with Johnnie, but rather back with Desmond—and more especially with Tom. She could remember childhood holidays at Rathbeg, being driven alone with Chris to Mass on a Sunday morning and her feeling of neglect and slight bewilderment that Tom and Harry did not come with them. And there were memories of the nuns along the garden walk of the convent where she had been to school, how the long black habits had billowed in the gusts of wind; and how different and at peace they had looked later when she had seen them kneel in the chapel. Some of the earliest childhood memories had been of the awkwardness when her mother's brother came to the convent to visit her, and his children, older than she, smug, curious, a little amused, had questioned her about all the things that made convent life. It had made her shy before them, and—although she knew it was wrong, and felt the disloyalty keenly—she was half-apologetic for her Catholic father. It had always been so much easier for Desmond she thought, because he had never felt as she did, so pulled and pushed between two forces. As now she was pulled. He wouldn't understand all this—there would in no sense be a decision to be made. For him it was made already in the words she had spoken to Johnnie. He wouldn't have stood here clinging to this shoulder. The coldness of it all appalled her—the feeling that there was no will of her own involved here, and no right to answer yes or no. She was caught inescapably in this attitude which had been built up such years ago. Class-rooms of little girls sitting correctly, and her long-ago

terror of the Bishop who came for Confirmation. Desmond
had given her a silver rosary then. She could remember
a visiting church dignitary had laughingly called her 'our
little theologian'—they had afterwards written on a report
card that she was head of the class in apologetics. And
where did it all lead to except this very hour, and all
that Augustine and Aquinas had made her aware of was
the inevitable certainty that for Johnnie there was going
to be only the one word—never. One didn't sweep away a
lifetime of practice, of reasoning, of habit in an hour.
She was never going to see Johnnie again, never going to
talk of him again. She must even try never to think of him
again. It was always never. Would the silver rosary
help over this? She could read Evelyn Waugh and
Graham Greene again, and it was still going to come
back to the same thing. And could Johnnie understand
any of this, or would it be to him merely a spiritless assent
to maxims she had never questioned? Did Johnnie know
that she was convinced, and yet still swayed with desperate
revolt? And a silver rosary was not a compensation. And
did he know the chances that she would go away from this
interview finding peace no longer in the sight of kneeling
figures in chapel. She looked at his face and wondered did
he know he might destroy the convictions which now turned
him away? Did Johnnie know how much power there
was?

'But nothing, Maura, can change this decision about
Irene. She knows about you and me—as little and as
much as there is to know. And the times I've seen you alone
she could count on the fingers of one hand. We could go
on with this marriage, and it wouldn't be any worse than
these last months have been—but she won't have that.
She knows what has happened to me, and everything that's
going to follow.'

She raised her head quickly. 'What's going to follow?
What do you mean?'

'That I'm not going back to the firm.'

'Johnnie!'

'What's the use?' he demanded. 'Where would it get

me? In six months I'd be gone again.'

'But I thought it was settled—you were going back, and you were going to stick, whatever happened.'

'Whatever happened didn't include the eventuality of loving you. Or the way that I love you. God, Maura, I didn't want it. You were the last kind of woman I imagined myself loving. But what you are, or what I am, doesn't seem to enter into this at all. I wouldn't have chosen this —I love you because I can't help myself. It's something I'd wish myself well out of, but yet I'm helpless. Until you came I was almost certain that I could go back home, and dig in where my father wanted me, but this last month has seen the end of all that. It's the end of everything—even of you.'

He put his hand on her hair, pushing it back from her forehead, talking in accompaniment to the gesture. 'I've known all along that a divorce from Irene wouldn't give you to me. I knew you wouldn't marry me. But it's all part of this thing, that not being able to have you, whom I want—I want nothing else. I haven't the least idea of where I'm going, or what's going to happen to me, but Irene must be freed from this torment of uncertainty. Whether she wants it or not, she's much better away from me. It will hurt her, but not half as much as she'll be hurt if she spends the rest of her life attached to someone who never knows what's happening next.'

'Johnnie, I'm to blame . . .'

'Who's talking about blame? You didn't ask to be loved. I didn't want to love you. No one takes the blame for the inevitable. If you were less your father's daughter you might have taken this chance with me—but then I mightn't have loved you. If I had been less renegade— more the sort of person I should be—I wouldn't have been in that pub waiting for you to walk right in. Things never plan out, do they, Maura? It's always the unexpected that knocks you flat.'

He pressed her face between his hands. 'I'm going now. I didn't have any right to come here—you would have been much better off without all this. But I'm too selfish to let you go free—if I was going to suffer you would know about it. And I wanted to hear you say you loved me. Say it again.'

'I love you, Johnnie. Always.'

They kissed each other, not tenderly now, but with full passion. The 'never' of Maura's imagining seemed to be close upon them, and gave their kisses desperation. Their separation would begin from the moment they stopped kissing, and so they clung to each other with all their fore-knowledge of loneliness, all their need of comfort. Their kisses were wild and sweet, and the feeling of their bodies and lips was not unfamiliar, but like something that had been known and loved for a long time. It was this familiarity which pained, this certainty that they belonged together. Finally the anguish of the moment touched them; it was no longer just the present of their loving, but the beginning of the future. They drew apart.

Without a word Johnnie turned from her and walked quickly across the room. She waited, with her back to it, for the sound of the closing door, but a minute of silence passed. She wheeled slowly.

'Johnnie . . .'

He was beside her again, his arms about her.

'Maura, come with me. What the hell does anything matter? You love me, don't you? Is anything more important than that? We could do a million things to-gether—we'd be happy together. I'd make up to you for everything. Maura, you can't send me away when we love each other like this. Maura . . . Maura . . .!'

He jerked back her head to take his kisses, and drew her to him tightly.

'Johnnie, I can't go.'

'You've got to go with me. How will I exist without you? I can't exist without you.'

'You mustn't ask me. You know it's hopeless. It wouldn't work—it wouldn't work, Johnnie.'

'You wouldn't be unhappy, my love. Say you'll come

with me. Say you will. Say you will!'

She began to weep uncontrollably. 'We can't—I can't.'

He grew angry, the sight of her tears unnerving him. 'We will. Maura, I won't leave you.'

Abruptly she drew away from him. 'This is useless.' She was rubbing her eyes with the back of her hand, a child's motion, frantic, clumsy. 'Go away, Johnnie.'

'You can't send me away. I won't go.'

'Please go.'

She turned her back on him, and buried her face in the curtains, and caught their smell of dust and soot, the London smell. She rubbed her wet cheeks in them furiously.

'I don't want to see you again, Johnnie. You're not to get in touch with me again. You're not to see me. Do you understand?'

'Maura . . .'

'Do you understand? I mean this.'

She waited during the intolerable moments of silence for his reply. She waited and tried not to let her mind realise what she was doing. It was not now the matter of a decision, but a blind obedience to the faith that she had accepted all her life, a habit too strong to run against. She clung to the curtain, wishing the slow minutes would speed themselves away, go past and leave her with their results when it was too late to revoke them. They dragged past, when the silence was a kind she had never known before and would never forget. She tried to imagine all the times in her life she would recall these moments, and how sick she had been, and weak and near to defeat. It was a perilous kind of weakness, that Johnnie would only have to suspect in order to fasten upon. If he didn't go soon, she thought, the moments would be stronger than her resolution.

At last there came the sound of his movements across the room, and she clung tightly to the curtain to prevent herself calling him back as the door opened and shut. She counted each step on the wooden stair, heard them loudly through the empty building. And then she saw the bright sun on his head as he passed beneath her, and through the archway at the entrance of the court.

The tall black cat had stirred in anticipation of his coming, but sank back into its composure when Johnnie did not look in its direction.

She waited only until she was sure he had gone, until there was little chance of his returning. Then she went to the phone on her desk, and rang the Hanover Terrace number.

Her father spoke to her immediately.

'Maura, I'm afraid you're working late. Leave it, my child. It can keep until Monday.'

'It's finished, Father. It's all right—I've left it on your desk. I wanted to tell you I'm going down to the cottage right away. I expect I'll be back on Tuesday—Wednesday at the latest.'

'This is very sudden.'

'Yes, it is. I'm sorry—but I just feel I want to go down there. I've had enough of London—I'll have to get away from it for a few days.'

'There's no one to open the cottage. *Rainbird* isn't ready for you.'

'*Rainbird* has been down off the slips for the last two weeks. There's always food in the cottage.'

After a short pause he said, 'Very well, Maura—if you feel you must.'

'I'm sorry, but I'm not asking permission to go down. I intended to go in any case.'

'My dear child, I wouldn't think of stopping you. You must do exactly as you please.'

'Yes . . . yes.' And then the pain she had fought crept over her, and her whole body was weakened by it. She wasn't able to talk any longer.

'I'll phone you when I'm coming back. Good-bye.'

She replaced the receiver before he could reply. She didn't weep any more as she sat there at the desk. She stared at the window, and tried to think of what she must do, tried to think of anything that would hold her control, and the little sanity which had enabled her to send Johnnie away.

'Oh, God,' she said aloud, 'what will I do? What will I do without him?'

She stayed there until it grew too dark to see anything except the outline of the window.

## VII

The first light had begun over the estuary at Harwich, far down to the horizon in the east. Grey flooded into the black sky, and the new green leaves of May in the trees around Maura's cottage were sharp against it. There was a solemn stillness, and only a quick, solitary cry here and there heralded the awakening of the birds. The trees were still, and there was stillness in the fields. There were no tracks in the dew across the corn. The scene as yet had no colour, only greys and darkness which was not black. The quality of the morning was sound, so hushed and subdued, it was almost silence.

Maura's canvas shoes made little sound themselves as she began her walk down from the cottage, but looking back she could see her own passage in the dew on the road. Gradually, but with increasing strength the bird chorus grew as she walked—a faint twitter, a fine piping note, answered, taken up, and then half-lost in the myriad songs it awoke. There was a beauty she thought she had forgotten in that shy beginning, a rapture which touched and hurt her in some way because it belonged only to these few swift seconds, and she might never have them back again. She walked softly, the less to frighten the rabbits who fed in the fields, the less to declare herself a stranger and alien to these early-morning phases.

She came to the silent anchorage when the colour of the morning was coming to life. Grey stretches of the river held, in places, the faintest pink, though under the banks the water was still black. The lime green of the trees was visible; small forming leaves showed the brightening sky between them. The colour of the bluebells on the far bank grew bolder—in a few minutes of watching the ground seemed to grow purple before her eyes. Yellow-milky faces of buttercups showed in patches.

She turned away from the sight at last, and placed her provision bag in *Rainbird*'s dinghy. It was drawn far up on the mud-flat, and it took her several minutes of tugging to start it down the slope to the water. The sounds travelled down-river to a heron who stood fishing in the shallows. The head of the bird shot up in alarm and the great wings were unfolded. Its slow, deliberate flight was entrancing; she watched to see its head drawn back and the long legs trail. The croaking cries of fright were soon lost.

*Rainbird* rode with the particular quietness of little craft at her mooring; the light on the ripples of the water reflected on her fresh white hull. As she rowed towards the craft, Maura noted her beloved, familiar lines with satisfaction and delight—neatly furled sails and new tarpaulin stretched over the cockpit. It was at least in things like this, in the grey and pink of the sky over the estuary, in the gentle slap of the water against the hull, in the powerful flight of the heron, she would find refuge from yesterday's scene with Johnnie in the Temple. Her drive down last night had been frenzied, her heart locked with pain and the sense of loss. It had tormented her all through the endless night when she had sat in front of the hastily-built fire of kindling, and thought about him. She held her head between her hands and remembered his voice and the thousand things about him that she loved. But she found room to pity his own torment, his longing to escape from every kind of bond which held him—even that of his love for her. But what was it Johnnie wanted?—something glimpsed briefly on his beautiful, heartless island in the Pacific, something discovered there in the months of waiting. Something lost irretrievably in his return to the old life. Johnnie, who had been brought up to live among people, now wanted solitude, wanted sweat-making bodily labour to satisfy the desire for simplicity and dignity. And he belonged to neither world—his own seemed to him irredeemably rotten; the world he longed for would not receive him because he had not been born into it. He wanted her as well. And he could have none of these things. Whatever he did now would seem wrong to him. Even casting off his ties he would never be free.

Before dawn the supply of kindling had run out, and she had gone, cold and wearily, to dress to keep this appointment—made when she had knocked up The Stag so late the night before—to meet Willa down here at the anchorage. As she slipped into the worn, comfortable garments, the sweater and slacks smelling of salt water, she recalled Willa's face, sympathetic and unquestioning when she had made her request for crew. Willa would come this morning, calm and matter-of-fact, turning this trip—which Maura saw as an escape swiftly planned in her moment of desperation—into something normal and usual, something looked forward to during the winter months. By the time they reached the French coast Willa's good sense would have prevailed; she herself would be more at ease, and the happenings of the afternoon with Johnnie would have begun to assume a different significance.

In the galley she made coffee. There was no fresh milk, but she found tinned milk left from last summer's supply. The loaf of bread Willa had given her was hardly touched, and when the sharp smell of the coffee grew strong, she realised how hungry she was. She opened a tin of jam because there was no butter. It was sweet and thick on the stale bread, striking her tongue like the syrupy sweetness of the coffee. She ate standing up, staring straight ahead through the port-hole at the bank opposite where the bluebells grew at the base of the trees. Now and again she glanced at her watch and wondered how much longer it would be before Willa came.

And then, in the lane above the anchorage, she heard the sound of a car, and knew it was not Willa.

She knew surely that it would be only one person, and she came on deck fearfully.

Johnnie got out of the car slowly. She saw each deliberate movement as a part of a whole—gazed upon the scene as if it had all happened before and was produced as an almost forgotten memory. It had the frightening quality of inevitability—and she experienced the feeling of being powerless before him and all these circumstances. The gentle lap of the water continued—strangely, because it seemed to her that all movement and sound should cease. But the birds didn't halt their song, and the colour deepened everywhere steadily. The trees had come out in their intense, bright greens, and the water was giving up its greyness.

Johnnie walked down the slope to the boat-shed. She recognised the water-stained flannels, the ancient sweater. He wore an old jacket, and fumbled now in the pocket for a cigarette and lighter.

'Where are you bound for?'

'Ostend.' She said it faintly, and her voice didn't carry across that stretch of water.

'Where?'

'Ostend.'

'What crew?'

'Willa is coming.'

He paused, and then said, 'I'll go as crew.'

She was weak and afraid, and yet not afraid as she had been the night before when she had seen him. His coming had shattered all the peace of the morning, and yet strangely he was a part of it. He had shattered it only as the flight of the heron had done—something natural and in its place against the proper background. She looked all around her—at the morning which now seemed a thing of incredible loveliness and mystery. From down on the mud-flats came the loud triple call of a redshank, the evocative, marshy cry she had learned to associate with these stretches of the river. She was conscious of a feeling of wonderful gladness that all this was so, that Johnnie was here and a part of it, that the sun was beginning to strike the tops of the trees, turning the foliage to soft green magic. She looked at the ease of his body as he stood upon the slope, and knew that he too was glad—and confident as well. There was no uncertainty any longer in Johnnie. A movement of pure happiness ran through her, a joy and lightness which had been dead the whole winter.

'You'll miss the tide, Maura.'

'I must wait for Willa.'

'You'll miss the tide.'

'We'll go out under power.'

'A good sailor doesn't use power.'

She took her decision quickly, knowing, as she hauled the dinghy close to *Rainbird*'s side, and climbed in to row it back to the shallows, that once he came aboard, they would sail without Willa.


# VIII


The day passed with the spectacle of little cargo ships in the North Sea. The wind was from the north, a fresh breeze which gave them good time. The sun had come out warmly, blazing white on the sails, and the hulls of other craft. They left the dipping East Anglian shoreline behind, and the slow laughter of the herring gulls. The sounds were the pleasant, familiar creak of the timbers, and the rhythmic swish of water against *Rainbird*'s sides. Occasional spray dashed upon them, wetting their faces and leaving the taste of salt water on their lips. The wind held steadily all day.

Maura prepared meals from the tins she had brought down from the cottage. The loaf was finished and they spread jam on hard biscuits. She made coffee, and they drank it together, Maura sprawled on the deck while Johnnie took the tiller.

'I phoned Hanover Terrace at ten o'clock last night,' he said.

She looked up at him. 'What did you hope to gain by that?'

'I wasn't prepared to accept what you had said. I thought if I could see you again it might be different. They told me you had gone down to the cottage. It took me until three this morning to make up my mind to follow you.'

The swish of the waves was like a lulling accompaniment to his words. The plunge and straightening of the vessel had a lovely, deep rhythm. Her body rested back against his knees.

He continued, 'I don't quite know what I expected to happen—I guess my only clear thought was that if we could talk again together you might see my point of view. Or I might be resigned to yours.'

She leaned back more heavily against him, feeling the length of his legs pressing on her shoulder blades and right down to her thighs. 'Was that all you came for—to talk? You wore your sailing flannels.'

He threw back his head and laughed loudly; the sound seemed to hit back at them from the spread of canvas 'I knew I had to be down for the early tide. And I brought my passport.'

They laughed together, and he leaned over and kissed her fully on the mouth. They clung closely like that, knowing the joy of it further, and forgot the tiller. The boom came round, and they were right into the wind, and the air was filled with the harsh, aggressive flap and crack of the slack canvas. They were thrown apart violently.

When he had righted *Rainbird* and they had stopped laughing, Maura said,

'And you've just missed seeing a fulmar. It's rare to see them here.'

'I've got the rest of my life to see fulmars,' he said, paying no attention to her arm pointing in the direction of the vanishing bird. His free hand he placed on the back of her neck, his fingers running through and tugging lightly on the short curls. 'But I'll remember that *you* saw a fulmar.'

For three hours that night there was no wind. They dropped the sea anchor, and lay together on deck, watching, as the craft rocked gently, the stars swing between mast and forestay, seeing, occasionally, the riding lights of passing vessels. The May night was mild, with a touch of the warmth of summer about it, a night out of season.

Johnnie said, 'The stars on this side of the world are small and far-away. They look kind of lonely to me. When I see them I remember how the stars looked in the Pacific. Big—much too big, Maura, and blazing away as if they'd come right out of the sky and knock you flat. It was all rather theatrical—like the background of a Broadway musical. When I came back I thought the stars were homely and plain, but familiar. They're nicer that way.'

'Do you ever want to go back, Johnnie?'

'Back where?' He asked the question carelessly. He lay with one arm beneath her, and his head against her shoulder, face turned now and pressed into her sweater.

'Back to the Pacific? Do you want to see it again?'

'I guess not. It wouldn't do much good.'

'Johnnie?'

'Yes?'

'What happened out there—I mean what happened to you?'

'Nothing much. At least nothing much in the real sense of things happening in war. I lost a few men I'd grown to trust, and I lost much of my feeling about all the things that meant being at home. I've never replaced them, somehow. I've been sitting inside a kind of vacuum ever since waiting for something to happen. This pushing round the world at a loose end isn't what I want, either.'

'Will you find what you want with me, Johnnie?'

'Heaven knows—do you have enough faith in me—do you love me enough to want to stay with me even if I don't find it? Maura, it sometimes takes more than a woman's love to redeem a man. Do you know that?'

'Yes, I know.'

'And you still want to go on with this?'

'Yes.'

He caught her closely in his arms in a sudden rising of passion or of fear. 'My love.'

'Johnnie. . . .'

The vessel swayed and moved in even rhythm as the gentle sea pushed against it. The dark horizons came and vanished on each side, and the small stars gave their uncertain light. There were the changeless noises of the sea, and their murmured words of love.

They made the harbour of Ostend when the morning sun had already gathered some of its early brilliance. It shone harshly on the shipping, on the rusted side of the cargo vessels, the screaming gulls, diving after refuse, were white in it, the washing flapping languidly on make-shift lines, was bleached in it. The sound of voices shouted in accents of ports all over the world. There were fresh smells to assail them every few minutes—the smell of dead fish on a pier, the smell of food cooking as they passed close to a tanker and as they came quietly, under power, to tie up at the bottom of a long flight of stone steps, the strange, greasy smell of wool bales. Far down on the farther pier a gang of dockers were going off a night-shift. Their voices were tired and infrequent.

'We'll go ashore for breakfast,' Johnnie said. He looked at her. 'I guess this is the stage where we stop thinking only about ourselves, and make some kind of plans. There's Irene, and your father—and Tom.'

She sat down suddenly beside the tiller; her hands were clasped together and pressed between her knees.

'Johnnie, I'm not coming.'

He laid down his jacket. 'What!'

'I'm not coming. I can't come.'

He said quietly, 'My dear, you've chosen the wrong side of the North Sea to tell me this.'

'I know,' she said wretchedly. 'Oh, Johnnie, I'm sorry. I'm a rotten little cheat—I've cheated you so badly, so completely. I thought I could go through with it, and I can't any more.'

She continued quickly: 'Yesterday—last night it was different. All that was one life left behind and another not yet begun. Johnnie, do you understand what I'm trying to say to you? My darling, I didn't know I'd be such a coward, such a cheat. You should have listened to me back in the Temple. You should never have trusted me in that mood yesterday morning. You should have known that because I loved you—yesterday, that time, that place—I would have done anything you asked.'

'So the bright light of reality is shining on us now, Maura, and you don't like what you see? Is that it?'

'Don't say that. I didn't mean this to happen. But I should have known that in the end I couldn't go through with this.' Between her knees her hands clasped and unclasped.

He looked at the hard sun on her black hair and on her face which had gone so suddenly white. Her eyes looked darker than he had ever seen them before. They had a stricken, glazed expression, and in her hunched shoulders he saw her misery.

He was touched and bewildered, not wishing to recognise that in this moment when he was losing her, he could experience love for her in a completely new way. She was simple and childlike now, and fighting to hold on to the things which had been her life until yesterday morning. She was vulnerable; anything he wanted to say to her could be said and she would make no effort to hit back, or defend herself. And she was tired, like the first night he had seen her sitting at the bar in The Stag with weariness in her face and eyes. He could be cruel now, lash her with words of his disappointment and regret which she would never forget. He looked at her finely-pointed face; the high cheek-bones were sharp in her weariness. They were both going to suffer over this; the suffering was never quite going to be finished with for either of them. She had cheated—all that she had said was true. But was she more of a cheat than himself? Who would not have known she would let him aboard yesterday morning; who would not have known that then, if at no other time, she would have agreed. They had both cheated in the excess of their desire for each other. He felt pity for her stir in him.

He came to her swiftly. 'Forgive me.'

She put her head against his, and he could feel her body shaken with the stress of her weeping.

'We'll both do a lot of this, Maura. We've been foolish

and mistaken. But so much better to weep for it now than later.'

'How could I have done this, Johnnie?'

'It's my fault,' he said quietly, 'because I should have known you well enough to understand that you meant all you said in the Temple. This could never have lasted between us because I had taken hold of, and ridden, your moment of weakness. I think all my life I would have waited for the time when you began to regret. But I'm blind about the things I want. And I did want you, Maura, more than anything in my whole life.'

They looked at each other, with the bright morning sun harsh upon their faces, and heard the confused laughter of the gulls overhead. From a cargo vessel nearby someone tipped a bucket of refuse overboard. It hit the water with a heavy sound, and the gulls dived after it.

She said then, 'What will you do?'

'Do?' He shrugged, but it was not in indifference. 'Stay here, I guess. I don't think I can face England right now. Or Irene either. I shall tell Irene all this.'

'Yes, you must. Tom must be told too.'

'Is that necessary?'

She nodded wearily. 'It's too late not to be completely honest. Tom has the right to know. It will be the end of us together, and he must know the full reason. I've cheated long enough.'

'Four lives,' Johnnie said, 'is a pretty big roll to count because I chose to wander about Europe searching for some sort of salvation. But I would have found it with you, Maura. We would have worked it out together. But no— perhaps you were—you are—my salvation. It could even be, possibly, that I was meant to love you, and even lose you like this, in order to feel the prickle again, the irritant, to drive me on. In some contrary fashion you've satisfied me. Perhaps I'll learn to live at peace with myself, or discover what my particular gods are. Or to know, finally, that there is no peace, and give up my probing. Whichever it is, I'll come to it soon.'

They kissed longingly, hardly believing that this was

the end of loving, and of themselves together. Maura's face was still wet with tears and when he bent close to her, she could feel the new dampness of the perspiration on his forehead. She drew back from him at last.

'Can you forgive me for this?'

'Is there such a thing as forgiveness for the error of love? Has anyone the right to forgiveness?'

She allowed her arms to slide heavily down his body, and she stepped back from him. The tears she had checked threatened to begin again.

'Johnnie, go quickly. I can't bear it any longer.'

He looked about him desperately. Still not quite relinquishing his hold of her, he looked about at the deserted piers overhead.

'I'll find someone to go back with you.'

She shook her head. He saw the wet on her cheeks glisten in the sunlight. 'I've managed *Rainbow* alone often.'

'You'll be in trouble if there's strong wind or seas. And you've had no sleep—you're not fit to take her back alone. I'll find someone. If I look into enough eating places along here there'll be someone who'll go back with you.'

He caught her back into his arms, and kissed her once, and this was only a shadow, a memory of their former kisses. It felt as if he had already gone.

'Good-bye, Maura.'

He turned and picked up his jacket. She watched him reach out and grasp the edge of the stone steps and swing *Rainbow* in close. And she watched him as he mounted them, jacket over his shoulder, and started along the pier.

She didn't wait to see if he looked back, but went down into the cabin. It was dark there, and hot, and the sun on the water cast little glancing beams through the port-holes, moving in wonderful brightness on the polished mahogany. Slowly she lay down on one of the bunks and her body seemed to tighten and shrivel and grow small in the apathy of her grief.

Her conscious need when she roused herself again was

for a cigarette. She found only her own empty carton in the pocket of her slacks. Even her fingers seemed to itch for the feel of a cigarette between them, and she was frenzied by the blankness of the packet. She tossed it aside, and moved swiftly to the galley cupboard. They yielded nothing; she started pulling aside the cushions, and found, pressed against the bulkhead, a package with two cigarettes. They were American, Philip Morris, and the cellophane and wrapping was crushed as if Johnnie had left them beside him as he sat there, and afterwards, forgetting, had leaned back.

She lit one and went on deck. The brightness smote her eyes, and putting her fingertips to them, she could feel the irritation and soreness left by her weeping. She looked at her watch, and saw that it was more than two hours since Johnnie had left her, and the sun now burned down strongly. The activity of the port was going on all about her, and she sat and stared unseeingly.

The two hours that were past, had, she prayed, burned out the great and worst pain of his going. Never again in her life did she wish to know the intensity of such emotion. She knew that it was by no means past her forever, that again and again there would be sudden visitations of it, fierce and terrible. But acceptance of the fact had been won; she would have to go on living with the aching loss of him, but she had wisdom enough to know it would lessen, if never completely die. The first thing was to believe the fact of his going, and belief had been reached in her two hours of torture. Now she believed this, it was possible to see how life would change. She would no longer nurse a continual thought of Johnnie, a thought that in the past months had been near a hope. The reality of him was vanished; she was going ahead to take up existence with a motive which had changed this morning from substance to shadow. Johnnie himself was lost to her; Tom was lost, too. She had thrown both away in the single action, and she was left alone to face the thought of continued life. It was loneliness like the quiet and isolation of this little craft in the tumult of the port and the laughter of the gulls.

She was lighting the remaining cigarette from the but
of the first, when a voice hailed her from the pier
She looked up and saw a fair boy of about nineteen in a
thick seaman's jersey standing above her.

He said, in accented English, 'You are the lady bound
for Harwich?'

'Yes.'

He said nothing more, but ran down the steps and
pulled *Rainbird* in close on the hawser. 'The American
sent me,' he said, as he climbed aboard.

She judged him Scandinavian, and his English was
better than a sailor's usually is.

'You are ready to go?' he asked. 'We should not delay
longer for this tide.'

'Yes,' she said, accepting him completely and finally
because he was Johnnie's choice.

The gale that sprang up when they were outside held
them in the North Sea for a day and a half, battling with
sea-sickness, and the futile hope of cooking on the galley
stove or keeping water out of their food supplies; Hendrick
was capable—Maura knew in her weariness that she could
not have completed the crossing without his skippering
of *Rainbird*. Wrapped in stiff oilskins they entered Harwich
harbour near to dusk on the next day, with a fine mist
drifting down under grey skies.

# PART THREE

---

## I

The village had not missed the fact of Maura's arrival three nights ago, or the presence of Johnnie's car at the anchorage. Maura pondered all this as she climbed the hill to the cottage in the rain with Hendrick. But its evidence met her plainly in the newly-laid fire in the sitting-room, and the tins of food waiting in the kitchen. There was no fresh bread or milk, but she saw eggs in a bowl, and butter and sugar which had not been there before. Village opinion, she thought, was undecided about her return, when it would be, and for how long. Nor would they know, with any certainty, that Johnnie had come alone in his car. And if anyone had marked her return with Hendrick on *Rainbird*, speculation would rage back and forth on his identity, and the matter of Johnnie's or Irene's non-appearance would be argued happily for months. She recalled with faint wonder the time when she had considered this an easy price to pay for her acceptance in the village. It had grown up around her until now a curtain could not stir or a fire be lit out of season without this narrow world knowing of it.

Hendrick, beside her, stirred impatiently and gestured towards the eggs.

'I will cook them,' he said. 'I cook very well.'

She remembered their hunger and their sickness on the passage back. 'Yes, if you can.'

And at the same time she was aware of the discomfort of her wet clothes, and grateful for the bodily tiredness that would make it possible to sleep without thoughts of Johnnie.

They ate Hendrick's supper of omelette and biscuits, with tinned peaches and strong black coffee. He took her praise of it calmly, as if he were already old and there were many years of such meals behind him. But his youth showed also in his quick smiles which he seemed unable to subdue, and the glances he threw at her when he thought they were unnoticed. They were silent while they ate because he would volunteer no information about himself, and she was unwilling to start the chain of questions which would lead back to Johnnie and the circumstances of his leaving *Rainbird*.

There was a gravity about him that rested strangely on his young face, and aroused curiosity even in her tired and defeated state. But he was young enough, and naïve in his embarrassment about the pyjamas she brought down to the sitting-room along with a pile of blankets. His English almost deserted him when he tried to protest that they would not fit.

But she pressed them upon him, and wanted to laugh when she saw how awkwardly and unhappily he took them.

'I suppose,' he said grudgingly, 'for a woman you are tall.' Unwillingly he tried their length against him. 'Thank you,' he found it possible to smile again, and she was reminded of the very youngness of Peter Brown who sailed with her in the summer, and some of this boy's toughness and shyness belonged to Peter, too.

'Hendrick,' she said, when they were banking up the fire, 'do you want to go back to Ostend? There are steamers from here to Holland.'

He laid the coal on carefully, then looked at her. 'Do you go to London?' he asked. 'You have a car?'

'Yes. I'm going back to-morrow.'

'Then I would be very pleased to go with you.'

She nodded. 'When you get to London what will you do?'

'I will manage, thank you. There is always something for a sailor to do.'

She could ask him no more questions, but said good-night and left him crouching before the fire.

They went before six next morning. The rain of the past two days had gone, and in the orchards and along the roads the moisture on the blossoms caught the sun in thousands of points of brilliance. The cornfields were growing bright with their tender green, and Hendrick was happy and sang snatches of songs in German, and made faces of mock distress at her when the car laboured badly on the hills. Occasionally they saw trees and gentle bits of cloud reflected in stretches of water, and the ducks on it seemed to float absurdly among the clouds. Everything pleased Hendrick, not just the bright, glittering morning but the dreary miles of suburbs through which they passed. Suddenly, as they turned off the North Circular Road he asked her how he would get to Newport.

'Why Newport? There are jobs in London.' She hardly would admit to herself how her affection for him had grown, and how impossible to think that she might never see him again. It seemed uncomfortably like putting young Peter Brown on a train and seeing him go out of her life forever.

'I promised, once, that I would see someone who lives in Newport. And then, after that, there is the rest of the world. There are small ships which go from every port.'

She said nothing in reply, but drove him through the thickening traffic to Paddington. He stood on the kerb to say good-bye to her, and flushed deeply with a return of his embarrassment when she offered him money.

'The American gave me all I need.'

She wrote her address clearly for him. 'Then take this, and write me . . . If anything goes wrong.'

He smiled. 'Thank you. Good-bye.'

She started the car and headed towards Tom's rooms in Chester Row. Her mind all through the drive had been filled with thoughts of this interview, but cutting between her and it was the memory of Hendrick walking down the ramp. She wasn't ever going to know what it was that took him to Newport, who he was even, and where he came from; but he would be memorable for his own sake, for the feeling of youth which hung over him, and the fact that he had been with her during these most urgent hours of her life.

## II

She found Tom at breakfast. He rose from the litter of the newspapers to greet her.

'Maura, come in. Have you just come from the cottage?'

She nodded and dropped into the chair he drew up. 'Yes, I left very early.'

He was unshaven, and still wearing pyjamas and dressing-gown. He sat down again, with a gesture offering her coffee. She shook her head and he poured his own. His movements, adding sugar and milk, seemed to her maddeningly deliberate when she had primed herself for what she would say. But he seemed rather to control the situation, as if he knew he would speak first, and not she. And he did.

When he had finished stirring the coffee he said, 'I've been expecting you.'

'Why?'

'You went away rather suddenly, Maura.' He gave the faintest shrug. 'God knows, I'm not the sort of person who asks for explanations—particularly not from you. But I felt that you would come and tell me why you went down. I wasn't surprised to see you here this morning—though I'd hardly expected you before the end of the week.'

'Tom, I . . .'

He cut her short. 'Before you say anything, I should tell you that I know Johnnie hasn't been in London since he telephoned Hanover Terrace on Saturday evening and found you'd gone to the cottage.'

She said dully, 'Did you think that had anything to do with me?'

'I was almost certain it had a great deal to do with you. Johnnie is in love with you.'

She looked at him steadily. 'You say "almost certain." But that's all. How did you know it was the truth? There was nothing in my life for you to discover, nothing that I had hidden for you to find out. You know as well as I do, Tom, that I never saw Johnnie outside of Hanover Terrace when there weren't at least four other people with us.'

'Have you never thought it was possible to fall in love in the middle of a crowd? Johnnie is in love with you all right. I've seen it all the winter.'

'If you saw it why didn't you do something about it—why did you wait?'

'I'm not a child, Maura, full of momentary jealousies. And in any case I wasn't certain about what you felt—I knew there was something there, but how strong it was, or how deeply it touched you, I didn't know. I've spent the winter adding up all the pieces.'

He sipped at his coffee, and she, watching him, saw the agitation which he had brought under control, saw him gathering together his thoughts to say what he wanted, and make it clear and simple. She thought suddenly how handsome he was, with the lines that had been there since Italy, deepening each year in his dark, thin face. There was a streak of grey across his hair from the place where the wound had been. But he would go grey early, she thought, like his father. In ten years no one would be able to distinguish the present grey from the rest.

'There are only two reactions,' he continued, 'to the person you love. One is to be at ease completely—to fit each other like another part of oneself. The second way is how you and Johnnie reacted upon each other. He was irritant and stimulant to you. You had only to be in the same room as each other, not close or speaking, but you both became different creatures. I don't know if you wanted to love each other, but I began to see after Christmas, how the attraction never left you alone. You talked to different people, but it was always for each other; you avoided looking at each other, but you were always aware of every movement. I began to see that you were pulled in a way that must have been almost impossible to resist.'

'Then you had no right to wait, Tom. You were wrong to wait even a day after you knew all this.'

'Perhaps you're right. But I knew, besides that, you weren't seeing Johnnie alone. I knew you were as honest as you seemed to be. And I was going to take fright over a situation which wasn't really a situation at all? I preferred to wait and to trust you. And to go ahead with our plan to get married in July.'

She looked away from him, through the window to the spring sunshine washing the cream fronts of the houses opposite. Then she turned back and said, 'I haven't been worth that much trust, Tom.'

'Tell me.'

She hesitated, then did as he asked. 'You were right,' she said, 'in believing that I have never seen Johnnie alone. I hadn't—not until last Saturday. He came to the Temple when I was there in the afternoon.'

And she told him, struggling with her desire to hold it to herself, all that had happened. 'After he had gone,' she added, 'I went down to the cottage. I planned to make the trip to Ostend with Willa.

'Believe me, Tom, that was what I had planned,' she said.

'But Johnnie came. While I waited for Willa that morning he came. When I saw him it wasn't even making a decision any more; it was nothing like the questioning and the decision that day before. I knew I just had to have him with me—that was all. At that time nothing else in the world counted. We sailed without Willa.'

She couldn't look at him any longer. 'Tom, it wasn't meant then to be just a few days together. I was never capable of planning that kind of thing. I was going to stay with him. We would live together. While that mood was on me I was prepared to do anything, be anything, just to keep him by my side. I was mad, Tom, crazy with my love for him.'

Her voice dropped, the life appeared to drain away from her with the memory of that bright morning on the other side of the channel, and the laughter of the gulls.

'But it wasn't permanent madness. I became sane too soon for myself—and much too late for you and Irene. So, you see, I'm back. And Johnnie—Heaven knows where he's gone.'

'Is it all finished between you, Maura?'

'Quite finished, Tom. Quite finished.'

'Does Johnnie understand that?'

'He understands as much as he can be made to that it's impossible for me to marry him while Irene is alive. As for living with him—he's had experience of how long that lasts.

'It is . . . quite finished.'

She got up, pushing her chair back slowly; she walked to the window. The street below her was quiet—it had little activity in the morning and during the day, only waking to a swift life after six o'clock when the small groups of two and three cars began to gather. Drifting over from the river came the sound of Big Ben striking nine. She gripped the curtain tightly.

'I'm sorry, Tom,' she said. 'I knew that I loved Johnnie when I promised to marry you. I don't expect your forgiveness for that. The only thing left for me was to tell you the complete truth now, and then go and tell Father that we aren't going to be married after all.'

He was silent for a very long time, and motionless. She listened to the silence and waited for him to end it. It seemed to bank up behind her, but it was neither surprised nor charged with any reproach. She wished that she could say more to him, but her words had all been said, and this telling of her love for Johnnie had hurt her more than she had expected. Until these moments of telling Tom that it was at an end, there had still seemed a fantastic, foolish hope left to her. But now that was dead. How much that morning at Ostend had cost her —both Johnnie and Tom. They were cast away, together and swiftly. She wondered how long it could go on hurting as much as this.

At last there was the sound of Tom's chair scraping on the floor; he came and stood beside her. She turned to face him.

'Maura,' he said, 'do you remember I once told you about the girl I loved, the Italian girl, Gena?'

'Yes.'

'You must understand there wasn't anything unique in the way you loved Johnnie. I have felt it for Gena. There wasn't anything I wouldn't have done if she'd wanted it. I would have stayed in Italy, given up every ambition, every other love for her sake. Yours wasn't a new experience, Maura, but a rather rare one. Not many people love to the exclusion of everything else, and even you didn't succeed in that. You didn't succeed, and you're back here, and you're throwing all your future life away in futile atonement for this mischance.'

'Mischance?'

'The mischance,' he said, 'of loving Johnnie when you can't marry him—of his loving you. The mischance of Gena being killed in Florence. She's dead, Maura, and you might as well make up your mind that Johnnie is as much lost to you as if he were dead also.'

'Tom!'

'You've got to get used to looking at it that way. He *is* gone, you know. You can't ever have him.'

She was silent. Feeling the tight aching in her throat she turned away from him. But he caught her arm and pulled her back.

'Maura, why shouldn't we go on just as we were?'

She made to answer him, but the words died in her throat.

'If you come to Rathbeg with me—if you marry me, you'll forget him. Time wears out one's tragedy. And I understand about it. I wouldn't force you to forget him, or blame you for remembering. It's your chance of peace.'

'Is peace all that one can hope for from marriage? Isn't there anything else?'

'There would have been something else if you had married Johnnie. But you can't have him, Maura, and without him peace is as much as you can hope for.'

She said passionately, 'But, Tom, why? Why all of this? Why do you keep offering me second chances. I've been unfaithful to you. I've broken promises. How can you know I won't do it again?'

'Because,' he said, 'you're like myself. You'll only be in love like that once in your life. It doesn't happen again.'

She suddenly reached out and caught the sleeves of his dressing-gown. She gripped the cloth tightly in her fingers and pulled him close to her, as if she knew, as if she had waited for this moment, that there could no longer be any barriers between them. They were forcing each other into revelation from which they would never be able to escape.

'Tell me, Tom, truthfully, what you feel about me. I don't want half-truths—it's important that I have the whole. It's the most important thing left to me.'

His own hands sought her shoulders, held her there in a gesture that was full of affection, and a little tenderness also. There was a suggestion of sympathy, not obtrusive. He didn't pity her.

'You know that I don't love you,' he said. 'Not in the way I loved Gena. But if there is any other kind of love—then you have it. You've always known that, Maura. But I'm selfish about you—I want all the things that you have to bring to our marriage. We suit each other so well, you and I. I like you, tremendously—I like to talk to you. And I admire you because you're elegant and controlled, and you have quite a lot of wisdom.

'And when you came back from the cottage at the end of last summer,' he said, 'you were changed. I couldn't have known anything about what had happened to you—I didn't know about Johnnie—but you'd lost your aloofness, that trace of . . . it was almost an inhumanity which you seemed to wear. You *were* always a little smug and too wrapped up in your own life. But you'd suddenly then come down to earth, and you didn't mind the earthiness of the rest of us any longer. And if you have broken your heart over Johnnie, it's made you more lovable to the rest of us.

'You were Desmond's daughter, and he'd always grabbed too much of your life. You didn't have time or patience, as he hasn't, for the commonness and simplicity of people. You didn't understand people, or why they behave as they do. It was good to see the change in you. I'd known, for a long time, as you knew, that I wanted to marry you. But when you came back I had a sudden picture of our lives together, how it would have been at Rathbeg . . . and, well, it fitted perfectly.

'It still fits,' he said.

'Still—even now?'

'Perhaps more than before. You're not faultless any more; you've had to ask for forgiveness for something. You've broken away from Desmond. Even if it didn't last, you've made a break, and he can't ever possess you wholly again.'

She said, 'But I'm not the only woman who could give you those things. There could be others, Tom—without complications!'

He shook his head. 'I don't imagine that. Other women would expect the sort of love I couldn't give—and I'm tired of explanations. And I wouldn't want a woman who is insensitive to the absence of love . . .'

He broke off, saying quickly, 'Maura, does this seem unnecessarily brutal and clear-cut? You've asked for the truth, and I'm giving it to you, because if you marry me you'll never have to doubt again that you didn't hear every side of this.

'I'm not offering you the sort of love you should be offered. It doesn't exist in me any longer. I could give you affection and loyalty—and love in a kind of fashion. You've got to make up your mind whether you want that or not.

'And as for yourself—well, you're Desmond's daughter. You'll be far closer to Rathbeg for that reason, than any other woman could be. Will you come?'

'I don't know.'

'You must decide now.'

'Give me time. I don't know.'

'The decision won't be any easier in a day or a month. What you've got to decide is whether, right here and now, you'll make a step to forget about Johnnie, or whether you'll let yourself drift God knows where. It's as simple —and as drastic as that.'

She had no answer for him. He looked at her pale face, intent upon his own, and saw its bewilderment. She had not been afraid or uncertain when she had entered the room. Defeated, almost lifeless—but not like this, without confidence in him or herself or anything else. He guessed that his words had destroyed the last of her hope about Johnnie. She had lived through emotions in these months that all the years of the war, all her life with Desmond had not given her. He could pity her—even if she did not see his pity—but he was conscious of gladness and a feeling of relief that this was past her, and he need not fear it again. And she was awakened by her suffering, and never again would she gaze at the things about her with that blank, naïve look which seemed to shut out all knowledge, even a desire for knowledge, about them. She had been awakened, he thought, and he would now have to watch what would come of the awakening.

'Maura, can I put it like this—I might have loved you if it hadn't been for Gena. You might have loved me if you had never known Johnnie. We're quits. Could you marry me on that?'

Still she did not answer him, turning her head to the window in a kind of frenzy of desperation.

'We won't wait until the end of July. I could finish up this job in two or three weeks. Will you marry me—in six weeks from now? In five weeks, Maura?'

'If that's what you want, Tom . . . then, yes, I will.

'I'm not going to tell you any more all the things that are wrong with me, the bits of the bad bargain. If that's what you want from me, I shall behave as if Johnnie never happened. But you and I know that he did happen, and that's going to colour our lives, no matter what the rest of the world thinks. It's your bargain, Tom.'

He relaxed his grip a little. She was aware of his great firmness, a strength displayed where she had not formerly sought it. He made the future alarmingly clear; it contained only himself and Rathbeg. There would be no compromise on that, and he would be unsparing of her; in spite of what he had said, she thought he would be hard in his judgment if she failed. Because he loved Rathbeg more than he loved her. But he was honest, and he had told her that much, offering her the fullness of that life to overcome her useless, endless want of Johnnie. He would give her kindness and tenderness, and never in her heart expect her to forget these months. If he was prepared to have it that way, then he was as much responsible as she.

He dropped his hands. 'I'll shave and take you home.'

And as he turned away she was conscious of the thought that Desmond was saved from his disappointment.


# III

But they went instead to see Desmond in the Temple, and even in his surprise at their arrival, Maura could see him look with disfavour at her wrinkled flannel skirt and stained raincoat she had worn during the drive up from the cottage.

She sat down in the chair facing her father; Tom remained standing behind her.

'We thought we'd come and tell you,' Tom said, 'that we want to get married soon—in a month.'

Desmond looked from one to the other, and his heavy eyebrows twitched.

'This is rather sudden—might I ask why?'

'Why? Why?' Tom said. 'Because we've decided we want to. That's good enough reason.'

'I see. You've been constantly together for four years —you've been engaged since last autumn, and now you suddenly decide you'll be married in a month.'

'Surely it's our own concern if we want to do it?'

'Oh quite. But I happen to need Maura just now. I don't think she can be spared so soon from work here.'

'I happen to need her as well.'

'I'm prepared to admit that perhaps you do, Tom. But what about your job?'

'My job? There are dozens of men to fill it as soon as I go. I've never pretended to anyone that it's been in any way important—except that I'll know more about running Rathbeg economically by having stuck it out here at the Ministry—but the job itself . . .'

There was much more of it between them, the words flying back and forth across her head, and it seemed strange that Desmond, who had always wanted her to marry Tom, should fight to hold her just these few weeks longer. There was talk of money.

'It takes some time getting these things drawn up, Tom.'

'Is it possible you imagine that's a valid reason for postponing the wedding?'

'Maura's mother was a wealthy woman. There are a great many arrangements . . .'

'I've always supposed,' Tom said stiffly, 'that whatever Maura did about her money after she was married was her affair and yours, not mine.'

And there was talk about going to Ireland.

'The Ministry would let me go in a couple of weeks if I wanted to press the point,' Tom said. 'I could go to Rathbeg and settle things there—come back here for the wedding. Perhaps Maura would like to come with me?'

Desmond turned to her. 'What do you say to that? Would you like to go with Tom to Rathbeg?'

'Yes,' she said, suddenly knowing how much she wanted it. 'Yes, I'd like that very much.'

'Then,' he said, 'you must suit yourself.'

She watched him finger his pen, lying on the desk before him, and wondered why she could feel so detached. It seemed to her that she had sacrificed Johnnie for love of her father, and now he seemed no longer worthy of what she had done. She looked at the tall magnificence of him when he fussed over wedding invitations and who was to make her gown, and she saw him as the farm boy who had come to Trinity, made ambitious and excited by the brilliance he occasionally glimpsed. She wished she might tell him he was made a little ridiculous with his plans, that he revealed all the foolish snobberies which the years had grafted upon his original simplicity and energy. But he would be hurt, and even if the former height of her love for him seemed like a memory, at least it had a power to restrain her, and she said nothing.

But Tom delivered her from the plans.

'Maura and I would like to be married quietly,' he said.

Desmond looked up from the notes he had begun to make.

'It seems to me,' Tom went on before the other could answer, 'that if we can't have just a moderate-sized wedding, we'd better have the smallest one possible. I don't see the point in having hundreds of acquaintances obscuring one's few friends.'

Desmond glanced at Maura. 'Is that what you want?'

It hadn't occurred to her that there was a possibility of having anything but what Desmond himself wanted over this matter until Tom had spoken; now she grasped the opportunity he had made for her.

'I'm tired, Father,' she said. 'I want a rest much more than the strain of a fussy wedding. Give a party if you like when we come back from the honeymoon, but I'd rather dispense with the trimmings beforehand.' She rested her head against the back of the chair and looked away from him.

His gaze went from one to the other—from Tom's set expression to Maura's one of aloofness. For the first time she saw him outclassed. He shrugged his shoulders crossly.

'Well, of course, if you've decided that, there's nothing more to be said.'

He shuffled the papers on his desk. He was defeated and angry, and as with everything that was his personal life, he was bad at hiding it. Maura looked across at

Tom, who now stood with his back to them both, gazing through the window down into Pump Court. She was aware of affection and gratitude for him, and the feeling of wonder that he could defy Desmond in this fashion and remain unconcerned. Tom was stronger than Desmond, and that also amazed her. She began to see, as Tom had told her, that if once she could remove herself from her father, a great many things might be different.

## IV

A breath of agitation, something close to fear, crept through the room at the sounds of the voices. They could hear the footsteps on the stairs. Chris laid aside his book, looking towards the door. Before it opened Tom had stubbed out his cigarette and restrained himself from turning sideways to glance at Maura's face. But he could see her hands, the tense, betraying hands which clenched and unclenched in the few seconds which remained to her. Then he stood up as Simpson opened the door and announced Irene.

Maura rose slowly, because she hadn't the courage to pretend that she wanted to see Johnnie's wife. In the ten days since her return from the cottage she had half-believed that this interview would come, that in honesty and fairness she would have to seek it, but now with Irene before her, the situation was too unreal to admit belief. She thought that somehow the conventions would prevail, and they would say nothing of consequence to each other, but the hope died instantly with her reading of the other woman's expression.

Irene stood now before them, not replying to their greetings, but looking from Tom to Chris.

'Would you mind if I talked to Maura alone,' she said.

Chris smiled at her, his affection for her in his smile. 'I would have had to ask you to excuse me, in any case, Irene. I've got all this stuff to read through this evening.'

As he spoke he collected the books and papers that had filled the sofa beside him. He nodded to the others.

'Good-night, Tom.' And to Maura, 'I'll see you afterwards.' And then another smile to Irene. 'Good-night.'

When the door closed behind him Tom spoke.

'Maura, I'll phone you in the morning.'

She appeared to hesitate, then was abruptly moved to a protest. She turned to Irene.

'I'd like Tom to stay. Do you mind . . . we're going to Ireland to-morrow, to Rathbeg. I don't think there can be anything you want to say that he shouldn't hear.'

Irene answered slowly. 'Tom might not want to hear it all.'

'I think I've heard from Maura as much as you can tell me,' he said. 'I'd like to stay.'

She looked from one to the other, the firm line of her mouth slackening a trifle, as if she was in doubt. 'It makes it all so much simpler.' And to Maura she said, 'You're right to tell him. Yes . . . it's much better.'

Then she sat down, her movement unconscious, so that they remained standing and gazing down upon her. In that position the folds of her black coat fell almost to her feet. She pulled at her glove nervously, looking at the dying fire and trying to find her first words. In the midst of her own fear Maura felt pity and admiration stir for her, because she had come to meet the situation while dreading it, and was conquering it. And now, again, as if she could never be accustomed to the fact, Maura thought how beautiful she was, and wondered how she would appear to a man. The emotion on her face increased her beauty; she had the appearance of a little black-clad statue as she sat there.

She raised her head at last. 'Do you know where Johnnie is?' she said.

Maura was aware only of her utter reluctance to say anything, to attempt to answer the question. In an instant her mind sought other things, remembering deliberately the hot sun that morning in Ostend, the confusion of the gulls diving for refuse from the ships, and the figure of

Hendrick on the dock above her. Her eyes left Irene's face, rigid now after the effort of saying what she had come to say, and bright with a painful kind of exultation in what she had accomplished. Her gaze moved to Tom, and he was looking at her, and not helping her, just waiting. She despised her weakness and could not control it. Tom was expecting more from her than this—at least as much courage as Irene had displayed. She was conscious that much depended upon her words, much and perhaps more than she could now fully realise.

'I saw Johnnie last in Ostend,' she said. She shrank from the words, and they fell lamely.

Irene rose to her feet with a gesture of protest. 'But Johnnie has been back. I saw him the night before last.'

Her animation left her. 'I counted so much on his seeing you. I didn't believe that he would have gone without seeing you once.'

'Gone where?' Tom said, before Maura could speak.

'Where?' she repeated. 'That's what I don't know. I don't suppose Johnnie himself knows where.'

She added dully, 'But he's gone.'

She drew in breath deeply and said, 'Maura, he told me about you—about him coming down to the cottage, about going to Ostend. Johnnie didn't take it very well. He doesn't understand how anything can be more important than the person you love. I don't understand very well, either. For Johnnie I would have done anything. And yet you say you love him.'

She talked in a curious, monotonous tone, as if she had no listeners and was speaking aloud the thoughts that obsessed her. Maura wanted to cry out and halt the words that came from her unchecked. They hurt and wounded, brought up too vividly the memories of Johnnie's bewilderment. She couldn't crash through them, or go round them. And if she herself suffered, didn't Irene suffer much more in the loss of something that had been her possession for so long. It was cruel for them both, cruel also for Tom and the newly adjusted balance of their relations. And yet it had the quality of inevitability—the action that demanded to be done, the energy that must be spent before a hope of peace.

'But then you do love him,' she went on. 'You and Johnnie . . . I suppose you're the kind of people they say are made for one another. The kind of love that doesn't need a reason or an excuse—it just happens to be that way. No one else'—she broke off—'Do you realise this Tom? No one else stands a chance against a thing like that. I often think about it—two people who were meant to come together and no chance or mischance on earth is going to stop them. That's what happened, I guess, with you and Johnnie. The people who stand on the side-lines—like myself, like you, Tom—should know there's going to be a crash and get out of the way as gracefully as possible.

'I supose when you marry a person you know doesn't love you in the way you love him, you're never free of the fear that this may happen. You go on in the usual way, never knowing, always wondering, and one day you see a look on his face for another woman you've always wanted for yourself. Marriage is finished after that—it's only a muddled pretence. That's what I've seen all winter. And when Johnnie asked for a divorce he seemed to think he'd got to explain all this to me—as if I didn't know. He tried to tell me what his love was like—as if I didn't know it all, as if I hadn't loved him like that since the first time I saw him.'

Her face was stern with the effort to say all this, leaving out nothing, so that they should understand Johnnie, understand herself. It was compelling and awful to watch her as she talked, forcing herself to go on until it was all said.

'But that is finished for Johnnie also,' she said. 'When I saw him two days ago he had only his love left to him. There was no hope any more—he knew there could be nothing from you. You were gone, and he knew it was final and absolute. I think he talked to me more than he ever has, saying the kind of thing he was driven to say, and yet wanted not to say. And I couldn't help him, only listen. I've never been able to help Johnnie—never. I've been patient and gentle and quiet when he's needed that; I've been pleasant to have around him. But I've never helped him, never forced him to be something different just because I was there. I wanted to be everything in the world to him, and instead I was only a negative kind of habit.

'You know that way you love a spaniel—because you can always depend on it to put its muzzle against your knee, or throw itself at your feet? That kind of love's very comforting—very. It makes you warm and secure. I guess that's the way Johnnie felt about me.

'He told me about you in the Temple, and on the trip to Ostend. Johnnie cried to me that he loved you, and you wouldn't go with him. And now it's all gone, and he doesn't care about another thing in the whole world. He doesn't care whether I divorce him or not, whether he goes back to his job. He doesn't care about a damned thing but what he can't have. I can go on calling myself his wife if I want to, and that doesn't matter to him, either.'

She pulled at her gloves, and now tossed them beside her handbag on the chair. It was a movement of some passion; she had, just in this brief transition, forsaken her gentleness, thrown away the reserve that characterised her. Her face, which had seemed pale, was alive with colour and feeling. She was clear and sharp, a person with mind and will and power as she had never been before. Tom wondered if, having lost Johnnie, the fear of losing him was already lifted, and she was set free of it. And now, set free, she didn't understand the sensations, and reached forward, tasting this excess of emotion and allowing such licence to it as no normal person would. Sometime, he thought, she would achieve a balance. This would come much later, when even hope of Johnnie had gone, and she was grown accustomed to her unwanted liberty. He wished that the balance would be found somewhere between the lovely, subdued woman she had been during the winter, and this extraordinary creature, talking as if her existence depended upon them understanding what she must know they already understood too well.

Her ungloved hand stretched out and gripped the mantel-shelf.

'I'm going away,' she said. 'I've made up my mind since I saw Johnnie.'

'Where?' Tom said.

She lifted her head a little in surprise. 'I'm not sure. France . . . I think.'

'Why not America?'

'I don't think I could go back,' she said slowly. 'Besides, when Johnnie has come to his senses a little, when he has shaken this mood off, he's sure to go back. Although he doesn't know it now, I think it's certain he'll go back. For me . . . I think France is best.'

'Does Johnnie know?'

She shook her head. 'I suppose I should have told him then—the other night. Only I don't think I was sure of myself—and then he had no thought for anything but the things he'd got to say to me. He wandered out of the flat, and he seemed dazed. And then I realised he wasn't coming back that night. I didn't know where he'd gone.

'So I came to ask . . . Maura.' She addressed all her remarks to him, not looking much towards the other woman. She behaved as if talk with her would have snapped her control, though each word directed at Tom was meant for Maura.

'Johnnie should know that I'm going,' she said.

She seemed as if she expected no reply to this; her eyes wandered from Tom to Maura, and back again. And then Tom made certain of an idea which had taken him when she first entered—that this seeking of news of Johnnie was merely a pretext, half valid, half false, because she had been determined to see Maura. She would have come without a reason if she had needed to. He guessed that in her confusion and pain she had not completely believed in her final parting from Johnnie until she had confirmation of it from Maura's own lips. Had she hoped, Tom wondered, that somehow Maura would deny Johnnie's story of the trip to Ostend, was she still searching for a grain of comfort somewhere in all of this? She fought her tendency to hysteria and despair bravely, but it showed in actions like these.

'But you don't know where he is, do you?' she said, her voice rising a little. 'Nobody knows.'

She turned and her other hand gripped the mantel. Because she was small, her bowed head rested in the space between her hands. They were white beside the darkness of her hair and the black material of her coat. It seemed to them, watching, like an attitude of prayer.

Still with her back to them she raised her head and said, 'I must know where Johnnie is, because I have to tell him I'm going to have a child.'

She knew they would say nothing, and she went on:

'I'm three months pregnant—and Johnnie doesn't know. He hasn't even guessed. *You* haven't noticed, have you? Even Sir Desmond—and he notices me more than anyone else—hasn't seen a difference.'

Tom came nearer to her, tentatively touched her outstretched arm.

'Why haven't you told Johnnie? If you had told Johnnie . . . even two weeks ago you would have changed all this. He would never have gone to Maura . . . Johnnie would never have done that.'

She said with passion, 'Would you, when a man is asking you for a divorce because he loves another woman —would *you* cry to him that you were going to have his child? Would *you* hold him to you because he was honourable, because he wouldn't desert you? I've got more guts than that. Don't you think I knew I could have tied Johnnie to me more firmly than ever simply by telling him? If he loves another woman, then a child can't make a difference.'

Tom gripped her arm more firmly, as though he might be tempted to shake her. 'Irene, you can't think of going away. You've got to give Johnnie his chance. You can't make plans until you've seen him. No one behaves like that, Irene.'

He saw her fingers grip the mantel with extraordinary

force. 'What Johnnie says or doesn't say can't make any difference. I'll see him once—and then the divorce can go through. Do you suppose I could live with him now? Why, Johnnie wouldn't even notice whether I did or not. All I'd be to him now was the spaniel he occasionally tripped over.'

Tom said, 'Irene, for God's sake . . .'

'Oh, what's the use,' she cried. 'Why bother talking about it? You know as well as I do that it's all finished.'

Maura and Tom gazed at her in the silence, at the black-clad figure which clung to the mantel in a fierce struggle for restraint. She was so lonely in that struggle, so much by herself in her decisions, and sticking to them with cold stubbornness. She was magnificent and foolish at the same time; admirable, but like a child who does a deed of outrageous daring for no purpose. But it was terrifying for them to watch it, because her decision was not a child's to be abandoned when enough attention had been paid to it. But it was something she would carry through in loneliness and fear. The sacrifice of herself was deliberate—and with all of that, Maura thought, so unnecessary and wasteful.

She ran her tongue over dry lips, looking towards Tom for help.

'Irene,' she said, 'you must think about it more. You must let Johnnie take you back to New York.'

At her words Irene turned abruptly; the soft hearth-rug twisted with her movement. Her hands were now still by her side It seemed as if Maura's voice, after so long a silence, had shattered the force of her restraint.

'I can't go back with him,' she cried. 'Oh, damn you —can't you see why I can't go back with him? Because Johnnie's child may be coloured!'

They didn't want to look at her face. It was terrible, with tears running down it. She looked almost ugly when she cried, and older. There was such pain in her face, and a different, older knowledge than it had ever betrayed before. She didn't care about them; once her control had gone it didn't seem to matter to her how much of her suffering they saw. They saw all of it then, heard the raucous sobs that were almost as loud as shouts. She wept on and on, making no attempt to check this weeping. Her hands remained by her sides, in a kind of primitive gesture of despair and misery. The weeping was like a gigantic and useless protest against its own cause. They knew that her grief could never be gentle and resigned.

Her passion gradually spent itself, worn down by its very force. She took a handkerchief and wiped her wet cheeks, looking in rather a surprised fashion at the streaks of powder which showed on it. With her weeping the rigour of her control was broken. She appeared dazed, her courage not touched, but subdued and less aggressive. She kept looking from one to the other while she wiped the tears, as though she hoped she had not said her last words aloud, that they still belonged to her, unspoken. But she had, and she couldn't take them back. She sat down.

'Of course, Johnnie doesn't know,' she said. 'I've never told him.'

She suddenly flung her hands wide—the first appeal she had made to them.

'It didn't seem wrong at the time,' she said. 'I didn't think of it as wrong. Since I was sixteen doctors had said I could never have a child. Believing that, it didn't seem wrong to marry him without telling him . . . and I loved him so much. He said he didn't mind about having no children—and he didn't know how glad I was. Johnnie didn't deserve to be cheated like that.'

Pity held Maura almost tongue-tied; not so much pity because Irene was still too brave to pity. Not pity, but fear of wounding and injuring beyond what had already been done. But she needed reassurance.

'You didn't mean to cheat . . . this isn't your fault.'

Some of the apathy left Irene; she straightened in the chair. 'Oh, yes, it is. It's all my fault. I cheated by not telling him, and now it's caught up on me. I guess I was just too sure of what the doctors had said. After all, I'm not the first woman who's been told she couldn't have a child, and discovered that it wasn't right. It happens all the time . . . and I'm one of the people it happened to.

'I guess it was my fault, all of it. But I loved him in a way that made me a little crazy. I hadn't had much of a life, and just when I knew Johnnie I wanted to have a little happiness—and it didn't seem wrong to cheat for something I wanted so badly.'

She twisted the sodden handkerchief, pulling at it with the frenzy of her hands. Desperately she needed to talk. Now, with the first words spoken the rest came out, seeking vindication of her action, defending it and still blaming herself. Her hands kept up the ceaseless rolling and releasing of the handkerchief.

When she began her story she set out her facts neatly, as if they had been thought out and even rehearsed many times. Maura recognised this and it saddened her to see how Irene's mind must have played over this part of her defence since she had married Johnnie, wording it to herself in fear and apprehension against the time when it might be necessary for him to hear it.

'I've lived all the part of my life I can remember in the town called Moreton, in Georgia. I think I went there when I was five, after my mother and father were killed in a street accident in New York. My grandfather lived there in a clap-board house three blocks from the Negro grade school where he taught. He was half-caste, the son of a Negress and a white, whose father had left Ireland in the potato famine. Grandfather's people worked hard enough—but all they'd ever got was a few acres that produced a poor-quality cotton, and you can't get far on that. Grandfather had brains—I suppose he was a pretty good teacher, but he was coloured and poor, and there never is much chance for people like that. I remember how kind he was to me—unbelievably kind, and because my mother had married a white man, he knew long before I did how tough things might be for me. He was a simple man, Grandfather, but he always seemed pretty fine to me.

'I remember it so well,' she said. 'When I was old enough I went to school where he taught. I played there with my cousins, the children of his son. Uncle Henry had married a full-blooded Negress and the children were as dark as if there was no white blood in them. I saw the difference, of course, but it hadn't begun to matter to me then. But it did, eventually, and Grandfather watched for it, and tried to help me over it. But he couldn't protect me completely—no one ever can.

'He had ambitions for me, in a mild way. Wanted me to go to college—I think he wanted me to teach, because he believed that teaching was a pretty fine thing. I was supposed to do all the things he hadn't done. But I was afraid of it, and when I finished at high school I worked in a bookshop in Moreton. He had been ill for about a year before I left school, and he lived about a year longer. He'd given up teaching, and he was in pain pretty constantly from a growth in the chest. After he died I went to live for about three months with Uncle Henry's family. But we didn't suit each other much. As long as Grandfather was alive I wouldn't have left Moreton, because we loved each other as sometimes an old man and a kid do. But with him dead there was nothing to hold me there. Someone had told me once I could be a model. So I went to New York.

'I wasn't tall enough to interest the dress designers, and Moreton hadn't taught me how to wear clothes, so I got jobs when they needed pictures of a girl in a cotton dress. Fortunately they needed a lot of girls in cotton dresses, so I made enough money to live on. But I was so lonely I wanted to die every night when I got back to my room. I used to go to the movies, but that's all. I hadn't got any friends, and I didn't make dates—New York seemed very big and very expensive. I missed my grandfather a lot.

'After I'd been there a while, a girl at the model agency asked me if I wanted to share an apartment. She didn't ask if I was coloured, or who my people were, and I'd had enough of living alone. I hadn't the courage to spoil it by telling her. Four of us shared the apartment and I was living there when I met Johnnie.

'I met Johnnie because he almost ran me down one

Sunday morning on 58th Street. The wind had blown off my hat and I ran in front of his car to chase it. He swerved and went into a lamp-post. The front of his car was smashed in, and he was very angry with me. And I was so frightened I sat down in the gutter and cried. I think my crying made him worse, but he waited until they came and took his car away, and then he took me back to the apartment in a cab. He was trying to be kind, and to stop saying what a fool I'd been. There wasn't anyone in the apartment, and he discovered there wasn't much in the ice-box, either. He made me come and eat lunch with him. I suppose I fell in love with him that first day.

'I knew Johnnie didn't love me in the way I loved him, but I imagined we would be happy together. I knew his family and what Johnnie felt about continuing as head of the business, and in all of that I was prepared to agree with whatever he wanted. I suppose all along I knew that his people didn't altogether approve of his marrying me, and that made Johnnie all the more determined to do it. I'd never known anyone as kind and simple as Johnnie, or anyone I wanted to be with as much. I believed I could make him happy, and if I cheated about not telling him I was coloured, it was because I thought it could never matter to us.

'My child may be coloured,' she went on, 'and that fact—even if Johnnie had never fallen in love with you—would make it impossible to go back to New York. There isn't any reason why Johnnie should suffer for a situation he has never sought. By not telling him that I was coloured I took away from him the right to decide whether he wanted to run this risk or not. And I don't expect him to stick by a decision which wasn't his own. This had always been my own problem, and Johnnie shouldn't have to bear it for his children.

'If the child is coloured I shall never take it back to the States. Whatever its problems are going to be, I don't want it to grow up with the feeling I knew—of being a part of two worlds and belonging wholly to neither. Whatever decision it may make later, I want it first of all to have known a world that operates no prejudice against a person whose skin is dark. There's so little I can do to compensate a child for this kind of mess, but it has at least the right to that much.

'And now I've got to see Johnnie and tell him. And I'm afraid of that—oh, God, I get sick when I think of facing him and telling him what I've done. It could be easier if I didn't love him as I do, but he'll be kind to me. He'll want to make plans for me, and stay with me. And all the time I would have died to save him from this kind of thing. If only he'd abuse me—but I know he won't. He'll go on being kind, and I don't think I can stand that. It's all his damned kindness about the little things that makes it so hard.'

She began to gather up slowly her handbag and gloves. Now she spoke directly to Maura.

'I wanted to talk to you. Perhaps more than I quite understood myself. I suppose I wanted to come again and see you, and understand what it was that made Johnnie love you. There were things to say to you . . . and, of course, I've told you . . .'

She turned swiftly to Tom. 'I've told you far, far more than I ever intended you should hear. But you, Maura, you haven't said anything. You've said nothing of Johnnie, nothing of yourself. The way I think about it, you're unworthy of him because you don't love him enough. You love other things more—but, of course, Johnnie doesn't see that.'

She got to her feet. 'I want to go before Sir Desmond comes in. And you must promise never to tell him anything I've said to-night. He'll think me ungrateful—I don't intend to see him again. That's one of the things I can't make myself do. He's been so kind—all the winter—and thank God he doesn't know he's responsible for this. He will be sorry about me and Johnnie, but it's *you* that he adores, and he wanted your marriage so much.'

Tom said, 'Maura and I are being married in three weeks.'

Irene looked at him. 'You know, don't you, that she is

still in love with him? Even if she has sent him away she still loves him.'

Tom said, 'We thought there was more than just that fact.'

'There isn't anything more than that,' she said. 'Believe me there isn't anything. She loves him, and because she can't have him she'll go on loving him as long as she lives.'

They didn't try to stop her leaving.

At the door she said without turning, 'Good-bye.'

They stood still and listened deliberately to the sounds of her going downstairs, and the final slam of the front door. Maura even half imagined she could hear the sounds of her footsteps on the pavement outside, but she knew this was not so. Then she sat down and stared into the fire, hands clasped before her, not speaking to Tom, and not moving, until later, much later, Desmond came home.

## V

Maura undressed mechanically, and lay on the bed in her dressing-gown. About her the sounds of the household gradually diminished, and died away altogether, leaving her too much alone with the ticking of the clock and the circle of brightness which the reading lamp threw on the ceiling. The traffic outside grew less; she lay waiting for the time of absolute quiet when there would be nothing to hear at all. But she had forgotten the rain. For the past hour it had come in occasional gusts against the window, like the rattle of gravel. She could remember seeing it glisten on Desmond's hair when he had come in. He had stood in the centre of the room, after greeting Tom, handsome in his dinner jacket and flushed with the wine he had taken, and had asked about Irene's visit. He ran his household in that fashion—the telephone calls and visitors to Maura and Chris he regarded as his own. This evening he had been rebuffed by Tom, not pointedly or coldly, but in a way which suggested that Tom had never recognised Desmond's right to such information.

Once again, as in the days just past, Maura had stood aside and witnessed Desmond's withdrawal before Tom.

She had said good-night to them both there, and left them alone. Desmond followed her upstairs soon after, and the house settled into unbroken quiet.

Maura listened to her own even breathing in the stillness of the room; listened to that and at the same time remembered the sobs of Irene when in the end she had begun to weep. She tried to draw back from the memory, and couldn't. It was impossible, even as she knew it was impossible to put out the light and sleep. Her eyes circled the pale walls, and instead saw Irene with head bowed over the mantel. Along with the ticking of the clock and the rain, she heard her say that she, Maura, was undeserving of Johnnie's love because she had not loved him enough; and her frightening little story again, the Negro grade school, and the girl who hadn't learnt to wear jewels and furs in Moreton, Georgia, for people to photograph in New York. She twisted on the bed and prayed to escape that spectacle of Irene's solitary and lonely courage. And downstairs, in the stillness, the door bell rang.

She got up immediately, and went and stood on the landing. Desmond came out, tying his dressing-gown cord. He leaned over the banister, waiting, as she did, in silence. They heard Simpson's steps in the hall, and then two voices together. Desmond started downstairs. As he did so the clocks all over the house started a slow and erratic chorus of half-hour chimes. She followed him down.

She stood on the last flight of stairs and saw the little group of her father, a policeman and Simpson—and the sight of Simpson in an unexpectedly vivid dressing-gown seemed part of the strangeness. Long afterwards she could remember that ill-assorted trio there, and remembered that the clocks had barely finished chiming.

'Father, what is it?' she said.

They turned and looked at her, upraised faces turned towards her pale in the single light which burned in the hall.

'They've come from Great Portland Street,' Desmond said to her.

'It's about Mrs Sedley, Sir Desmond,' the man began again. 'I presume she's a friend of yours.'

'Yes, yes,' he said.

'I'm afraid it's bad news, sir. She was run down by a bus near London Bridge. They sent me to the address they found in her handbag. There was no one there, so I . . .'

'Is she alive?' he demanded.

'Yes, sir, she's still alive, but I'm afraid they don't expect her to live long.'

Chris had appeared on the landing beside Maura. She heard his light breathing close to her, and then Desmond turned and spoke to him.

'Chris, will you dress quickly? I'll want you to come with me.'

Desmond faced the policeman again. 'Which hospital?'

'Guy's, sir. She was knocked down south of the bridge —almost beside Guy's. We have a patrol car here for you, sir. The hospital told us it was urgent.'

'How long ago did it happen?'

'She was admitted a little more than an hour ago, sir. They phoned through to our station. I went round to Great Portland Street—they told me that Mrs Sedley's husband hadn't been there for some time. And then the porter mentioned your family as regular visitors there. I thought you might perhaps . . .'

'Yes, of course,' Desmond said. 'You were quite right to come here. It won't take me more than a few minutes to dress.' He made to turn away.

'Sir Desmond?'

He looked back. 'What is it?'

'It's about the lady's husband, sir. Do you know any place I might get in touch with him? There isn't much time.'

Desmond stopped short. 'No, I don't know.' Then he looked towards Maura. 'Do you know?'

'No.'

144

Desmond didn't wait any longer. As he passed her on the landing he called down to the policeman. 'You could try the office of the *Financial Times* in the morning—and he has friends at the American Embassy.'

He went on a little farther, and then called out, 'Try them all—but it will be too late then.'

The policeman stood in silence and some uncertainty, looking from Maura to Simpson. Then he made quick, deliberate little notes in the book he held. 'I'll see what I can find out from these people, Miss. There isn't anywhere else you can think of that I could try to-night?'

She shook her head. 'I don't think there is.'

They stood about in uneasy quiet, not talking, until Simpson said suddenly, 'This is a shocking affair, Miss Maura. And Mrs Sedley here only a few hours ago.'

'Yes,' she said slowly. 'Yes, Simpson, it is. Very shocking.'

They said nothing more until Desmond and Chris came down again, dressed, both at the same time. Simpson had their coats ready.

'Go back to bed, Maura,' Desmond said as he struggled into his. 'Try to get some sleep. There's nothing you can do by waiting up. We may not be back until breakfast time, perhaps later.' He took his hat and put it on. 'Quickly, Chris.'

Chris, who had been standing waiting for him by the door, only said, 'See you later, Maura.'

When they were gone with the policeman and the last sounds of the car had died away, Simpson closed the door quietly.

'Is there anything I can get you, Miss Maura?'

'No, Simpson, nothing.'

She suddenly knew that she had the worst of it, waiting here alone in the heavy quiet they had left behind them. Better for them the speed, and the rush, the feeling of urgency which would accompany and stay with them. For her there was nothing but the empty house, and the imprint of Irene's back still against the cushions in the drawing-room, and the twisted hearthrug where her foot had caught.

Simpson stood with his hand on the light switch, waiting, and on his face, as she looked up, she caught an expression, something more real, more personal than she had ever seen there before. So even Simpson . . . The power of beauty, the depth of quietness and sweetness that had been Irene's, left no one untouched. And strangely, with her heart full of pity, she could still feel a tug of envy for the other woman's power. Was he thinking of that beauty destroyed, the terror of that kind of death, the pain that she suffered now, while they stood there? Oh, God, where was Johnnie?

And then, with the thought of him, another thought occurred. She turned to Simpson.

'I've remembered somewhere I can phone . . . about Mr Sedley. Will you bring coffee into Sir Desmond's study?'

She waited in his room, sitting at the desk, for the call to come through. The room was cold—it had not been used that evening, and the fire was laid in the grate. She stared at the rolled up newspaper, the small sticks, while she listened to the voices repeating and repeating the number. She thought about Irene, and the wet shiny surface of the road, and the pain, if she were conscious of any pain; and she thought of the child. She wondered if Irene were lonely, or had loneliness already gone? And she imagined the terrible loneliness of that night walk through the city to the other side of the river. The loneliness was the worst thing about it.

Then she heard Willa's voice.

'Willa? It's Maura here.'

'Maura? What's wrong?'

She edged forward in the seat; she didn't know how to say all the words that came to her. She waited a long time, trying to think how to say them.

'Maura, are you still there? Can you hear me?'

'I was wondering about Johnnie's car, Willa . . . Has he come down to collect it? No one knows where he is. I thought he might be with you . . .'

'Yes—yes, he's here. *Maura, what's the matter?*'

'Then, Willa, tell him—tell him there's been an accident. Irene has been in an accident—here in London. They say there's very little time, so he's got to come as quickly as he can.'

'Maura, you talk to him. I'll go and get him.'

'No, no, there isn't time. Willa, it's urgent. He can't waste a second. She's at Guy's.'

'Yes—I've got that. But, Maura, talk to him—Maura, please.'

'No, Willa. Just get him on the way as quickly as possible. That's all.'

When she put the receiver down the silence was worse than ever, and the thought of Irene waiting to take hold of her. But there wasn't escape from it anywhere in the house—or anywhere else. She put a match to the fire and prepared to endure it until Desmond should return with the news that she was dead.

The rain finished at dawn. She drew the curtains and watched the light grow in the little square, bricked-in space. It was grey and still, with the brightness of the fire leaping out across the room. With the rain gone, it was a soundless morning, nothing yet stirring through the house or about it. A gentle dripping still continued from some guttering or roof above her, but finally that also finished. She sat with folded hands and listened for the sound of the car.

The sky had cleared when they came. She stood by the open door and watched them get out of the car. The sun would come through later, she thought. She could see her father's weariness as he walked towards her and up the steps.

Desmond looked at her with a grey and angry face.

'Irene's dead,' he said. 'Her husband reached her before she died. But she wasn't conscious long. Just now and again. She asked for me . . . spoke to me. Nothing much, poor child.'

He sank down on a chair in the hall. It was the first time Maura had ever seen her father with stricken eyes.

'She went under a bus. Tough, brave little soul—but

147

there was never any hope that she'd live. Much better if she'd given in and died right away.'

He straightened. 'There was a miscarriage as well as her injuries. They told me she was about three months pregnant. And where was her husband?—what was she doing wandering about London alone—what was she doing in that place? Maura, why did she leave here and go off like that? What happened to her?'

Chris swung the door behind him. The noise of its closing seemed to echo in the house.

'I don't think Maura has got to answer questions like that,' he said. 'Whatever Irene had to say when she came here was for Maura alone—or else she would have said it to all of us'

They were each side of her. Chris leaning against the door, his face tight and fine-drawn with fatigue, Desmond clutching the chair and breathing heavily.

'No, damn you! I won't be answered like that. Irene left my house last night and now she's dead. I have a right to know what happened to her here.'

She looked from one to the other—Chris's gaze upon her with sympathy, Desmond staring at her with his anger and wretchedness. She thought of Irene who was dead now, and of how little right they had to talk of what she had revealed—she remembered the promise Irene had wanted from them that Desmond would never know about the child. But Desmond knew, and he was angry and blaming Johnnie. He didn't know anything of Irene's misery, was making wild guesses at what might have compelled her on that headlong flight through the city, ending, probably, in some terrible kind of despair there near the bridge. Desmond had got to know about this because half-truths would satisfy no one.

'Irene came here this evening,' she said, 'and told us she was going to have a child.'

'Yes, yes,' Desmond said, and she recognised it as the way he had answered the policeman.

'But that wasn't all. Irene was afraid the child would be coloured. Her grandfather was a half-caste Negro.'

'Oh, God!' Desmond said. 'Poor child.'

'It wasn't her fault. No one could blame her for not telling Johnnie about being coloured. When she married him she believed she could never have a child. Johnnie never knew she was pregnant. There were so many mistakes we all made. Because Johnnie didn't know she was going to have a child he asked her for a divorce. And after that she wouldn't tell him. She was afraid—because of what she'd done.'

Desmond's head had jerked up suddenly. 'A divorce? Why should he ask for a divorce?'

She said slowly, 'Johnnie and I love each other.'

'Maura! What are you saying?'

'Has it never occurred to you before, Father? Johnnie and I love each other. I tried to go away with him—only my courage didn't last long enough. I came scuttling back here because you, and religion—and Irene too, I suppose— got bigger than my loving Johnnie. So you can look at me and know what a rotten little coward I am—afraid to stay away from Johnnie, afraid to go with him.

'Father, I'm always afraid. I suppose you, and the life I've always led, tied to your house and your purse-strings has made me that way.'

Desmond said, 'I don't want to hear any more.'

'You've heard as much as there is—you've heard all that I've done to Irene, and to Johnnie and to Tom. And if you've got any pity left over from Irene, you might spare a little for what I've got to go through.'

She turned away from them and began to walk towards the stairs.

'Maura, come back. I want to talk to you.'

'Talk? What's the use of that? You know the facts as they are, and those you can't alter. I'm going now to phone Tom and ask him to come here.'

The porter closed the hall door behind him slowly, the full measure of his curiosity displayed in that action. Maura heard the sound, felt the man's thoughtful, interested eyes as if they were still upon her, and from that moment felt she had no right to be here, in Johnnie's sitting-room. The room was darkened, the curtains still drawn tightly across the windows, and yet as she moved to pull them apart her movements were reluctant. She felt as if she were disturbing something that was beyond her sphere, a tampering, prying action with possessions that were not her own. And yet when the strong light flooded the room it was normal and ordinary—and yet not as she had ever seen it before. There was dust, for one thing; on the table beside the window she could see it, the dust of several days undisturbed. The faint motion of the air as the curtains swished back had started the flutter of dark, dead rose petals to the table. She stretched out her finger to touch another bloom, and it also, papery and dry, fell with its tiny but distinct sound. There were white roses among the red; they had opened fully but the brown had only just begun to stain the edges, and they stayed firm under her touch. She didn't like to see the yellow hearts of them exposed like that, or the stiff ugliness of the stem when the petals had been swept clean in one movement. She had seen before how the red flowers of a species died before the white, as if all their strength had gone in the making of the colour. But red roses had been Irene's favourites, and all winter long she had sought out the expensive, artificially-cultured blooms to decorate this room. They looked alien, these things, sitting stiff and dead in the sunshine, when all over the country the first buds were beginning to open.

No one had cleaned here, no one had opened a window or emptied the ashtrays since Irene had left to come to Hanover Terrace four days ago. Nor had Johnnie himself, she knew, been here except for a few minutes to take some clothes. And the flat seemed to react—it had taken on the air of desertion that was thicker than the dust. She looked at the roses again, thinking with a sense of shock and grief of all that had happened since they had been fresh. Four days only, but time enough to change and alter the course of their lives, and time, even, for them to have grown almost accustomed to the change. And still the change wasn't complete. She waited now for the click of Johnnie's key in the door.

Each detail of the four days was unforgettable; and this was the first time she would talk with Johnnie since they had said good-bye on the deck of *Rainbird*.

There couldn't be any forgetting of Desmond's fear, alone when she had told him that she and Johnnie loved each other. He had not let her alone that morning, not wanted sleep after his night at the hospital, until he had pleaded and persuaded, begged her to consider what she was doing. Because it had dawned on him at last that Johnnie was free, and that she, his daughter, would do whatever Johnnie wanted. Desmond was stricken because he saw visions of her life at Rathbeg destroyed, and she herself, beyond his reach and influence.

So now she sat in this desolate room, looking at the things she had seen many times before, and waited for him. It was the typical London flat, furnished with the uniformity which depressed when one had seen it too often. Irene and Johnnie had inhabited it without interest or curiosity about it, certainly no affection, and it had remained much as it was the first time they had seen it. Irene was strangely unconcerned about the places she lived in—unconcerned save to indulge her passion for beautiful flowers. The daily maid had waded fretfully through their untidiness, the careless manner of their living. Books and flowers and a monstrously large radiogram were all they had ever added to the original style.

And nothing more would ever be added, because to-morrow Johnnie was flying back to New York.

She heard his key in the door, and when he paused in

the doorway, she turned slowly to look at him. She stood up, but they didn't move any closer to each other, the full length of the room separated them, and, it seemed as well, their consciousness of the happenings of the last few days. He didn't look any worse, she thought, than he had appeared at the inquest and funeral; the tan from sun and exposure hadn't left him; his lean body had never yet betrayed sleeplessness. He wore a grey flannel suit, the jacket of which hung open—he always wore his clothes like someone who had no vanity. She could see that the sun had bleached streaks on his hair.

'Hallo, Maura.'

'Hallo, Johnnie.'

He thrust his hands into his pockets and came into the centre of the room. Their greetings had been tentative, almost shy, like children's.

'I'm sorry you've had to wait here,' he said. 'I couldn't think of anywhere else we could talk without dozens of other people interrupting.'

'Yes, I know. I didn't mind.'

The talk died. They were too much aware of all that had got to be said before the interview was ended, and neither had the determination or strength to start.

Johnnie gazed about the room. 'I'm sorry it looks like this for you. I told the woman not to come—it can all be done when I've gone.'

He moved with apparent aimlessness to the window, closer to her, and she watched, fascinated, as he suddenly withdrew a hand from his pocket and touched one of the brittle red roses. When the petals lay in the heap with the others on the table he stared at them for a long time.

'There's so much about this flat I never liked,' he said. 'Usually I never care where I live—it's never mattered to me if a house looks like a furniture shop with the labels off. You know I have no taste, and I don't care if people want to put Louis Seize beside Early American. But this flat is much worse than bad taste—it's unfriendly. Irene and I always have been careless. We always leave stains on things, and the handles come off. Nothing like that

152

ever happened here. Her unhappiness started from this flat. Even the flowers never lived as long as in other places.'

She watched his finger tracing designs in the dust.

'What will happen about the flat?'

'The flat? Oh, its lease has another month to run. I'll see that it's cleaned when I leave—and then it's not my affair any more.'

She said 'yes' slowly, looking down into the narrow street. To where they were, on the third floor, the bottled sounds of the traffic in Great Portland Street rose sharply. Maura felt them pressing on her, through the closed windows, heavy, ceaseless sounds that accompanied her own wild thoughts. She knew she was helpless in the face of his assertion that he was returning to New York. Above the buildings opposite, and stretching away to the park, the sky was a bright May blue, the very day was polished to a kind of brilliant optimism that always belongs to bright days of the spring. The kind of day, too late to catch one unawares, and still too early for the worn glory of summer, that made winter clothes seem shabby and every young face in the street seem beautiful. Away and apart from this sense of optimism she and Johnnie stood here, talking to each other in dreary commonplaces.

She said, 'What time are you leaving?'

'Plane goes at nine-thirty in the evening.'

As he spoke he moved abruptly away from the window. 'Would you like some coffee?'

She nodded.

He led the way into the kitchen, and she watched him, quick and skilful as his movements always were when they had an aim. But he was unfamiliar with the lay-out. She put water in a saucepan on the stove, and waited while he searched about for the coffee; and then he went to the wrong cupboard for the cups. She knew that there had been very few times in these past months when Johnnie had prepared food in this kitchen.

While they waited for the coffee to heat she saw him begin a slow search of his pockets, and presently he drew out something and handed it to her.

'I bought it in Amsterdam,' he said. 'I thought it looked like yours.'

It was a ring of bright green jade.

'Put it on,' he said.

The mounts were tiny gold hands that grasped the stone; the jade was polished and dazzlingly brilliant.

'The dealer told me it was made about four hundred years ago. The little princess who wore it had her name inside.'

She slipped it off, turning the inside of the band towards the light. In the gold were the almost obliterated Chinese characters. She put it back on.

'Johnnie, I love it.'

'Thought you would. I've been carrying it round in my pocket since then. I suppose I would have posted it to you.'

Then he turned his attention to the coffee.

They drank it standing up. Johnnie leaned back against the sink. The kitchen had a swept, frigidly clean appearance like the inside of a hospital, but even here the days of disuse had laid dust in a film over the enamel tops of the tables. It was quieter here, on the side of the flat away from the traffic, much quieter except when the refrigerator motor started up, and that, like the traffic, they didn't notice after a while.

Maura went to the stove and poured more coffee from the saucepan.

She turned and faced him.

'Well, Johnnie?'

He put his cup down on the draining-board, and she watched his hands go into his pockets in the familiar gesture.

'I didn't mean to see you,' he said. 'If Tom hadn't told me . . . what he did last night, I wouldn't have seen you now.'

'Why should you go to see Tom—why not me?'

He shrugged. 'I wanted to thank you in some way—all of you. There was only Tom or Chris to whom I could go. Tom seemed easier.'

'And Tom told you? Tom told you everything that I wouldn't have told.'

'About Irene? Yes, he told me all that. He has more pity than you, Maura. More common sense.'

'More pity? Is it pity to torture you with what she suffered? I would never have told you.'

'No,' he said, his hands searching deeper into his pockets. 'You would never have told me.'

Back in her mind as he spoke were the painful, raw scenes of the inquest, and her memories of a solitary plane tree—dust on its new leaves and bark darkened with years of London grime—which struggled for its life in the narrow little passage outside the court window. They had all sat there rigidly—stiff fingers frozen into the kind of stillness Johnnie had taken unto himself and imposed upon them all. The court had been hot in the afternoon sunshine, and they were uncomfortable in their dark clothes, and somehow ashamed of their discomfort. In the beginning she had winced when they had called Irene 'the deceased,' and later was shocked to find that she didn't notice it so much. The unpleasant became familiar, she thought, and soon passed over into the forgotten. But she doubted that she would ever forget the manner of Irene's death, or the fact that for the first time she had seen Desmond overcome by the atmosphere of a court-room, and wanting to break through it, wanting to plead for a little more humanity when a woman he had loved was spoken about. There was Desmond's fear to see as well—a terrible fear that her, Maura's, relationship with Johnnie, would be dragged to the light. He twisted and squirmed under his fear, and more than once she had seen him take his handkerchief and wipe the sweat from his forehead.

'Think of the courage it needed,' Johnnie said. 'Not the sort of courage one expects from a woman—waiting until it was close enough. And she had the bad luck not to die right away.'

Almost from the beginning they could see that the verdict would be suicide. That is, from the time the bus

driver had stood there, miserably anxious and faintly indig-
nant at finding himself in a coroner's court, and said,
'Anyone who does what the lady did is either mad or blind.
Waited until I was on top of her, she did, then stepped
out in front of me.'

'There was no chance of avoiding her?'

'I tried to swerve, sir, but you got to have room to
do that. First she was on the footpath, and then she was
under my wheels.'

Tom had stood up and calmly told them about Irene
when she had come that night to Hanover Terrace. He
told as much as he wanted to tell—Irene was disturbed,
had told them that she and her husband were separating,
she had refused to go back to America with him—and she
had told them that she was going to have a child.

'Did she say why she would not return to America with
her husband?'

'For some time the marriage had not been a happy one.
She believed that separation was the only thing.'

'And she still, you say, had not told her husband that
she was going to have a child? Have you any idea why she
didn't?'

'Because she knew that he would make it difficult for
her to leave him.'

The questioning of Tom went on for a long time, a
wearyingly long time, but nothing could drag from him
the truth of what had taken place in Hanover Terrace.
Maura knew that it was not for Johnnie's sake that he
lied, but for her own sake, and for the memory of Irene in
tears, turned with her face against the mantel-shelf, and
his pity for her loneliness. Not from Tom would anyone
else hear Irene's story of her life in Moreton, and the
meeting with Johnnie when she had been so much in love
that the truth had not mattered beside it. They all knew
what the verdict would be—the bus driver and policeman
had assured that. Tom could be forgiven his perjury because
he had seen and believed in Irene's courage, and had
courage enough to protect her. And when she, Maura, was
called, she had added nothing to his statement, corroborat-

ing everything he had said.

Johnnie's face, when he took the stand, was as composed as Tom's own, but he grew impatient under the pressure of the questioning and his anguish showed plainly. She could remember the misery in his voice when he had faced the coroner and said clearly:

'I am aware that whatever unhappiness my wife suffered was wholly my fault. Whatever she was driven to do was because she knew I had ceased to love her—that the unsettled life I led would never give her any peace.'

They had waited quietly during the few minutes which the coroner needed to collect his notes. The small room had grown hotter. Maura kept her eyes on the branch with its leaves shining in the sunlight. Then the coroner began his summing-up with economy and terseness which seemed habitual, and the verdict—'the deceased had taken her own life while the balance of the mind was disturbed'—was nothing more or less than they had expected. It softened the words to hear that impersonal voice pronouncing them; the smooth routine tones of it destroyed the image of Irene and her desperate, foolish, courage.

Johnnie had had the explanation from Tom last night, and had phoned Maura to meet him here, at the flat. This had broken the silence of two days after the inquest, days in which she had been minute by minute hoping and praying for his call. And yet she had stood before him here, this morning, hardly able to credit her sense at hearing him say that he intended to leave London without seeing her. The pain of it went past belief.

'Cigarette?' he said.

'Thanks.'

He lit them both, and leaned back against the sink. She looked at him closely, carefully, in a way she had not done since he had stood above her on the pier at Ostend, in the blazing morning sunlight and the clamour of the port. His face was a little worn with strain, but he seemed more fully in possession of himself than she had ever seen him. She felt a wonder again at the constant change in him, recalling the person she had met at The Stag, and that dulled, vague impression of the winter months, and then the passion and realness of him on the passage to Ostend. What he was now she didn't know, knew nothing except that he was different, and was conscious of wonder in the discovery that she could love him through all these changes.

'Tom has more compassion than you,' he said, picking up the thread of their talk. 'He wanted me to know that it wasn't myself alone—simply the knowledge that I loved you and not her—that drove Irene to killing herself. You knew that yourself, but you wouldn't tell me.'

'I suppose I was wrong,' she said. 'I hadn't thought that you would make yourself responsible for her. I think I just wanted to spare you the knowledge of all the rest of it.'

'And who else would be responsible? I knew Irene loved me—what else was I to think? What else would I have gone on thinking except that Tom had the sense to tell me the truth?

'And yet,' he continued, 'the truth was almost worse than what I had believed. She was afraid to tell me about the child. Imagine what it must have been like—carrying the thought around with her all this time, and afraid to tell. What sort of a person must I have seemed to her— in fact, what sort of a person was I? Irene was afraid of me.'

'Don't, don't!' Maura cried. 'She wasn't afraid of you. She had begun a deception years ago . . . and she found she couldn't live with the consequences of it.'

The ash spilled from his cigarette to the floor.

'Why are women so hard on one another?' he said. 'What Irene did was human and natural—concealing from me a thing which she thought could never matter. But with the years we've been together she hadn't built up enough trust of me to be quite sure I'd understand why she had done it. It's so foul to think of what I must have been to her. She'd seen me walk out on everything else in my life—and that's why she didn't trust me.'

'That's not true.'

'Not true? The truth is I'd walked out on every other

important thing, and she believed I'd walk out on her, too.'

'It's not true—it's not true!'

'It's true, and you know it! And you know that's why I'm leaving you.'

'You're leaving me?' she repeated. 'You're *leaving* me?'

'Yes.'

'I didn't believe it,' she said slowly. 'I didn't believe it when you said you didn't mean to see me. You *don't* mean it, Johnnie.'

'Yes.'

'But, why? Why?'

'Why? The reason must be clear enough, Maura. You've seen what happened. Irene killed herself because of me. Do you think I would have that happen to another woman?'

'But Irene isn't you and I. We love each other. *I* love you.'

'Irene loved me, too.'

'For God's sake, Johnnie!'

'I'm sorry.'

She came closer to him, caught his arm.

'Darling, doesn't it mean anything to you any longer that we loved each other? Has that ceased to mean anything?'

He took her in his arms gently. 'It could never cease to mean everything in the world, Maura. I love you. It hasn't stopped.'

'Then, why . . .?'

'Why, my darling? Because I've ended one woman's life. I'm just too scared to think about messing-up another.'

'Johnnie, don't you see that there's no parallel between Irene and myself.'

'I'm the parallel. I'm no different.'

'No different?'

'The same person who married Irene. The same one who used to leave her alone for months—or uprooted her life to take her with me. I'm the person who runs away from things. I haven't changed, not a bit.'

'But I love you.'

'Love isn't the only thing.'

'It's all that matters.'

'You didn't say that in Ostend. Other things mattered more. Your religion, your father, Irene. All these things were more important than loving me. Don't think for a moment that I've forgotten what you said.'

'But I can have these things and your love as well.'

'Having your cake and eating it?'

She flushed. 'Yes—if you put it that way. Having my cake and eating it.'

'I'm sorry, Maura. It wouldn't work. I'm not the person to marry anyone.'

She dropped her arms away from him. 'You're finding an easy way to say you don't love me?'

He pulled her close to him again.

'I can't make you begin to know how I love you. I want you with every moment of my life. I *need* the love you have for me.'

He said passionately, 'But I won't keep you with me and see it all destroyed. I won't see myself killing it the way I killed Irene.'

She cried, 'You couldn't kill it, Johnnie. It's there forever, part of me. I'm not alive without it.'

'Then, would I let you live with me and see your love give you no peace, no happiness? Would I want to watch the lines coming into your face year by year and know that if your love was living, then you were dying?

'God Almighty—I wouldn't!'

'Johnnie—Johnnie,' she wept. 'Don't leave me. Take me with you. Don't go. We'll be all right, Johnnie. We'll be all right. We love each other.'

'Love isn't enough. I'll never be anything more than I am now—wanting freedom from every tie that a reasonable man expects. Go and marry Tom. He'll make you happy. I'm no good for you.'

'Please, Johnnie, please! Don't leave me like this. Don't leave me. I'll follow you—yes, I'll follow you.'

She clung to him, her face on his shoulder, her weeping

unrestrained. He held her close, not moving, saying nothing. At last she looked up.

'Johnnie!'

He didn't reply.

'Johnnie, you mean it, don't you?'

'Yes—I mean it.'

She suddenly stiffened in his arms. 'I don't believe it,' she said. 'You can't just send me away like this. You're my life—I can't live without you.'

Then she stepped back from him.

'But you do mean it. I begin to see it. God knows why —but you do mean it.'

'Yes.'

'Is there nothing I can say—nothing to do? Have I got to see you go and do nothing?'

'There is nothing—the fault is with me. You can't make me any different.'

Her arms dropped to her sides. With the wild tears still on her cheeks, she experienced for the second time the loss of him. She had thought, back in Ostend, that she would never know a greater pain, but this was far worse than anything she had believed possible. And with it went her rebellion against the stupidity of it, the needlessness. Johnnie was wrong—and it seemed certain that he could never be made to see it in any other way. 'I can't stand it,' she said, and she turned and walked out of the room.

# PART FOUR

## I

The mountains were like jewels in the distance behind Rathbeg, and the thin thread of the road from the shore twisted and wound through the country for more than three miles before it reached the house. Maura's eyes could follow it only a short distance, losing it then between banks and hedges laced over with tall green. All the country was in its full tide of green, the mad, lush green of Ireland before the age of high summer darkens it. The shadows of the mountains were purple, and she thought if she looked behind, the sea would be the colour of a pale amethyst in the evening light. She did look back, and it was there, exactly as if someone had held the pale purple stone, moving it slowly and lovingly to catch its brilliance. She could feel the stickiness of dried salt water on her hands. The evening was calm—as calm as the gentle tide that lapped the shore; and the roofs of Rathbeg in the midst of this beauty were more peaceful than anything else.

Tom, she thought, had been sure of what he was doing when he had brought her to this kind of peace. She slipped through a gate into a field, following the path that skirted the young corn. Out of the nightmare of London he had taken her here—they had been at Rathbeg even before Johnnie's plane for New York had left London Airport. Tom had taken her away quickly, thinking and acting for her when her own mind refused such decisions. And he had known all the time that she would have left him in an instant if Johnnie had wished it. He seemed to know, as well as if he had been present, the horror and agony of that interview in the flat; he seemed to know her utter disbelief that Johnnie had meant what he said. Tom accepted it all, her numbed grief and distress, the shock—accepted it and appeared to understand it. He had brought her to Rathbeg and said nothing, leaving the peace and beauty to accomplish their own work, proving to her, but never indicating, the compensations that existed for the loss of Johnnie.

Desmond had seen them go with immeasurable relief. And now a week had passed since Johnnie's departure, and her father's letters had begun to take on an air of certainty, as if he were quite sure, at last, that the danger was gone. When he was moved to it, Desmond's letters could be powerful, and they spoke to her now of his happiness. She was doing the thing he had prayed for, he wrote; there was security and peace at Rathbeg, there was permanency. But Desmond was happiest because she still belonged to him. She looked about her, at the little fields with the cowslips among the green, at the buttercups on the banks, and whispered to herself that if Johnnie had been hers to love, it would have been the love of her whole soul and mind, and there should have been nothing left over for Desmond. She wanted to fling herself down in the corn, and bury in the earth the cries of her treachery to Tom—to call aloud that passion doesn't die because its object is removed, that love can go on forever.

But she didn't do that. She followed the narrow paths that led through the fields to the house. The evening was coming down from the mountains quietly. It was a quiet sky, no over-bold patches of pink upon the blue-grey. The brief heat of that early summer's day had gone long ago, and even the last of the workers in the fields were leaving, leaving with the jerk at their caps and an entrancing smile for her—their smiles full of curiosity and a readiness of affection. She smiled in reply, and thus escorted she came to the wall that skirted the park.

About the house the gardens were tranquil and rather formless—not exactly neglected but kept without much interest from year to year. At the side of the house was a rose garden. Maura paused by it, and the scent of the June roses was languid on the air; they climbed in a wild race over a trellis. At this time of the evening the house and garden had a deserted air—there was no movement, no sound of voices calling to one another, all was still and a little waiting. The long windows of the drawing-room were open, but nothing stirred inside—there was no breeze just now to ruffle even the curtains. Her footsteps made no sound on the grass as she walked nearer. She stood here, looking into the room; saw the undisturbed order of the place. All was order save for that one corner by the fireplace where Gerald's pipes and papers lay close to his chair, where his footstool, thrust aside quickly, had wrinkled the rug.

He felt her shadow darken the window and sat upright. 'Is that you, my dear?'

'I've just come from the shore,' she said quietly.

'Ah, yes. It's a beautiful evening for it. I often do the walk myself. You didn't bathe?'

'No. I took off my shoes and walked along the water's edge. It seems such a long time since I did that—I imagined I was back to the first time I came to Rathbeg.'

'The first time . . . you were such a long-legged child then.'

She laughed. 'Then?' She stepped farther into the room, staring into the tall gilt looking-glass that reflected back almost the whole scene. 'I haven't changed much.'

She turned to him, spreading out her hands, indicating the room, the garden beyond the windows. 'Nothing changes very much here.'

Gerald shrugged. 'Perhaps that's not a good thing, my dear. Often I've been . . . negligent. Things have gone on here as they always have done because I've shrunk from changing them. I've never been able to make myself do the things that changes demanded. Some people aren't made for it. Now, Tom—he's different.'

'Yes, Tom's different. But will he want things different here?'

Gerald suddenly looked bewildered.

164

'I don't know. I've always liked things as they are. But change is bound to come. We can't hold it back. Even here in Ireland taxes and this quiet revolution keep pace, you know.'

Maura looked at the light of the summer evening on the gardens. 'I shouldn't want it to change.'

Gerald shifted, following her gaze. 'Yes, it's lovely, isn't it? All my life I've thought it was lovely, and I've been content with it. But Rathbeg needs Tom more than you and me. Tom must make the farms pay as they've never had to before, or the place would only last as it is within your lifetime—there wouldn't be much for your children.'

Something in his voice made her turn and look at him. He met her gaze steadily. 'Rathbeg will be all right because Tom will never spend his winter afternoons dozing over a fire when he should be in the office doing accounts. That's how different we are—and it's a good thing.'

'Yes,' she said. But she walked back towards the window because she didn't want to stay and hear what further things he might say; she didn't want confession of real or imagined negligences. Gerald would not change himself, and it was only a vicarious kind of satisfaction he found in declaring his failure—not any desire or intention of being different. He merely wanted to dramatise his quiet little world of inaction, and looking across the mown lawns to the wall of the rose garden, she thought that prosperity had not suffered much while he dozed by the fire. What he probably would never admit was his genius for leaving things alone—as valuable in its time as Tom's knowledge and efficiency were necessary now. But he liked to think all this a tragedy—with that bent the Irish have for exaggeration skilfully drawn out. But one could not help loving Gerald for the faint air of sadness on his beautiful face, for his tall, stooping figure and the gentle hands.

She looked towards the westward sky over the mountains.

'Will to-morrow be fine, do you think?'

'For the Coolnaven races? The forecast is for rain,

165

but if there's a hint of sun in the sky the crowds will be out, and Merry Lady's price will drop. Sheelagh will bring her in all right, though. Have you met Sheelagh?'

'Yes—years ago. I remember her when she used to come over here as a child.'

'Grand girl,' Gerald said softly. 'Rode a couple of winners for me last season. Of course, she's always glad to rid a horse from their own stables—Merry Lady is from Drumknock. It's a good advertisement. But it's not the whole thing with Sheelagh. She'd do anything I asked.'

Gerald said nothing more, though she waited for him to go on. This slightly-known girl, Sheelagh, was an accomplished fact in his mind, a fondness which he expected Maura would share with him in time. With Gerald there was no haste in anything. Without turning to look at him she knew his thin, haggard face, much older than it should have been. The years went uneventfully for him, a long spread of time in which there was no need for hurry. The shades of this room were peaceful, and so was the evening light around the windows. But a life of such peace, bounded by the house and farms, the far mountains and the shore, had not worn him any less harshly than other men. He was not as old as his stooped figure, or the lines in his face. He was no older than Desmond, and one would have put the difference at ten years.

'Tom will be at the stables, I suppose,' she said.

'I expect so, my dear. One usually gets him there last in the evening.' He had picked up his paper again.

She made her way through the hall to the back of the house where they did not like her yet to go. The hall had an air of unexpected tidiness, and she could remember Tom's voice raised in the back passages in complaint about the littered table, the rain-streaked windows, the rugs that were seldom moved. And now the wood floor gleamed softly with great beauty and new polish, and Tom had said he would hang red curtains there because the view towards the mountains in the winter was too grey and cold. She passed the kitchen, and there was no sign yet of the evening meal beginning, only the loud, flat ticking of the kitchen clock. Later the meal would be served almost on time, with a sense of breathlessness and a faint amazement at the achievement—it would bring with it the clamour and haste of the last half-hour in the kitchen.

From the vegetable garden there came the sounds of voices in lazy dispute—not so much dispute as a device for getting through this, the slowest, longest hour of the day.

'You'll never tell me there was a horse in the county to touch him. Sure, he was a great lepper, that lad.'

An older voice now, languid with contempt. 'Ah, go on wid you. Sure that fella couldn't jump the border of me own garden.'

'You've got the wrong horse. Didn't me own father see him on a bank that'd wither the heart inside you to look at. . . .'

She passed out of earshot; the voices faded, blurred and became part of the evening air. A little wind stirred now among the apple trees at the edge of the garden, then touched her face and blew her hair about her. She could hear the muffled stamping of a horse in its box, and all the quietness of small sounds. Tom was with a groom in the harness room, the place smelling of brushes and leather soap. It was orderly and kept in a way that things seldom were at Rathbeg.

The man touched his cap to her.

'Good-evening,' she said. She did not know his name.

'Good-evening, Miss de Courcey.'

He watched her with that frank and not unkind curiosity which had remarked all her words and actions since she had come to Rathbeg this last time. If Tom had not been there she felt that he would have smiled.

Tom turned. 'You've been away a long time, Maura.' His glance took possession of her.

She smiled and said nothing. They went on talking.

'Tell Connolly when he comes that the price is too much.'

A look of concern spread across the man's face. 'And

won't he just say, sir, that you've never yet clapped eye on the mare, sir? Such a beautiful lepper she is, even if she does come from the old man's stables—I've seen her meself, sir. A lovely critter—fit for a queen, I'd say. Couldn't I just see Miss de Courcey now on her. T'would be a grand sight, sir. Oh, a lovely sight.'

'Just tell Connolly the price is too much.'

'T'would be a sacrifice at less, sir.'

'He'll have to sacrifice something if he wants to sell her,' Tom said shortly.

The man watched them go with the pained expression heavy on his face, but when they were half-way across the yard they heard his whistle, low and clear. It was the end of the day, that whistle; the end of work, the beginning of the clamour in the kitchen—there were no more voices in the vegetable garden. The mountains had taken all the colour out of the evening sky.

'Connolly is his mother's cousin,' Tom said when they could no longer hear the whistle. 'He won't get what he's asking, but he'll probably get a little more than he hoped for.'

'Even when you haven't seen her?'

'I saw Harrington's daughter-in-law on her during the winter. No great goer, but a gently-mannered, good-looking creature. I thought you might like her.'

'I don't know, Tom . . .'

'We'll see her. There's no hurry. We could have a run over and have a look at her.'

Maura said nothing. They took the path across the lawn towards the house. The wind came in soft little rushes, leaving patches of stillness in between. There were no lights yet in the house.

Tom suddenly caught her arm. 'Come and smell the roses. It seems a long time since I smelt the roses at night.'

The garden was deeply shadowed, with the trail of white roses over a trellis standing out sharply. But they knew it was the perfume of the red roses they smelt. It was heavy and indolent, much warmer than this early summer's night.

'I missed you,' Tom said.

'When?'

'After tea—when you went to the shore.'

'I wasn't far away.'

'I know. It's foolish. I was glad to see you back though.'

'You might have come to look for me.'

'I knew you'd come eventually.'

'Yes.'

The wind came down off the mountains—a little cold now. It caught her hair, whipping it sideways across her face, the flying ends stung her eyes.

'It's beautiful, Tom. The mountains are beautiful.'

'Yes. They're more beautiful in a way than the Italian mountains—they're kinder. Not the sort of beauty that makes you almost wish you'd never seen it. Perhaps . . . it's only that I've known these mountains all my life and I'm used to them.'

'One always knows where one belongs in the end—or to what one belongs.'

'Yes.'

She caught his hand in her own. 'Come in now. It's cold.'

On the way back to the house they said nothing, listening to the piercing, insistent song of the crickets which had started up in the boggy ground at the back of the rose garden.

## II

Gerald liked to leave the dining-room unlighted as long as possible. The windows were closed now against the chill of the evening, and a little wood fire burned in the stone hearth. He spoke very seldom at meal-times, needing only things like the view of the mountains and the fire with its growing pile of white ash on which to fix his attention. Silence was a habit grown on him since the time when Tom and Harry had first gone to school, and then the war years, when there was little visiting among his friends to be done, had confirmed him in it. He had always known that it suited him better than speech, but since Tom's return with Maura it had seemed to hang about him like a net which he made only feeble and half-hearted attempts to break through. This strange and unaccountable shyness engulfed him now, as he listened to their quiet talk.

How dark they were, the two heads leaning towards each other. Their talk was that of two people who know each other as friends, with the tolerance and humour that new lovers do not have. He had never questioned Tom about this long wooing of Maura, nor would he have dared to. The truth was, he thought, he did not want to know. By his own choice Tom had been away from Rathbeg for four years—and this was no sudden flowering of love at the end of it. And yet he could see no hint of calculation about it. They were kind to each other, these two, a kindness that was deep and undisguised.

Gerald was suddenly saddened and amazed because he loved them so well, and understood them so little.

'I walked past the other point—the side we never go. There's a cottage on that bay, but no boat.'

Gerald leaned towards them. 'Mary Stanley lives there. You remember her, Tom?'

'Yes, I remember her. I haven't seen her since before the war.'

'You'll see her occasionally in the town on market days to sell the pigs—but nowhere else. And don't expect her to be overjoyed to see you, either. She's always so afraid one might want to visit.' He looked at Maura. 'Her father owned linen mills in Belfast and lost all his money. They came down here to that cottage, just the two of them. When he died she stayed on alone. I've often felt I should do something—but she so obviously doesn't want any attention or notice. It's a pity that being neighbours is so impossible, sometimes.'

He wondered, when Maura's gaze had turned upon him, if she knew the fascination of her face. Not beautiful—but it had the effect of arresting one's attention. Sometimes he saw it chased across by shadows, and lonely, and then it had for him the same quality of a solitary figure of a heron standing in still water. Now in the filtered grey evening light it was strained and carried a hint of sadness. She was truly a daughter of that brilliant man, his cousin, Desmond; in her face was that same seeking expression but without his touch of ruthlessness. She would be a good woman with children, not demanding or aggressive.

After dinner, he thought, she might play for them—he might persuade her to play Chopin. It was more to his taste than the Brahms and Beethoven she favoured. He had realised, since their arrival, how much he looked forward to her coming permanently to Rathbeg. He wanted many evenings like this, and it was comforting that Tom had wanted to marry Maura above anyone else. He did not have to feel his way with Maura; they were used to each other, and tolerant. Nor was she too young or timid. Her whole life had been spent with a formidable man, and she carried the stamp of elegance and assurance which Desmond had given her. He had once thought uneasily about her children being Catholic; time had removed the strangeness of the idea, and he found himself without any real opposition to offer. Tom had already faced and decided the issue.

He hoped that she might have children soon because the house had been dull and quiet for so long. He believed no one had ever guessed how he still grieved the loss of Harry, how much he went on missing him. The memory of the day when he had the news of his death could move him still to terrible pain. Harry had been such good fun. Less striking, less good-looking than Tom, he had been more of a companion. He had been more ordinary, more easily understood in his passion for fishing and his quiet, unremarkable love of farming. Harry would never have done as Tom had done—leave Rathbeg for four years to learn how a Government farmed in England. Harry would have stayed at home and farmed in his own fashion. He would have married Sheelagh Dermott, and there would have been grandchildren now instead of the mere hope of them. He suddenly felt aggrieved because Tom had waited so long to marry, and aggrieved because Harry had been killed before there was time to do all the things planned for him.

He looked sideways at the mountains, a swift, secret look like the one a man gives his mistress when they are in company. He listened in a half-hearted fashion to the talk—it was about a play they had seen during the winter. It troubled and annoyed him to discover how little interested he was these days in what went on outside his own home. He was forgetting the world that lay farther than ten miles from his door, and he knew he didn't intend to do anything about it. Except for a day in Dublin he didn't want to leave Rathbeg again. It was terrible to admit that, even to himself. Now that Tom had come back, he could hand over everything and be at peace. He knew he had been careless in his management of the place—he was not a failure, but he felt it. But it had been cruelly lonely here, and Tom had stayed away four years longer than he need. One did not cease to be made unhappy by a child's wilfulness. But Tom would not do all the things he, Gerald, had meant to do—clever Tom who spoke French and Italian with a lover's fluency and passion, who shared eagerly with Maura all the new magazines and books that came from London, who talked about having the library put in order—Gerald had winced at this because he loved the library as it was. They were ordering records, and he knew that Maura would never send her children to Miss O'Reilly in the village for piano lessons.

He could remember a time when he had been like Tom; when he had come down from Trinity his home had been well beloved, but there were other things. He could remember vaguely his ambitions to look at great pictures, and, because he liked singing, had cherished rather self-conscious visions of himself in the opera houses of Europe. But he had married Laura, that lovely, tempestuous woman who had taken him on gay shopping trips to London and Paris, where he had ventured half-heartedly into galleries and returned gladly to her inconsequential talk. Ambition died before her fascination. He could recall with certainty, the way she had filled the house with her exciting, excited presence, and his days with delighted attendance upon her. When the children were born she would not leave them, and he was too indolent and contented to desire change in any form. Change had been thrust upon him that day she had come back from hunting wet through and shivering. Two days after that she was dead, and himself faced with the unaccustomed quiet of the house and the fear of his two young sons. He had never grown reconciled to missing her, but somehow the years had been got through—he had farmed and hunted and fished, and taught them to do the same. It was the end of a cycle to see Maura here with them, and know that she had come, quieter—a very different woman but no less remarkable—to take Laura's place.

They left the room when she did, following her into the drawing-room where the fire was the only brightness. It coloured the soft-looking marble of the Adam fireplace to bright rose. There was still a pool of light before each window.

'Perhaps you'll play for us, Maura?' he said. 'Can you manage without the lights? It's so much nicer this way.'

### III

The flags were fluttering at the end of the first race when they edged their way among the pack of standing cars at Coolnaven. There was an immediate swarm of small boys upon them, and a man with race cards through the window. He greeted them merrily, and was off like a streak of good humour to the next car which turned into the parking space. Gerald delegated the most pushing of the urchins to mind the car, and followed after Tom, who moved through the crowd, impatiently.

Gerald murmured to Maura. 'I always think it's so unfair to always choose the biggest . . . but what can one do?'

The threatened rain had come early that morning. The ground was soft and damp, and in the parking space tufts of longish wet grass brushed wetly against their legs. They had driven from Rathbeg to the other side of the mountains, but the mountains themselves had not been visible. The mist had cut them off cleanly; its gentle, vague curtain brought the horizon much nearer, and threw up the mad brightness of the summer greens. The sticky, damp air was full of sound, and there were the little moods and waves of excitement which attend an Irish race meeting.

Maura recognised its particular feeling, glimpsed briefly at that one meeting to which she had been with Tom at the end of the war, and dimly remembered from her childhood when a groom had always come with them to— as Gerald had put it tersely—keep them from under the horses. She recalled the freedom of those days longingly, when the people of Gerald's acquaintance, seeing Tom now, crowded about them. Inevitably there was talk of the wedding, and little side glances and looks of surprise when the date was mentioned.

They examined her carefully and frankly, all of them, not now with the glances kept for distant cousins from England but as a person who would affect their relationship with Tom. A man beside her, no older than Tom, gazed at her appraisingly, deciding that she was no beauty but she had a certain look about her. It irritated him, just a little, to find that he could not, on this meeting at least, quite fit her to an easily recognised pattern.

He said, 'Why do you have to be married in England, Miss de Courcey? We looked forward to dancing at Tom's wedding.'

And Tom, hearing him, as he was meant to, turned quickly. 'It's the bride who matters at a wedding, surely —not the dancing?'

The group broke apart then, a little ruffled, a little uncertain how the words should be taken. Judgment of her, Maura thought, was perhaps reserved until a second or third meeting, but some of them had already decided. She could imagine the last man labelling her 'a cool enough bitch.'

Tom was hurrying them on to the saddling ring.

'Good God, look at the time—and Sheelagh will take a pretty poor view of us asking her to ride a mount and we not even there to see her off. This bloody crowd . . .' Much louder he said, 'Could we get through, please?'

They found her beside Merry Lady, a weight cloth over her arm, while Gerald's groom fussed over the saddling —a tall, lovely girl, her face bright with anticipation of the race and pleasure at the sight of them.

Gerald took her affectionately by the hand. 'My dear, I'm so sorry. Tom has been cursing us up hill and down dale for our tardiness. And then everyone in the whole of Ireland wants to stop us to talk about the wedding.'

Sheelagh turned then to Maura. 'And I haven't said how glad I am about it! I wrote Tom when we first heard —I wonder did he ever tell you? I remember you and Chris at Rathbeg—oh, ages ago. And you came several times to Drumknock.' She gave her quick smile to Tom. 'And you, Tom—how wonderful to have you back for good. Your father's been very patient all this time.'

She talked on—the conversation now of the race, and Merry Lady, a little bright bay mare who eyed the crowd nervously. Maura was apart from it, remembering Sheelagh of years ago, a tall, dark child, even then possessed of great kindness and great courage on a horse. She had been Harry's chosen companion for fishing days, and a favourite with Gerald. She could dimly recall, too, that the house where she lived was always full of people, so that Sheelagh had as often as possible bullied the groom into going with her on the long hack to Rathbeg, where there were only children and a peculiar kind of peace.

They had her up on the mare now, she was slim and straight, splendid-looking and excited in Gerald's racing colours. The swift little wind whipped pink into her cheeks and pulled the blue shirt close about her.

'There now,' Gerald said, handing the bridle to the groom, 'the race is a gift to you if you go out ahead. The mare hasn't much power, but she's game and as clever as a dog over the fences.'

They watched Sheelagh down to the start, the groom leading through a crowd at which Merry Lady's ears went back. Then Gerald hurried to place the bets, and Tom took Maura to the point on the rails from which they could see the best of the race.

For Maura the race went past in quick flashes of silk, and the quick comments from Gerald and Tom, rather stern-looking both, behind their field glasses. It was a quick-run race, and Merry Lady went out to the front and stayed there. They were on and off seemingly tremendous banks with ease that deceived until one saw three of the eight starters lose their mounts.

'A very ignorant horse, that thing of Rose Cassidy's,' Gerald said.

'A goer, though—but the next's a soft field and may quieten him down. Look, the O'Day girl's off! Thought she wouldn't stay. Nerves like wire and no head on her at all.'

They rode into the finish at a pace—a hot class of horses, and the last two fences took little doing. Sheelagh was well to the front, and she came in first. She was so great and accomplished a horsewoman that she was quiet when she came back to the saddling ring.

'Oh, a lovely ride,' she said, not boastfully. 'Merry Lady's improved on the fences—a great little thing.'

And she smiled on them, Tom and Maura and Gerald, and slipped into the coat which Tom held.

'I've got a terrible hunger,' she said, and began to lead them back through the crowd and the congratulations to where the cars were.

The rain had swept back over the mountains again as they approached Drumknock. Heavy rain, dashing against the windscreen, flooding the road, obscuring behind its curtain the little bedraggled villages through which they passed. Sometimes they saw people in doorways, and occasionally one or two in the road, with the shoulders of their coats soaking, hats and head-scarves dripping water. But mostly the doors were shut and nobody moved about the deserted landscape. Maura felt the sense of its desolation creep across her, and in the car there was only the rhythmic whir-whir of the windscreen wiper, and the crash of rain on the roof.

'Have you got a cigarette, Tom?' she asked.

He felt in his pocket, and gave her cigarettes and lighter. 'Light one for me, will you?'

The lighter wouldn't work. In the back Gerald stirred and produced matches.

'I wish I'd gone back with the horse-box,' he said, a little thinly. 'I don't care to go to Drumknock these days. And an afternoon like this . . .' He let his voice trail off because there was nothing any of them could say about the sheets of rain which tore at them.

'I don't see how you could refuse,' Tom said. 'Sheelagh had just ridden a winner for you, and her mother told her to ask us.'

'Yes, yes,' Gerald said. 'Sheelagh's a splendid girl. I wish that race had been for prize-money, not one of those damn cups. She probably could have done with it to buy some clothes. Though there's always money for appearances at Drumknock, and very little else. I don't know how things will be when Margaret dies.'

Tom said, 'I haven't see Lady Margaret since—— The last time I saw her was at the party before Harry went to join up. Do you remember—I came over on leave at the last minute? She wanted Harry and Sheelagh to get married then, didn't she?'

'We all wanted it, Tom, except them. They were going to wait, they said. There wasn't even an official engagement. I think, with the way things turned out, Sheelagh regrets it. But she's only twenty-seven—Harry's age—and she'll probably get married when her mother dies.'

'How is she these days?' Tom asked.

'Margaret? They don't say very much. Sometimes she's too ill to see one at all—will never let you near her when she's in bed. They can't operate, you know. Heart's too bad. I shouldn't think she has much longer to live. Sheelagh told me about the growth more than a year ago. It's hard on the girl.'

'That sort of thing happens to people like Sheelagh—the sort who are tough enough—and brave enough, I suppose —to take it.'

'There's one thing certain, though,' Gerald said. 'She's made of different stuff from her father.'

Maura, listening, was disappointed to see the lodge gates of Drumknock come into view, and the nearness of the house now silenced their talk. She could only vaguely remember Sheelagh's father, a gentle-voiced man who had sometimes driven over to Rathbeg. But any fact and reality of him was vanished completely, and the reason why it should be a good thing that Sheelagh was not like him was lost on her.

Sheelagh's car stood before the front door; she must have driven like the wind, Maura thought, to get here before them. Its canvas hood was soaked and sad-looking. The rain hissed on the gravel. A young manservant appeared with an umbrella, and Sheelagh herself stood in the doorway. She was wearing tweeds of a beautiful colour and cut, and possibly of some age, Maura guessed. They came into the hall, shaking the rain from themselves, and taking off coats; two spaniels came forward inquiringly. Gerald called them to him, and they came immediately but with no show of eagerness.

'My mother asks me to apologise,' Sheelagh said as she led them into the drawing-room. 'More especially since she thought she'd be well enough to see you when I left this morning.'

Tom said, 'How is she—I mean, generally?'

'Not well, Tom. She has a good deal of pain. I'm afraid she looks very different from the last time you saw her.'

'Yes. We talked about it in the car—it was just before Harry went.'

'Yes,' she said. Her face was quite still, and no one could have read either pain or indifference into it. But her movement was stiff when she turned and rang for the tea to be brought in, and that betrayed her as nothing else might have done.

Maura sat back in her chair, looking about that white, high-ceilinged room, and remembering that it must be close on fifteen years since she had been here before. It was beautiful, undeniably, but time and lack of money was taking just the edge off the splendour this room had once possessed. It was fantastic, of course, that it was inhabited solely by this young woman and her mother, who stayed in her room most days. Age-darkened mirrors reflected back the room dimly; the fire was warm and reassuring—but still there was the impression of disuse and anticipation. The spaniels had curled conventionally before the fire; they were as sad as the rain outside. Maura was beset by her few memories of this house. It had been gay, even noisy. She recalled she had played tennis here once, and there had been many people—people over from England, and the women had looked expensive and cared-for in dresses as pale as flowers. There had been a war in between, she thought, and Lady Margaret was dying, but somehow all of this didn't account for the change she sensed about her. This was the feeling of things lost, not gradually occurring. Harry's death perhaps, and Sheelagh's father. She couldn't remember what Sheelagh's mother was like—except that she was as tall as her daughter, and Scottish. She wanted to see Lady Margaret again, wanted to pull the past close to her and see how it really was. But that was impossible, for she had never truly known Drumknock. Fourteen years ago she had been unnoticed by the rest of the party here, except perhaps for Sheelagh's father, and she herself shy and young, accepted things as they were, unquestioningly. Indeed, fourteen years ago there had been no need to ask questions of Drumknock.

She listened to the gentle sounds of spoons against the

teacups, and watched the dogs come to ask automatically for the last piece of cake. Sheelagh and Tom were talking; names of people they had met at Coolnaven passed between them. Maura could see now how great Tom's pleasure at being back here where gossip was of familiar things. And she knew, for the first time, how great had been his wisdom in putting four years of London between Italy and his return. His love for the girl, Gena, was not forgotten, but placed in perspective, and Rathbeg was not now the unwanted alternative to Gena, as it must once have seemed to him, but a life to return to gladly, something mercifully kept apart from the heart-sickness of those years. Maura knew that Sheelagh also was glad he was back—as she would have been if Gerald had returned after an absence. But Tom was closer to her in years, and Harry's brother.

Gerald flicked his fingers at the dogs, but they, now that tea was finished and cleared away, had time for no one but Sheelagh, lifting their heads occasionally from their paws to gaze at her with eyes of adoration. When she got up to find cigarettes they were with her, and when she sat down again they lay close to her, as still and beautiful as painted dogs.

Maura, listening to Sheelagh and Tom, felt little urge to join in—it was still the past, and she was only a part of the future. She lifted her eyes to Gerald, and he, somehow, understood her restlessness.

'Sheelagh, might I show Maura the trophies? I imagine it's something she hasn't had an opportunity to see here.'

She looked at them both. 'Of course. But I hope you won't find it dull.'

Gerald stood up. 'When I set about inventing a story to go with each of them she won't find it dull.'

He took her across the hall to a long passage which led off it, lined with glass cases along one side. There were shields and cups there, all as bright as if they had been polished yesterday.

'They probably have,' Gerald replied when she said this. 'Margaret can't bear to have anything neglected which mere work will keep looking as she wants it. She has a ridiculous staff here for just the two of them, and won't close any of the rooms. A very foolish woman—as I often tell her.'

He made no attempt to explain the trophies, pacing slowly, his hands behind his back, to the tall window at the end of the passage. She came and joined him, and memory served her well enough to make her certain that there were gaps in the line of cedar trees at the fringe of the lawn But it was lovelier now when one could see clearly to the park beyond, and see the young horses who stood, wet and dark, in the shelter of the clump of elms. The rain slanted down against the blue of the cedars more fiercely than it should on this summer's day, and Maura began to wonder if it were not perhaps the rain and the evening drawing in close about them too early that produced this feeling of stricken apathy about the house.

Gerald found her thought as surely as if she had uttered it. 'You'll see changes, no doubt?' He was still looking at the horses.

'Not immediately,' she said. 'Remember I'd been to Drumknock not more than three times. It was full of people, I know—but Lady Margaret is ill.'

'Yes, the illness could account for a lot of things but not for such a feeling as there is about the place these days. It's so sad for Sheelagh—so wrong because she's young.'

He pressed his hands on the sill before him, leaning close to the window. 'Did Tom tell you about her father's death?'

'Tom mentioned it from one of your letters some time ago. I remembered him, but not clearly.'

'It's over two years since he was killed. He was driving down from Dublin and crashed through the parapet of a bridge. It was a shock to us all—somehow one had always believed that if a man like Richard was to die violently it would be on the hunting field, or with a gun. But we weren't surprised any more when we heard the truth of it all.

'I suppose the beginning of it lay with Richard and Margaret themselves. They always spent too much money

—his father had made it from English coal mines, though I think her family had very little. There was no kind of expense spared here—even for what money would do before the war. He was Master of Hounds, and started the strain of hunters Sheelagh breeds from now. I don't know how things went with them during the war—I suppose as with most of us. Nor do I know how many shares were left in the mines—though all that finished with nationalisation. They never cut down their scale of living, and suddenly he found he needed more money than he'd got. He put everything that was available into gold mines in South America. They failed, and he learned about it that day in Dublin. I suppose, poor fellow, he'd only got quarter of his mind on the road, and it was a foul winter's evening.

'It was a long time before they discovered how little there was left—and Margaret was tardy about putting the place on the market. She sent some of the servants away, and lived off the money she'd got. Sheelagh knew as much as her father, almost, about horses, and she kept the best of them. I think they considered selling Drumknock and running just the stables—though they never actually got round to that. It was all knocked on the head when Margaret finally saw a doctor about her cancer. Or rather it was Sheelagh who took that decision. She was frightened at first, and came to me about it. But she didn't need her mind made up for her. She said she would keep the house as long as her mother was alive.

'I suppose she's right—she loved them both dearly, impractical as they were. But it's damned hard on her—and she's not over Harry's death before all this happens. But then, women *are* brave about those kind of things. Your mother was a brave woman, Maura. I remember her well, though I only saw her the once.'

He gazed out into the rain in silence. On his face was the kind of backward glance she saw there too often, and she wondered if he were thinking of Sheelagh and Harry, or of the woman lying upstairs.

He moved abruptly. 'Let us go back, my dear.'

# IV

Maura listened to Gerald's footsteps along the passage. She put down her pen and waited for him, because he would have come to this part of the house in the afternoon for no other reason but to see her.

He called to her. 'Are you there, Maura?'

'Come in.'

He stood with his back against the door frame. He looked old and handsome in a tweed coat of a marvellous colour.

'Sorry to break in on you, my dear.' He indicated the writing paper before her. 'Margaret Dermott has just talked to me on the phone. She'd like to see you if you'd go this afternoon.'

'She's better?'

'Better than yesterday. She's up and apparently well enough to see you.'

'Yes . . .'

He pressed her gently. 'You don't want to go, Maura?'

'It's not that I don't want to go.' She pushed her chair aside and stood up, still not facing him, but shifting the paper uncertainly.

'That's not right,' she said. 'I don't want to go because there's too much waiting to happen there. I hate the thought of Sheelagh there alone—coping with it.'

'It would be a kindness,' he said. 'Margaret asks to see so few people these days. She says she remembers you when you came there all those years ago. I'm afraid, too, she thinks she may not be alive when you come back here again—though God knows she surely won't be taken as soon as that. But, then, she won't let anyone see her really ill, so perhaps it's just as well . . .'

'Yes,' Maura said again. Then she turned and faced him. 'Of course, I'll go. I think it's because she's ill and probably more sensitive . . . and I remember I was shy of her before. She used to be so gay she made me tongue-tied.'

Gerald sighed. 'Ah, well, she's a foolish and impractical woman, but she has great charm—both of them had. So many people loved them for it.'

He fumbled in his pocket. 'Here's the key of the car. You'd find Tom's easier to manage but he has the key on him, I think. You know the way well enough to get there? I think she'd find it less exhausting to see you alone.'

'Yes—I'll manage. She expects me for tea?'

'Yes. No need to hurry. Finish your letter first.'

But when he had gone he left behind no desire to finish the letter. It was to Desmond, and only begun. Gerald, with his talk of Margaret had taken away the mood of it. She gathered the loose sheets and laid them in a drawer.

She changed her dress and made up her face carefully, the memory of that smartly-dressed pre-war crowd still with her. She sat and stared before her into the mirror, wondering, in a brief second, what it would have felt like to have seen beauty look back at her. Desmond would have approved the faint red in her cheeks and the sun-tan. It would have been Johnnie who approved the cut of the linen dress, and told her the colour suited her hair. Johnnie always knew about clothes in a way that made it worth dressing for him.

She turned angrily and blindly away from the dressing-table. But the thought of him would not be denied, altogether. With a kind of madness, and feeling no sense of betrayal to Tom, she pulled open the top drawer and searched for the box in which Johnnie's ring was kept. She drew it out and put it on, seeing, as she stood up, the richness of its green in the mirror. It was as foreign and as strange as the mood which held her now.

She took a cardigan and handbag and went downstairs.

The hall at Drumknock was washed with the sunlight from the open door. She rang the bell and stepped inside, blinking a little at the dimness of the part where the sun did not reach. Yes, truly, it was a lovely house, she thought. It was white and high; there was a staircase that made you glad just to look at it, Hepplewhite chairs stood against the walls, the green of their brocade much paler than the lawns she could see through the windows. Above the mantel there was a portrait of a dark young woman who was just vaguely like Sheelagh—Lely might have painted it.

It was the dogs who came first, the gentle scraping of their paws against the wood. At the foot of the staircase they halted and waited for Sheelagh who followed them down.

'Maura! Everyone's kept you waiting! Mother will have my head—she's been wild to see you ever since you arrived, and now such bad manners when you do come. She'll tell me for certain you'll never come again.'

Lady Margaret sat in the drawing-room, a forest of blue and green tapestry rising behind her. She leaned forward in her chair and stretched out her hands. Maura saw a woman she didn't recognise except for that remembered blueness of her eyes. She looked vainly in that yellow, shrunken face, drawn in thinly with the lines of pain, for the beauty that had been there.

'My dear, how good of you to come and see an old woman! It's only my old loves, like Gerald, who remember me when I was pretty, who ever come now.'

Maura, taking her slim hand, remembered the coquetry which would never leave her.

Margaret pointed to a chair close by. 'It's such a long time since I've seen you—you were a mere child. Of course, it doesn't seem as long as that to me—once one's past forty time goes by unnoticed.'

She stopped talking suddenly, and stared into Maura's face, as if searching for the signs of what the years had been to her.

'But I'm so glad,' she went on, 'that you're back with us. Gerald has lived too long in that house by himself. I know he must have wanted Tom back with him, badly. I remember Tom coming home for the first time after the war, and Gerald came to me complaining that he wasn't able to understand him wanting to go and do agriculture in England. I heard that you were over with him, too. People had lost the visiting habit during the war. You didn't come to see us.'

'Tom was convalescing after his wound,' Maura said, gently.

'Ah, yes . . . that terrible head wound. Then, too, I remember because he brought you over, everyone tended to leave you to yourselves. We expected an engagement. I should have known my young Tom better than that—he was never one to do things hastily. That must be over four years ago. Ah, well . . .'

Maura smiled at her, and was quiet, thinking with faint amusement of Tom whom she had claimed to know and understand, who was never rushed. If Tom had had what he wanted he would have brought Gena with him to Rathbeg with no second thought, and let them all make of it what they would. Or would have remained behind with her in Florence, lost to them, to this small, solid world forever. But one only defended Tom's integrity in one's heart, silently. There was no need to say any of this.

'I'm sorry the wedding is in London—so many people here would have liked to be at it. But perhaps you're better out of it all. Weddings are all so self-important. Sheelagh says it's to be a small one.'

'Yes. Both of us have been working pretty hard all winter. We didn't feel like bothering with the fuss.'

'You're right, I'm sure. It's only the very young who enjoy the fuss of their own weddings. Later one suits oneself.' She said it with the faint malice of a woman who has married very young herself—and also from the conscious knowledge that Maura and Tom had waited four years.

Tea was brought, and she delegated the pouring to Sheelagh, her attention never leaving Maura for very long.

'I hope you won't find it dull here after London.'

'I don't expect to find it dull.'

'My dear, how can you tell? You've only been here for holidays.'

'I lived in London because my father lived there, and my job's there.'

'That's what I mean, exactly. Your job wasn't just a little job you'd be glad to give up any time. It was a man's job and had all the excitement of it.'

Maura permitted herself a slight smile, remembering the often wearing monotony of the days in her father's rooms in the Temple. If she had been given excitement it was second-hand, through him. 'More often than not it was simply routine. In a law firm if there's excitement, it generally belongs all to one person.'

She nodded quickly. 'Yes, but you're clever—you're like Tom in the things you enjoy. You've had the sort of routine that won't fit you for the routine, or lack of it, you'll find in a country house buried in Ireland. There aren't plays and concerts and clever people dropping in every two minutes.'

Maura felt herself tighten with mild annoyance. 'I think you're hardly just to the Irish, Lady Margaret.'

'Yes, child, but tell me what there is to do here except ride—and you don't ride, do you?'

'No, I don't—but I'm bringing *Rainbird* over from England. We shall use her.'

'Yes, I expect you'll have things enough to fill in the time. Though what I can't see is any child of Desmond de Courcey's settling down in the country.'

'My father loves Rathbeg.'

'He loves it all right, but does he stay there long? He does not! Your father is too fond of the sort of life he's made for himself to stay in a place where he doesn't see a fresh face from one end of the month to the other.'

Maura was almost forgotten while she pursued her memories of Desmond. 'I met him, I think, twice at Rathbeg, and once Richard and I went to dinner in your house in London. A remarkable man, your father. It never surprised me that he didn't marry a second time. It would take a remarkable woman to keep up with him— or one of his own flesh and blood, like you, Maura.'

Maura didn't know, just then, if she had intended this as a tribute.

'He is very fond of you and Chris,' Sheelagh said, speaking, Maura noticed, for the first time since they had sat down. 'I remember when you were all at Rathbeg together he wanted to do everything with you—the whole day long he stayed with you.'

'He won't like your leaving him,' Margaret said. 'Does he like Tom?'

'He's very fond of Tom.'

'That's a good thing—then it's hard not to like Tom. Though goodness knows it's too long since I've seen him to judge now. The middle of the war, it was. Well, it's pretty certain that Tom will never be rooted to this place like poor Gerald. He'll get about and see things—Gerald never did, you know.'

And so they went on talking while the shadows moved in that white room. She talked on and on, her talk was all that of a woman who is ill; of people and places Maura did not know, of things that had happened before she was born, bringing it all out because she had spoken like this to no one for so long, and because Maura was almost a stranger. It was like casting one's past, written out on scraps of paper, into a stream, and knowing that it was being borne away—could never come back. She talked of visits away from Ireland, of stupid, unthinking flirtations, of mad extravagances. In her talk she excused herself lightly, without believing seriously that there might be blame for her. And yet, Maura thought, how could one know what was right when it was all so lost in the past. Only Sheelagh, sitting there silent with the dogs at her feet, might know the truth of it. But Sheelagh loved her mother, and love distorts the truth.

Abruptly the flow ran out; it ran away from her like sand slipping through her fingers. She was exhausted and empty—perhaps a little frightened, Maura wondered—by the emptiness to which she was forced to return. Memories were only memories, her eyes told them both. She was flushed with her talk, and the flush died on her cheeks, leaving them hollow and drawn again. It was pleasant enough, she indicated to them, to talk of things one had enjoyed, with one's eyes fixed upon the summer gardens beyond the windows, but inevitably one would go upstairs to that bedroom for the last time. It was hard then to keep the panic away.

Her hands stirred like frail yellow claws failing to grip their object. She motioned to Sheelagh.

'Darling, would you go and get the silver mirror from my dressing-table—I've suddenly thought that I'd like Maura to have it.'

She brushed aside Maura's small sound of surprise, watching Sheelagh as she left the room.

'Sheelagh's a good girl. I know I'm difficult very often —but she's kind. Much kinder than one deserves. She would have made a good wife for Harry. You knew, didn't you, that she and Harry were going to marry?'

'Yes.'

'I had wanted that so much. Sheelagh was never the child that Richard and I might have expected. She is good —and we were merely charming. Sheelagh always knows what matters most in the end, and I—I don't suppose I've ever wanted to think beyond the next five minutes. She and Harry suited each other—neither could have lived happily for very long with anyone more exciting.

'But that,' she said finally, 'like other things, isn't in our hands. Sheelagh will marry eventually, I suppose. But that's one of the things I regret most—never knowing whom she will marry.'

She said no more about Sheelagh, merely stared before her at the lawns—but she was restless, and she kept moving her gaze about. Finally, it fastened upon Maura, taking in the whole of her.

'You're not like your father, are you—except that he was dark once. You and your brother are much quieter. He's been with you too much, I expect. Like Sheelagh said—he never left you alone.'

Abruptly her eyes moved. 'You've got good hands— yes, they're quite lovely hands. And that green ring. That looks good on them. Did Tom give you that as well?'

'I saw it in a window in Bond Street,' Maura lied uneasily. 'I liked it.'

'Yes,' Margaret said absently, as if it was already forgotten. 'Will you play something for me? Sheelagh tells me you play.'

It wasn't that she wanted to hear her, Maura thought, but only that she was exhausted; wanted to be left alone and yet couldn't bear the silence between herself and her guest.

She nodded and stood up.

'Of course,' Margaret said, 'your father is a brilliant pianist. Somehow one doesn't expect it of him—he doesn't appear to have the body or hands. And one wonders where on earth he gets the time for it.' She talked but she hardly even listened to the words herself.

Maura sat down at the piano. She slipped off the rings and laid them side by side. The one Tom had given her, and Johnnie's ring.

She played for about twenty minutes. Sheelagh had come in as quiet as a cat and taken a seat behind her. Margaret sat quite still, looking straight before her at nothing. The minutes had moved past them gently while she played, and when she was finished and took up the rings again, and turned about on the stool, it felt no longer afternoon in that room, but evening.

Margaret stood up. 'Thank you, my dear. You play well —but it's too twilight. At my age one's learned to believe it's not as hopeless as that. Now, come here. I want you to have this.'

She placed a small mirror in Maura's hands. The frame was a filigree of thin silver, so delicate it seemed as if it couldn't bear the weight of the age-spotted glass within.

'This is not a wedding present,' she said. 'I'll find something for you and Tom later. This is just for you because I've taken a fancy to you. It was my own, you know. It was given to me in Florence. I've always thought it was something that should be given, not bought or left in a will.'

And Maura looked at it and saw that it was a love gift—the thing that a man gives to a woman because she is beautiful, because he wants it to be close by, something that she will touch and look into.

'It's beautiful,' she said. 'I don't know how to thank you.'

Margaret said, 'I'm glad you're having it. It is beautiful, isn't it? It's always been one of my best-loved things.' She did not say if her husband had given it to her.

She bent forward and kissed Maura's cheek with her dry, papery lips. 'Good-bye, my dear. Thank you for coming to see me.'

Maura saw, as she moved towards the door, that her walk was still graceful and light.

When she returned to Rathbeg through the quiet, beautiful evening, her thoughts were numbed and still by what she had seen that afternoon. Her mind seemed a vacuum in which only existed the calm of the evening, and a faint uneasiness thrust upon her by Margaret Dermott's talk. But Tom cut across her mood. He waited for her on the porch at Rathbeg. He rose from the step where he sat when the car turned the last bend of the avenue.

He opened the door. 'I've missed you,' he said. 'I've got used to having you here, Maura.'

She smiled a little at him, and thought of all the times ahead when Tom would say, 'I've missed you.'

V

She felt the sharp, hot splinter of sunlight, which came through the gap in the curtains long before she opened her eyes. She lay there, perfectly still, distinguishing one by one the sounds of the stirring household, and breathing in the scent of the garden below. It was the scent of dew drying on grass and flowers. It was the feeling of heat before the heat itself was evident.

It was more than that. She opened her eyes and sat up

abruptly. She looked around her, wondering why this sense of disturbance and agitation should suddenly oppress her. But there was no reason for it—the small noises about her were the ordinary peaceful noises of the morning. Her room was just as she had left it last night; Margaret Dermott's mirror stood on the dressing-table; the tail of that beam of sunlight caught its frame and it shone with a kind of mad brilliance. But it was not that. Nor was it the ticking of the clock beside her, nor the soft, brogue-thickened voice of a young maid in the passage. It wasn't any of these things.

She flung the bed-clothes aside and went to the window, tugging at the curtains; the full burst of sunlight was hot on her face and bare shoulders. Yet the air that met her was soft still, but changing quickly with the heat of the morning.

She went back and stood before the dressing-table, looking at a face from which the sleep was not yet gone, at her disordered hair. Thoughtfully she touched the silver looking-glass, feeling its thin frame between her fingers lovingly. And then in a second her eyes had fallen on Johnnie's jade ring, lying where she had placed it last night.

She caught it up, held it out before her—held it out to catch the sun. All the disturbance of the morning was contained in it.

'Of course,' she said aloud. 'Of course—it's Johnnie!'

She put it down slowly, and yet she was full of excitement. Her eyes went back to her reflection in the mirror. She pushed her hair back from her forehead.

'You fool!' she said to her own image. 'You fool! Did you think you could keep him out like this?'

She turned away. With a kind of detachment she saw that her hands were shaking slightly as she began to dress. The room was growing warmer from that constant stream of sun. The zip of her cotton dress stuck, and she left it as it was, half open. As she took up the comb the young maid knocked and opened the door.

'Good-morning, Rose.'

'Good-morning, Miss Maura. You're dressed very early. But sure, it's a beautiful day.'

She laid down her tray, and began to pour milk into the cup.

'Rose, I don't want any this morning. I can't wait.'

'Will you not have it when it's poured, and all? Sure, t'will not take more than half a second.'

'All right.' She finished combing her hair while she drank the tea. It had grown almost cold from the girl's long dalliance in the passage with whomever had delayed her.

'It's cold, Rose,' she said.

'Is it, now, Miss Maura? Sure, I must tell Cook. Perhaps the range was not giving proper heat. And did you know, Miss Maura, that your dress is not done up?'

'Yes, yes, it sticks. I can't wait to fix it.' She put the comb down. 'I must go.'

The maid listened to her rapid footsteps along the corridor. Then her eyes fell on a pair of walking shoes she had brought freshly polished from the kitchen. She let out a little exclamation and rushed with them to the door.

'Miss Maura! Miss Maura!'

There was no answer for her, not even the last sounds of her footsteps.

'Gone off to Mister Tom at the stables, I'll be bound, and her in bedroom slippers,' she said, faintly shocked.

She didn't find him at the stables.

'Mister Tom's off exercising Lucy, Miss de Courcey,' the groom said.

'Do you know which ride he meant to take?'

The man pushed his cap back on his head. 'I couldn't say for sure—but usually on a morning like this when he's likely wanting some shade, he'll go along the path by the wall.'

'Yes . . . well, I'll try that way.'

She turned and made to cross the stable yard again.

'Miss de Courcey!'

'Yes.'

'Would you not go back and change your shoes? You'll get them wet and muddy on that path.'

She stopped and looked down at them. 'It's done already, I'm afraid. Can't make them much worse.'

She smiled at him absently, and went on. He pulled his cap back to its position on his head, watching her out of sight.

'Yes, and break her neck on them, most likely. Well, it's her neck.'

Beads of sweat had broken on Maura's forehead and neck by the time Tom, riding Lucy, came into view. He had turned at the farthest end of the bridle path and was coming back towards the house. When he saw her he waved and urged the mare into a trot.

She stopped and waited for him to come near. On the long grass each side of the path the dew lay like drops of rain. She put up her hand and wiped the sweat from her forehead. When Tom drew Lucy in beside her and dismounted, she could feel the pulse in her throat leaping with the excitement of her heart.

He didn't say anything until the mare was secure, then he turned and looked at her. She saw the knowledge that was already in his face.

'Well, Maura?'

'Tom . . .' His name choked strangely in her throat. She put up her two hands to it. 'Tom . . .'

'Yes?'

'I've come out to tell you . . .'

'Yes.'

'I've come to tell you that I'm going away. I'm not going to marry you.'

He seemed neither surprised nor angry. He raised his head and looked about him, as if he were thinking what he would do, or perhaps as if he were seeing the beauty of the morning for the hundredth time, and still finding it fresh. She had seen that expression upon his face before, when he was moved or touched—the emotions laid upon it that made her think back past his quietness and simplicity to the love that had been stronger than his love for home and the familiar things of his life. The girl who had loved him must have seen that look often, where she, Maura, saw it but rarely. She watched it fade from his face, and his eyes came back upon her.

He caught her gently and led her through the long grass that chilled her feet, to the stone wall which reached above their heads. He fumbled in his pockets for cigarettes and matches. She shook her head when he proffered the packet.

The smell of the smoke was keen on the morning air.

'Tell me about it,' he said.

'I don't know . . .'

'Just tell me.'

She stared ahead at the wall, old and mottled with green moss.

'It was when I woke,' she said. 'It suddenly felt like coming back from the dead. Nothing that went before it seemed real. Tom, try to understand—all these past ten days were a lost world. You know what that means . . . I've got to see Johnnie. I've got to go to him.'

'You've got to see Johnnie?' He leaned back against the wall. 'Will that do any good—after last time?'

'Last time doesn't matter,' she said. 'That's not the point. The point is that I love him still.'

'You love him very much?'

'Yes . . . you know what I'm trying to say? I love him in a way that makes living with anyone but him impossible.'

He looked round at her quickly.

The sameness of her expression broke, the line of her mouth fell loosely. 'Oh, God, I wish I didn't have to say it. But it *is* true. You've been kind—I haven't deserved such kindness. But one can't live on kindness. After a while I'd make you wretched because I couldn't stand the kindness when I wanted more.'

'You're obsessed with him, aren't you?'

'Obsessed? Call it that if you like. But if you understand that it's an obsession, then you know why I've got to see him again. What it will cost me doesn't count. I'll lose you, and all the life we planned together—and I'll lose my father because he'll never find it in his heart to forgive me. But I don't have any will about it—it's just there, Tom.'

He said nothing for a long time. She watched his face, turned sideways to her. He was hurt, but not surprised— not in his heart surprised or without understanding. It was the lack of surprise that gave him such calmness. She watched too, the hand that held the cigarette, the droop of it. There was a kind of defeat and patience there. But Tom could never be truly defeated again. That had happened too long ago. It was unwise, she thought, to be patient beyond ordinary human limits, as he had been.

'I have told you my reasons for wanting to go on,' he said.

'Yes, but ten days ago . . . I shouldn't have come here. I should have known that I would keep this sickness for him. Even if I were dazed I would sometime wake to it. It was unjust and unfair to you. But I've done it, and I'm going now. There are no amends I can make.'

He gave the faintest shrug. 'It was my mistake as well. There need be no amends for the kind of selfishness which made me bring you here. A marriage of convenience doesn't work when one of the people is in love the way you are with Johnnie.'

'It wasn't a marriage of convenience.'

'Well—a marriage of mutual affection and respect. Which doesn't make it love.'

He flicked the cigarette into the wet grass.

'I wish I could have loved you, Maura—could have made you love me. I think you're rather splendid with your obsession. Look at you now—your clothes half on you, and a silly pair of slippers that you'll never be able to wear again—running out here to cry to me about your love. You don't care about another thing in the whole world but that.'

'No, you're right. I don't care.'

'And I don't love you, do I? Even if I want to I can't love you. So you're quite free to go. There aren't any obligations or tears. There's been no crime committed.'

'Yes, but I blame myself.'

'Oh, don't pretend, Maura. You're a woman in love. You don't blame yourself about anything. There's room in your mind for only one thing now, and that's Johnnie.'

'That's true. But you're so matter-of-fact.'

'Why not? I'm not a romantic boy any longer. Ten years ago I would have protested and sworn that I loved you. I would have made a fuss. But the time to make a fuss was long ago, when I first saw you and Johnnie together. But even before that I'd lost . . . I'd lost you to him the day you met. Only a bloody fool makes a fuss over what's already cut and dried.'

He straightened. 'I'm going back to the house.'

She stayed close to the wall and watched him while he mounted the mare. Suddenly she started forward.

'Tom!'

'Yes?'

'What will you do?'

'When? Now?'

'When I've gone?'

'How the hell do I know?'

'You'll marry someone else?'

'Good God—what a thing to ask me! I'll look after myself, Maura. I always have.'

He wheeled the mare and rode quickly down the path between the trees. She watched until he had disappeared— the pale green light of the trees whose leaves his passage had stirred, washing the air after him. She followed him, conscious of wonder at what an awakening on an early summer's morning had done.

## VI

Maura waited for an hour in her father's room in the Temple. She sat in the chair before his desk with her hands limply folded in her lap. Now that the time for seeing him had come she was calm in a way she hadn't expected; it could have been fatigue from the journey which lent this calmness to her, or, she thought, a surfeit of emotion had killed her capacity to feel much more. Whichever it was, it had given her a sense of peace and order, a kind of balanced coldness which she knew would stay with her while she talked to him. She leaned back fully. The late afternoon sounds of the Temple were familiar. It was warm; she fancied she could hear the humming of insects among the tall fire-weeds in the bomb-site opposite Desmond's window.

She had sent him no message of her coming—and she was here before a letter from Rathbeg could have reached him. It seemed almost too far away to remember clearly standing on that bridle path yesterday morning, feeling the sweat on her neck and watching the smoke of Tom's cigarette. But his perfect composure afterwards she would remember; he had telephoned Dublin about her plane while Gerald listened in uneasy dismay. There had been no confusion in her departure; he had made it no more extraordinary than if she were a guest who catches an unusual train. Those last hours had been the end of passion in Tom; she knew that he would understand and forgive her, and his life would go on at Rathbeg. But he would be cooler and more remote than before, prudent and not given to impulse. But he had been kind; she grew ashamed when she remembered his kindness. He had taken the blame of it for himself, and eased her going, telling half-truths to Gerald for her sake. Kindness like that had almost need of forgiveness for its very excess.

The drowsy afternoon air, the sunlight which soaked the brown carpet and curtains, seemed to stir suddenly and move at the sound of her father's voice in the next room. She felt two spots of colour come to her cheeks; she leaned forward in the chair, watching the door. He came immediately they told him she was there; she caught the change in his tones just the instant before his impatient rattle of the door-knob.

He banged the door noisily behind him, looking at her at the same time.

'Maura, why are you back?'

'Please come and sit down,' she said. 'I must talk to you.'

He took no notice; he came and stood close to the desk, looking at her.

'Is there something wrong?'

She tried to hold him off with her gaze, but he pressed down upon her.

'Is there something wrong?' he said again.

'I've come back because I'm not going to marry Tom.'

It was only when she had said it that he shrank away from her. And it was not the expected anger she saw, but his hurt. He laid the hat he carried on the desk and turned away from her. He seemed not to know what to do with himself. She saw him walk to his chair and pull it out. But he didn't sit down; he went to the window behind and stood there. Seen this way, outlined against the summer sky, his body seemed huge and bulky. Both hands were in his pockets, his coat wrinkled unhappily across his back.

'I suppose it's this fellow Sedley?' he said.

'Yes.'

'Has he written to you? Has he been to see you?'

'No.'

He turned around. 'Then what has happened?'

She spread her hands. 'It's not as simple as all that. How can I tell you except to say I can't marry Tom.' She raised her head to him eagerly. 'Father, I've got to see Johnnie again.'

'You say he hasn't written you, and yet on some mad caprice you decided you won't marry Tom. Maura, what are you thinking of?'

'I've got to see him. I'm going to New York.'

'To New York . . . to New York?' He took a step towards her. 'Have you gone mad? This man has told you he won't marry you.'

'That was two weeks ago.'

'Two weeks ago—two years ago! What difference does it make? He said he won't marry you.'

'When Johnnie said that, Irene had been dead only a few days. His whole world was upside down. But look—he's had time to think since then. Time to come to his senses as I did.'

'Do you call this coming to your senses?'

'The real madness of it was allowing Tom to take me to Ireland. If I hadn't been in such a weak daze I would have followed Johnnie immediately. I wouldn't have left him alone this time.'

The incredulity was plain on his face. 'Have you no pride or decency? Irene is dead less than three weeks. What are you thinking of?'

'Irene loved him as deeply as I do. She couldn't live without him, either.'

He drew one hand out of his pocket and pointed at her. 'Maura, be careful! Up till now you haven't been able to push this man about. He has at least enough wisdom to know he ruined Irene's life. He's capable of ruining yours. What if he still refuses to marry you?'

'Johnnie and I love each other. I know if I go to him it will be all right.'

'That may be—but supposing he doesn't? What will you do?'

She didn't believe him and she shrugged slightly. 'In that case I'll come back here and try to make the best of it.'

'And that's all you can say?'

'Yes.'

'And what about Tom?'

'Tom? . . . Tom is all right.'

He lifted his hand in a kind of frenzy. 'Maura—why have you done this crazy thing? You can't even go back to Tom.'

'Go back to him? Of course, I can't! Do you imagine I could marry Tom when I love another man as I do?'

'Ten days ago you said you would.'

'Ten days ago . . . yes. When I was so sick and knocked about I didn't know what I was doing.' Her voice softened. 'Father, you love Tom as much as I do . . . you feel about him as you do for Chris. Could you honestly say that you would wish to see us married when we have no reasonable hope of happiness? Because there isn't a doubt that I would make his life wretched.'

'Isn't Tom the best judge of that? Didn't he still want to marry you even when he knew about Sedley? Tom loves you.'

'Tom doesn't love me.'

'Who said not?'

'He did. What you don't know, Father, is that he's been in love once in his life, and it isn't with me. Oh, he feels a great affection for me—as I do for him. But he doesn't love me.'

'Then whom does he love?'

'An Italian girl—she was killed during the war. Tom was so much in love with her he's never likely to love another woman again in his life. That was his whole passion—if she had wanted him, he would have given up everything for her; have never gone back to Ireland. No one ever loved more surely than Tom did—in a way that makes him understand why I must go to Johnnie again.'

'I didn't know,' he said humbly. 'Tom never told me.'

'There was no purpose in it. Nor would I have told you if it hadn't been necessary to make you see how things are with him. He wanted to marry me because we understood each other and, I think, because I'm the only person to whom he's ever talked about Gena. It seems as if he values the knowledge of her he's entrusted to me. We suited each other, Tom and I. We didn't make demands. And then he knew I had all your love of Rathbeg. He wanted to marry me because it was easier than finding someone else to marry —and because I didn't expect him to love me. But he won't grieve for me forever, Father. He'll marry in time— probably he'll marry Sheelagh Dermott, who was engaged to Harry. She's lovely, Sheelagh is. And it will appeal to Tom to know he's taking her away from a pretty miserable existence. In a way she'll suit him better than I. She's not Catholic, for one thing, and she's lived in

Ireland all her life. She breeds beautiful horses and knows how to manage Irish servants. She knows all the things it would have taken me years to learn. And Gerald loves her. Father, can you see that the happiness of both of them rests more safely with her than me?'

He was reluctant to answer. 'I suppose so.'

Then abruptly he was in protest again. 'But you would have forgotten Sedley in time. These things don't go on mattering forever.'

'Are you certain? Would you be willing to risk my happiness and Tom's on that?'

'Happiness? Ah, yes, but will you be happy with Sedley? That's no certainty, either.'

'Why not? We love each other.'

'Irene was a most lovable woman—and a pliant one. He couldn't make her happy. Don't you realise what this man is like, Maura? He's unstable. He's typical of the sort of people who have had their money made for them. The sort of person who hasn't the guts or strength to carry on the business which his father's energy created. He'd rather loaf around Europe, trailing a wife behind him, giving her no roots or permanency anywhere—killing her love, killing her—or both, before he's through. Is this the sort of person you want to marry?'

'Oh, you're not fair,' she burst out. 'You don't give Johnnie a chance. What does it matter if he doesn't want to make textiles? The firm is huge and greedy and cut-throat. There are other ways of living besides that.'

'Other ways? Spending one's life in Mediterranean resorts, I suppose.'

'Farming, for one thing. Johnnie wants to farm. Is it wrong to prefer to work with one's own hands than a push-button and dictaphone? Why shouldn't one have the life one wants if it's possible to choose? The truth is that you've never tried to get to know Johnnie. He wasn't a person to you—just the man Irene was married to. But he's more than just a person to me because I love him, and whatever sort of life he wanted his motives are straight. That's enough for me.'

He said slowly. 'You're deserting all the things that I've expected you would have. You'll live in a different country. If he takes a farm you'll never leave it from one end of the year to the other I'll never see you unless I go over there—and you know how I detest America. There's so much in your life I'll never know again if you go. I'll be just a name to your children—and you're a bad letter-writer, my dear.'

He said finally, 'Is it too late to tell Tom you've made a mistake?'

'It's much too late. It was too late last Christmas Day when we met Irene and Johnnie on the bridge. Do you remember that?

'You see, I do love him. Far more than you'll ever understand. I love him so much that everything else grows small beside that fact. There's nothing in the world beside Johnnie. It's just as simple as that.

'I wish you could see how I feel about him—share it in some way. Because it's my life, it should be part of yours also. I can't help hurting you by doing this—that's just the way things are. And if Johnnie won't marry me—and if I come back to England, it's going to make me sad to think of the way I've hurt you, of the way I'm ruining all the affection and love we have for one another all to no purpose. But you must see I can't help myself. I just can't help myself.'

He came and sat down in his chair. She saw him looking at her, his eyes resting on every detail of her features as if he were trying to discover the kind of person she was. She had never imagined that Desmond could weep, but it seemed that he might weep now. She thought of the years of his planning that had collapsed in this half-hour, and if he should weep his tears would at least have the dignity of this failure. She waited for him to say something, for his reproaches. Instead, he drew a piece of scribbling paper towards him across the blotter.

His voice was breathy and uneven. 'I won't have him separate us, Maura. No one is going to do that to me—after all, you are my daughter, and we've done better things together than most people.

He wrote something quickly on the paper. 'If you go to America it will be at least with my help. You'll want to fly—it saves time. And I must find someone in New York for you to stay with—the Treasury won't give you dollars for hotel bills. I'll think of something. You go home, now. I'll be with you in about an hour.'

She rose. 'Thank you.'

He went on making notes on the pad until she had left the room.

# PART FIVE

## I

Before customs examination had finished she heard her name being called over the inter-com. In the strangeness of that early hour the sound of it had a feeling of unreality; she looked about her and half-expected that some other figure would detach itself from the row before the customs benches and walk quickly through the swing doors. The voices were quiet, as if people were barely awake. The officer chalked her bags in a bored fashion.

'Looks as if someone wants to see you in a big hurry.'

'Yes . . . yes, I think so. Is that all?'

'Sure. You can go now.'

There was no sign of Johnnie when she came through the doors into the main hall—there was nothing familiar about the place except what is familiar to every airport. The trickle of people who had travelled with her were going towards the airline bus, or stood gazing about as she did. She turned and went to the inquiry desk.

'Have you a message for me?'

'What name, please?'

When she gave it the girl nodded in the direction of a row of lounges.

'The gentleman on the right is waiting for you.'

As she had spoken her name he had lowered his newspaper. Now he stood up and took off his hat. He came towards her and held out his hand.

'I'm Mark Brodney. Johnnie sent me.'

'Where's Johnnie?' she said. 'He cabled that he'd be in New York to meet me.'

'Sure, I know.' He was of middle height, and heavily

built; he had dead straight black hair and horn-rimmed glasses. His voice had a curious deliberateness as if he were waiting at the end of each sentence to see how she was taking it.

'Look,' he said, 'would you like some coffee, or would you rather go right on to town?'

'I'd rather move on.'

'Sure.' He touched her arm. 'We'd better stop by the bus and get your bags.'

They waited beside the bus, not speaking, until the luggage was brought out. He took her cases then, and led her towards a car.

As he started the engine he glanced across at her. 'Get much sleep?'

'Not much. I suppose . . . I was excited.'

'Yeah. I guess you were.'

They drove through streets at which she never looked. 'Where's Johnnie?' she said.

'Oh, yeah . . . about Johnnie. He couldn't be here, so he asked me to come. He said you'd probably remember hearing about me.'

'Of course, I remember. Why couldn't he come?'

'His father's pretty sick. In fact, he's dying. Johnnie's in Pittsburgh.'

'When? How long?'

'Two days ago. He didn't cable you because I said I'd be here to bow you in.'

'What's wrong with his father?'

'A kind of a stroke, I guess. The doctors say he won't live more than a couple of days.'

'I wish I'd come . . . some other time.'

'Why should you?' he asked. 'The one thing a woman's good at is making a man feel better.'

She didn't know what to say to him. He made her feel awkward and afraid because he made no attempt to talk to her the way a stranger does; he seemed unable or unwilling to manufacture conversation, and yet she sensed he was remembering each thing she said, and thinking about it. Johnnie had been only half-right in his description of Mark. This man beside her could make things move at a pace when it suited him, but in between he sat and let life ride by him—in the way he was taking everything about her factually, and with neither bias nor enthusiasm, until he understood the kind of person she was.

On the wide slope up to a bridge he spoke suddenly. 'If I thought there'd be even a few minutes before a copper would be down on us, I'd stop in the middle and let you look. This is the East River and the Queensborough Bridge, and that tight, sweet little joint ahead is Manhattan. People who come in on the liners dock in the West Forties on the other side, and most of them never seem to catch on that there is any other place except Manhattan—they've heard of Long Island because they've read Scott Fitzgerald, but that's about all. But still, it's almost worth a row with a copper to look at Manhattan from here early on a June morning. The only time it's prettier is on a June night.'

'Johnnie told me you were born in New York,' she said.

'Sure—but you don't have to be born here to be a New Yorker. It's just something you catch on to—and you don't ever stop being one. Every time I come back here—when my cab's bringing me in from La Guardia—I get him to stop on the highway down under the bridge, and I go and throw a nickel into the river. I call it my coin of tribute. The guys all think I'm mad.'

They left the river behind, and the viaduct approaching the bridge went straight past the tops of buildings in a clear line.

'Do you know the address I'm going to?' she said.

'Oh, yeah . . . the people your father wrote to. Well, you can take your choice about going there. I suppose you knew they were out of town?'

'Yes, but they cabled that they'd have the apartment opened, and I could use it while I was here.'

'That's your affair, of course. But if you want to inhabit a ten-roomed morgue on Park Avenue, you're certainly welcome to it. Perhaps you could amuse yourself by tossing a dime to see which of the four bathrooms you're going to use.'

'How do you know?'

'Went round there yesterday. Just thought I'd see what they were letting you in for. There was a woman there dusting the place because an English K.C.'s daughter was going to use it. She was making room on the mantel-piece for the signed photographs of Royalty. Do you think you'd like to go there?'

'Where else will I go?'

'I've got an apartment west of the Park that's got an extra room. You can use it if you want to.'

'Will that be all right?'

'Sure. I won't hurt you—I don't make a habit of it.'

'I didn't mean that.'

'Didn't you?' He grinned. 'Well, even if you didn't, it's still all right. At least you'll be within shouting dis-tance of someone.'

'But the other place?'

'I'll phone—say you haven't arrived. Or you've gone on straight to Pittsburgh. I'll say something.'

'Thanks.'

She leaned back in the seat and watched the eight o'clock city close in about them. They cut up west of the river and on Third Avenue the lights stopped them. She watched a train go by on the El. and recognised scenes from all the films about New York that she'd ever seen. In the streets the shadows were deep, and the buildings had a lazy, untidy aspect from the iron fire-escapes tacked on like rigid lace. It was dusty, and there were papers lying in the gutters. Even in the shadows it was growing hot. They crossed Park Avenue and Fifth, and reached the square in front of the Plaza where Central Park begins. She saw for the first time the sun on the tops of the buildings, and how they made wide canyons under the hard blue sky. The ends of the canyons narrowed in the distance, and the dead straightness of it didn't seem real to her—as if someone played with the model of a city. It was sheer and beautiful, if one found beauty in things like that.

The apartment Mark took her to was close to the Park on West edge.

'I've rented it furnished for two months, so don't expect a homey atmosphere,' he said.

The room he gave her was small and looked out on to another row of windows. Twelve stories down was the bottom of the light well.

'That's one thing about the English,' he said, watching her. 'Wherever they are they always make straight for the window as if they expect a view of fields and cows grazing. Now, me—I get lonely if I can't hear three radio programmes and what the people are saying in five kitchens. New York will scare you to death at first, but you'll probably end up liking it. Most people do.'

'I expect I will,' she said.

He laid her suitcases on chairs.

'When will we have news from Johnnie?'

He shrugged. 'Have to leave that to him. I don't imagine he wants to talk to you on the phone. You know Johnnie—what do you think will happen when his father dies?'

'He'll come here.'

'Yeah . . . that's what I figured. So we'll just wait.

'I suppose,' he added, 'you'd like a bath. See if you can get a few hours' sleep, too. I'm going to heat coffee if you want some.'

At the door he turned again.

'I guess you've heard the news?'

'What news?'

'About Korea.'

'No—what?'

'About eleven o'clock yesterday morning the Northern Communists crossed the thirty-eighth parallel into South Korea. They're screaming blue murder to United Nations.'

'What does it mean? What's going to happen?'

'No one knows. We just hope it's going to stay a local war.' He began to close the door. 'Coffee will be ready in about five minutes.'

## II

Their taxi drew into the parking line in front of the Plaza. The heat of the morning sun had grown into a midday fierceness, beating down on the tall buildings, on the sudden green break of the Park, on the bright paint of the victorias which waited in a line for customers.

Mark reached out and opened the door. 'Well, this is it. This is the money—the goods! Fifth Avenue and Bergdolph Goodman's and Cartier's a few blocks down. This is what you take your hat off to.'

She got out, raising her head to look up into the blinding sun at the distant tops of the buildings on three sides of them, and then to the fountains in the square. 'Well . . .' she said, 'you make wealth attractive.'

'Who gave you the idea that wealth isn't always attractive?' He slammed the door. 'Let's eat. My stomach tells me you must be starving.'

He took her into the shaded green, white and gold glitter of the Persian room. Maura felt the new coolness on her arms. He handed her the menu, and she read it for a few seconds and then laid it down abruptly.

'Something bothering you?' he asked.

'Yes. I think New York's magnificent, but I feel like the man who came to the feast without a wedding garment on. I haven't got the dollars to pay for this kind of food.'

'Forget it. I sold a series of articles to the *Saturday Evening Post*, and I'm getting rid of the money before my pants' pockets go up in smoke.' He pulled off his glasses. 'Besides, where else could I take a woman who wears a lime green dress and a hat as wide as that? Johnnie will want to know what I've been doing with you.'

'Johnnie, yes . . .' she said.

He turned aside and began to order for both of them. 'Do you think Johnnie will phone this evening?'

'He might. But we're not going to sit waiting for him.

You don't spend your first night in New York waiting on a telephone call. I don't think Johnnie will phone you —he'll come.'

'Has he been much in New York—I mean since he left London?'

'All the time until he got the news about his father.'

'Has he been living at the flat?'

'Sure.'

'Mark, tell me—what's Johnnie thinking? What does he think about himself—about Irene? Did he want me to come?'

'Hold on a minute, will you? I don't like talking on an empty stomach.'

He ate steadily through the lobster cocktail. Then he waited until she was finished and had laid down her fork.

'Mind if I smoke?' He grinned. 'It helps me to get things sorted out.'

'Has Johnnie written to you?' he said, when the cigarette was lit.

She shook her head. 'I only cabled him when I was sure of getting a plane passage, and when these people on Park Avenue had fixed up about the apartment. I cabled his Pittsburgh address that I was coming. He cabled back and said he'd meet me here in New York.'

'Well, now we know where we are.'

'What do you mean—"where we are"?'

'What I'm trying to get at is that you haven't any indication of what Johnnie's been thinking since the day in London when he turned you down flat.'

'Do you have to say it like that?'

'Would it be any softer if I said he refused to marry you? It all means the same thing.'

'Yes, I suppose it does.'

'Only you don't really believe that he did turn you down flat? Otherwise you wouldn't have flown in on that plane this morning.'

'No—I don't believe he turned me down flat. Johnnie loves me.'

'Sure, he does. Not all the people who love each other get married. If that were the case I'd have half a dozen wives right now.'

'We're not talking about you.'

'Oh, yes we are. We're talking about all the people who fall in love. Don't count me out because I'm not a golden boy like Johnnie. And don't count out the guy, Tom, whom you've just taken a run out on.'

'What do you know about Tom?'

'Take it easy, Maura. Do you think Johnnie hasn't told me everything that concerns you? Do you think that guy wasn't so sick to talk about you that I didn't hear about Tom, and your brother and your father? God Almighty, didn't I get the lot of it?'

'You must be tired of the sound of my name.'

'Funny—but I'm not. I like your name.'

'What about me?'

'My opinion of you can keep.'

'Until when?'

'Until later.'

'Look,' she said, 'Johnnie won't mind if you don't like me. Not everyone likes me.'

'Who said I didn't like you? Besides, I'd do anything I could for Johnnie when he's in a mess.'

'Is he in a mess?'

He stubbed out the cigarette. 'Do you call Irene's death anything but a mess? And Johnnie's father is dying. Just eat your lunch, Maura, and let me eat mine. I'm hungry.'

They hardly spoke again until the coffee was brought, and he gave her a cigarette; she inhaled and watched him light his own.

'Johnnie told me about you soon after I met him,' she said. 'We sat one afternoon on a hill, and he talked about you—I think I was even a little jealous then of the way he talked about you.'

He clicked the lighter shut and put it on the table. 'Are you one of these women who break up friendships?'

'Mark, I'm being serious.'

'Yeah, sure. So am I.'

'And when he came back to London he told me he'd seen you again in Venice. You'd been moving about a bit, and you'd finished another novel. Johnnie envied you then . . . you unsettled him so much. Your life belongs too much to yourself.'

'Are you going to blame me for whatever my life does to Johnnie?'

'No . . .. I can't blame you. But at that time I think I wished Johnnie hadn't see you. I didn't like you much. I went and got one of your novels then, hoping all the time it wasn't as good as Johnnie had said. But it was good.'

'If only enough women tell me I write well, some day I'll believe that myself. But go on—what else did he tell you?'

'He told me he first met you when he was at University —but it wasn't the same one. You were on a debating team that came to them.'

'Like hell it wasn't the same one—Johnnie went to Princeton.'

'And then he met you again in Leyte. He told me about your decorations.'

'I got my share because other guys got killed. But I didn't get far in the Navy. I wasn't promotion material.'

She looked away from him, reaching for the lighter which lay between them, watching the flame as she flicked it open and shut.

'Mark, why don't you do something about yourself.'

'What are you getting at?'

'Your writing, I mean. You're not putting in enough time on your work.'

'Listen, putting in time on law books made you a lawyer. Putting in time at a desk hasn't been known to make a good writer yet.'

'But it helps. You could do with a little more routine. You might even get married.'

'Oh, yes. Get myself a nice snug little outfit on Long Island, and buy a little English export car cheaply. Or perhaps I could commute from Connecticut every day. That would be fine, wouldn't it?

'Look, Maura, maybe this doesn't mean anything to you, but I was born on New York's Lower East Side. My old man was a Czech, who had to change his name because no one could pronounce the original one. The old man's great sorrow was my mother—she used to drink. She was happy when she was drunk. She was on top of the world. My father didn't like to make her unhappy by taking the drink away, so he used to sit with tears rolling down his face and watch her being happy. He used to go church and pray about it. He used to pray damned hard, my old man . . . and when I first began to realise that all the praying wasn't doing her any good, I began thinking that the Catholic religion—in fact, all religion—was phoney. I still think that way, only with added reason.

'All this doesn't create much of a taste for commuting each day from Connecticut, or living with a ball and chain round my ankle. And I've never yet met a woman who can live happily out of half a suitcase, so I'm likely to stay unmarried.'

He stood up. 'If you're finished we'll go. There's a picture in the Metropolitan I like to look at, and I haven't seen it for more than two years. Would you like to come?'

He lay back in the taxi as they drove down Fifth Avenue, saying nothing, until at 70th Street he stirred himself and pointed. Maura saw a large, squat building with a strip of formal lawn fronting the Avenue.

'It's closed on Mondays or I'd take you there. It's something none of the English miss seeing in New York. A millionaire called Henry Frick gave it to the city as a museum—but what it really does is stands there as a monument to British salesmanship in the person of Duveen.'

'Duveen!'

'Sure—your Lord Duveen of Millbank. He made a fortune this side of the Atlantic buying culture for American millionaires. I feel like heaving a brick in a

214

window every time I pass. It's not that I think it's a shameful thing to accept advice about pictures and sculpture—but Duveen patronised the Americans too long and too hard. At one time it wasn't worth owning a picture unless Duveen had sold it to you. Oh, well—what the hell! Why should I worry?'

He lay back again and didn't speak for the other ten blocks of the journey to the Museum. When they got there he led her quickly and without commenting through the entrance hall and up the long flight of wide steps to the picture galleries. The place was quiet in the glaring light of the sun on the glass roof, and their footsteps were loud and sharp on the floor.

'I hadn't realised before,' she said. 'The guards are armed.'

'Oh, sure,' he said. 'This is a tough country.'

He took her to the El Greco painting of Toledo, and sat down before it.

'I come and look at it,' he told her, 'whenever I begin to forget how it's possible to paint greens and blues.'

His action and abruptness were unlike Desmond in every respect, and yet he brought Desmond to mind. There was a unity of thought about the way he looked at the picture which might have been Desmond's own. He didn't regard it with the fondness of familiarity, but as if he saw it for the first time, as she did.

It had still for him the same power to startle and overawe. She began to wonder if it would have overawed Desmond, also.

He turned to her at last.

'Now let's get you straight.'

'About coming over here?'

'Sure.'

'Here?'

'Why not? Less noisy than other places—no one comes to look at pictures on a Monday afternoon. Besides, when you get tired of talking you can look at the Greco.'

She gestured with her gloved hands. 'Where do I begin?'

'That's up to you—what was the important thing before Johnnie?'

'My father.'

'Well, begin with him—not the things I already know.'

'Father was poor.'

'That much I know.'

She drew off a glove and began twisting it in her hands. 'He came to Trinity College knowing only what he'd learned from books to take his scholarships. I find it hard to imagine the changes that must have taken place in him during those Trinity years, because he was surely ignorant of most things he loves now. He discovered—or someone else did—a remarkable talent for music. My mother, of course, taught him about pictures. Or she began to—she died very young, you know. And in any case my father has a way of outstripping everyone else in learning once he becomes interested.'

'Your mother died . . . then what?'

'I don't remember much about the early part except that Father did everything with us—he made us like adults when we were still children. Many people must have thought us unbearable, and my father a fool.'

'University and the war?'

'Cambridge—I didn't seem to be away from him much. He used to take us abroad. We looked at pictures most of the time, and stayed in fashionable hotels. He never wanted things to be simple or cheap because he had a distaste for anything connected with the life before Trinity. I've never met any of his brothers, and when his nieces or nephews came to London he had them to tea—when no one else was there.'

'A snob?'

'Yes—in a sort of way. My mother had money, and Father is very successful. It's not surprising he should feel that way.'

'And what about Tom?'

'Tom was the one he always wanted me to marry—that was a return to the side of the family that had never lived in a little farmhouse. I think he wanted his grandchildren to grow up with a sense of belonging in a place where the family had been for a long time. What he couldn't do himself he wanted me to accomplish for him.'

'You could see all this—and were willing to go through with it?'

'Why not? I saw no reason why not . . . except that there was no reason why I should marry Tom until I met Johnnie.'

'Was that the only solution? Irene would have divorced Johnnie if he had asked her.'

'That wasn't a solution—I've been brought up as a Catholic. It would have broken my father's heart.'

He nodded, looking at her. At the end of the gallery a man stood before a picture in the corner. He left after a while, without coming any closer to them. A guard watched them idly.

'Tell me,' Mark said, '. . . that time you went with Johnnie to Ostend—was it the thought of Irene or your father or your religion which sent you back? Which point of the three did your courage fail you on?'

'You don't make it easy for me.'

'I'm just interested. Your father's grabbed so much of your life. I'm interested to know if he tipped the scales there, too.'

'I can't say.'

'Well, O.K. I didn't really expect you to. Then, after Johnnie said he wouldn't marry you, you went to Ireland with Tom. Tom knew about all of it, didn't he?'

'Yes. He knew. He thought once Johnnie was gone I'd be all right. When I told him I was coming here he said I had an obsession. I don't know if I believed that, but I know a week ago, when I decided I was going to see Johnnie again, it was like coming back to life. I think from the time he had said he wasn't going to marry me, I'd been half dead. I didn't know what was happening.'

'But you knew what was going to happen when you came back to tell your father?'

'I knew—or thought I did. I thought he'd be finished with me.'

'You wanted to go through with it even expecting that, even with only a fifty-fifty chance of Johnnie having changed his mind?'

'It was the only thing to do.'

'Sure.' Then he added. 'You're a strange woman.'

'Not strange.'

'Yeah—strange. You've lived in the shadow of your father all your life; he's kept you cut off from every other kind of life except what he wanted and planned for you. Have you wanted anything big that he hasn't wanted? —or done anything he hasn't done with you?'

'No.'

'Only Johnnie?'

'Yes—only Johnnie.'

He stood up. 'Come on. I've got to go.' He began to walk down the gallery.

'Mark?'

'Yes?'

'Aren't you going to tell me about Johnnie? It isn't fair. I don't know . . . what he's thinking.'

'Haven't time. I said I've got to go.'

Outside the Museum he found a taxi, and gave the driver the address of the apartment.

She leaned out through the window. 'Where are you going? Can't I come with you?'

'I'm going to see an editor who doesn't like women.'

'Do you have to see him to-day?'

'Look,' he said, 'a war broke out yesterday. Those who get there first get the jobs.'

'You're not going to Korea?'

'If I can get someone to send me.'

'I hadn't thought of that. Is it going to make any difference to Johnnie?'

'One way and another I think it'll make a hell of a difference.'

The driver turned round.

'I'm sorry, mister, but this isn't a parking place. There

218

are benches in the Park for those who want to talk.'

'See you later,' Mark said. He raised his hat. 'Get out one of those elegant English dinner gowns. I want to dine like a war correspondent on the eve of battle.'

## III

When they left the El Morocco, Mark stood on the pavement looking at the cab that drew into the kerb.

'It's five blocks, and round the south end of the Park,' he said. 'And it's a beautiful June morning. Do you feel like walking?'

'Yes. Let's walk.'

The taxi began to move. 'What are you trying to do? —give the lady flat feet?' the driver called to Mark.

'Sure. That's the idea.'

Mark took her arm and they began to walk. It was three o'clock and cruising taxis slowed expectantly as they came level. They didn't talk until they reached Fifth Avenue, and there Mark halted abruptly.

'You won't see another sight like that anywhere in the world,' he said. His tone was almost reverent. 'Look at it.'

The lights were dotted up and down the Avenue, and high up in Rockefeller Centre. They seemed hardly to have diminished since their early evening brilliance.

'Isn't it ever quiet?' she said. 'Doesn't all this ever shut down?'

'It's sweet music to a New Yorker's ear, Maura. It's the noise and perpetual blare of these motor horns, and the lights at night that make this town. I wouldn't want it any other way.'

Then he pulled on her arm. 'Let's find a drug-store and have some coffee.'

They found one in the next block—a long chromium soda fountain with three people at it, and a sleepy attendant wiping the lids of ice-cream containers.

'What's yours?' he said.

'Two coffees. Black.'

He slid them along the counter.

'Anything new about Korea?' Mark said. He nodded to the radio playing softly at the back of the counter.

'The capital—what's it called—Seoul—is being evacuated. The Government's leaving. Don't look too good.' He took up his cloth and began polishing. 'Well, I haven't grown too fat for my uniform.'

Maura stirred her coffee slowly.

'Will Johnnie want to go, do you suppose?'

'Hell, no. Neither will anyone else. If they do the job well enough, it won't grow into anything bigger than Korea.'

'The United Nations will send aid though?'

'They'll have to. The whole of U.N. will fall to bits if they don't back up South Korea now.'

'I wonder what Johnnie feels about it.'

'Afraid—like us all, I expect.'

'If you're afraid, why are you going out there?'

'Well . . . I guess no one's afraid of a local fight in Korea. But we're afraid that someone may drop an atom bomb too hastily—and after that the whole world will blow to blazes. Much of it depends on what the guys at Lake Success can do about it. And all we can do is sit and hope no one makes any mistakes.'

Maura raised her head and caught sight of their two reflections in the pink and black mirror along the wall.

'Mark, do you think I've made a mistake?'

'About what?'

'About coming.' She saw in the mirror his squarish dark face looking strangely familiar, and suddenly realised the number of hours it had had to grow familiar to her. 'Is Johnnie,' she said, 'going to wait until his father either dies or pulls through, and then come and tell me politely that I'd better go back to London? Mark, what is it going to be?'

'Is that what you believe?'

'I don't know . . . a week ago I refused to believe it.

Now I'm not sure. I'm not sure of anything.'

'What will stop Johnnie from marrying you?'

'What stopped him before,' she said.

'Irene?'

'Yes.'

He took out a cigarette and lit it. 'Do you believe that Irene killed herself?'

She nodded. 'Almost certainly. Irene would have killed herself rather than damage Johnnie. But he insists that he's wholly to blame. He thinks he ruined her, and he'd ruin my life as well.'

'I was fond of Irene,' Mark said. 'But everyone pays for their mistakes. She knew what hers was—poor little bitch.

'But two days after Irene's funeral,' he added, 'Johnnie would have believed he'd ruin any woman's life. It's possible he doesn't think that way any more.'

She swung round on the stool and caught his arm.

'Mark, for God's sake, tell me the truth. You understand Johnnie perhaps better than anyone ever will. Do you think he'll marry me now?'

'Even,' he said deliberately, 'if Johnnie weren't crazy about you, two things are throwing him into your arms right now.'

'Two?'

'Think,' he said, 'this is the time for Johnnie to take his stand one way or the other. When his father's dead he's either got to sell out of the business immediately, or stick there for the rest of his life. He won't get another chance.'

'What will he do?'

'I think, even if the Korean business hadn't blown up, that Johnnie would have hung on. You don't give up your claim to two generations' sweat and guts quite as easily as all that. I think Johnnie would have stuck, no matter what it did to him. But in a day or two Truman is going to order U.S. forces to assist the South Koreans. You'll see what it will do to set rearmament going again. Whatever way the affair goes we'll have to rearm—and Johnnie won't as lightly walk out on war contracts as he would on making nylon petticoats. If you've got a social conscience you don't start fiddling round like an amateur with a couple of acres of farm land when you should be getting from a plant all the stuff that can be squeezed out of it. He'll be making uniforms again before he knows what's happened.'

'It doesn't sound like Johnnie.'

'He's back in his own country,' Mark said, 'and his hand is forced. If I know Johnnie he's already kissed his dreams good-bye.'

'And where do I come in?'

'You're here—that's all that'll matter to Johnnie. Because he needs you he'll take everything you've got to give, and hardly stop to count the fact that you left Tom behind, and your father. He'll use you—Johnnie will. He'll marry you all right, and you'll be the buffer for his discontent. You'll see the side of Johnnie that isn't a success —the ugly side of the man who comes back from the plant fit to tear the place apart. And it won't be any use thinking he'll settle down to it in a year or two. He'll never settle down—he's going to be a misfit as long as he lives. He doesn't like his job, and he never will. So don't expect him to change or be any different. He's not going to be—not Johnnie. Either you get out now, or you're in for good—like he is.

'But I guess you love him enough to take even the particular kind of hell he'll make for you at times.'

'I think I do.'

'Sure, I know you do.' He got down off the stool. 'Look, my sweet, you wouldn't have stood much of a chance if you hadn't loved him like that. I've had you round me damn near twenty-four hours, and if I thought you were phoney I'd do everything I could think of to bust this affair wide open. I think I could have brought it off, too. Johnnie takes a lot of notice of what I say.'

He looked at his watch. 'I think we'll skip that walk. Central Park seems kind of bare at this hour in the morning.'

In the taxi he leaned suddenly across and kissed her on the mouth.

'I think you're pretty swell,' he said.

Then he lay back in his corner and closed his eyes.

She woke, even in the dimness of the room, with the knowledge that it was late—and with the sound of Johnnie talking to Mark in the hall. She got out of bed and opened the door.

'Johnnie!'

He took a step towards her, and Mark went swiftly in the direction of the kitchen.

'Your father?' she said.

'He died during the night. I got the first plane here this morning.'

He caught hold of her arm.

'I've only got two hours—I've got to go back. It's going to keep me away from you a long time, darling. I may not even see you for a couple of weeks. Can you wait here in New York, Maura?'

'I'll wait wherever you say—it doesn't matter how long.'

He drew her closer and began to stroke her disordered hair back from her forehead. 'It'll all take time. The funeral—and I've been away from the plant so long it'll take time to get the hang of things again. This Korean business is going to make things different. You don't mind waiting, Maura?'

He went on stroking her hair gently, absently. She knew from the feel of it that he took her presence there for granted, as one does of the person one loves, and he was perhaps, even at that moment thinking of other things.

# Fontana Paperbacks

Fontana is a leading paperback publisher of fiction and non-fiction, with authors ranging from Alistair MacLean, Agatha Christie and Desmond Bagley to Solzhenitsyn and Pasternak, from Gerald Durrell and Joy Adamson to the famous Modern Masters series.

In addition to a wide-ranging collection of internationally popular writers of fiction, Fontana also has an outstanding reputation for history, natural history, military history, psychology, psychiatry, politics, economics, religion and the social sciences.

All Fontana books are available at your bookshop or newsagent; or can be ordered direct. Just fill in the form and list the titles you want.

---

FONTANA BOOKS, Cash Sales Department, G.P.O. Box 29, Douglas, Isle of Man, British Isles. Please send purchase price, plus 8p per book. Customers outside the U.K. send purchase price, plus 10p per book. Cheque, postal or money order. No currency.

NAME (Block letters)

ADDRESS

---